Heirloom

a Kate Tyler novel

Heirloom

a Kate Tyler novel

Nancy Wakeley

Light Messages
Torchflame Books

Durham, NC

Copyright © 2020 by Nancy Wakeley
Heirloom
Nancy Wakeley
nancywakeley2@gmail.com
www.nancywakeley.com

Published 2020, by Torchflame Books
an Imprint of Light Messages
www.lightmessages.com
Durham, NC 27713 USA
SAN: 920-9298
Paperback 978-1-61153-373-6
E-book ISBN: 978-1-61153-374-3
Library of Congress Control Number: 2020907158

To my husband Dan
for his unwavering belief in me
and in the possibilities for this story;
to my daughter Michelle, always my cheerleader
and thoughtful advisor;
and to my sister Carol, who left us too soon,
but whose inspiration stays with everyone who knew her.

1

THE AISLE ON FLIGHT 902 into the Winston-Salem airport was jammed with passengers impatient for the doors to open. Kate Tyler pressed the back of her hand against her forehead, testing for a fever, then wiped the dampness from her flushed skin with a rumpled sleeve. Willful curls of auburn hair escaped her baseball cap and she pushed them away from her face. She apologized her way to an empty seat to get away from the suffocating clog of people in the aisle.

She leaned her cheek against the cool window, closed her aching eyes and took long, deep breaths to clear a lightheadedness that had plagued her since she left Rome. The line began to move, and she joined it again. She looked for a way to shift the weight of her backpack but there was no room in the crowded aisle to set it down. She hitched it further up on her shoulder and let the seats support her lanky frame.

Her trip to Italy had been a disaster. It was her first overseas trip for *Premier Travel Magazine*, a freelance job as a travel writer but one that could turn into a more long-term contract if she succeeded. Jack Starner had been the one to give her the Rome assignment, as he had liked the work she had submitted so far and was impressed with her experience traveling overseas and living in several European countries. The deadlines were demanding, and he had high expectations for her to deliver the copy needed to promote the popular, off-the-beaten-path experiences for tourists. "How To Become a

Gladiator" was one adventure that was on her list. But just after she arrived in Rome, she had been slammed with a flu that put her on her back for two days. She begged Starner to let her stay and finish the article, but he said he already had someone there in Rome who could take it over. As soon as she was well enough to travel, she was to fly home.

For Kate, the urge to wander the earth was instinctive, primal, imprinted early in her life. She and her twin sister Becky counted twelve cities, seven states and three countries as "home," going where their father's job in the military placed him. Kate grew up rootless and loved it. She collected nothing as a child so that she would have to leave nothing behind. She jettisoned friends and neighborhoods easily and quickly and without regret. As her fraternal twin, opposite in both looks and temperament, Becky approached their lifestyle differently. She kept in touch with all of the friends she made growing up by writing letters and sending photos; she kept souvenirs from each location in decoupage boxes marked with the name of each city they lived in. Unlike Kate, Becky's dream was to settle down. Everything she did pointed to that single goal, and she wound up choosing a career in law. After graduation from the University of North Carolina at Chapel Hill Law School, she took a job at a law firm in Winston-Salem, a city in North Carolina that she loved for its charm and history.

Kate's ambitions were different. She wanted to continue to travel, to return to the cities she had lived in and find new places to visit. So, with a degree in journalism, she began freelancing for small travel magazines, writing for meager pay but always getting enough work to develop her craft. Her co-workers labeled her the "gypsy journalist" and she lived up to the name.

But after six years of living from job to job, and not living much in between, she realized that she wanted more. She loved the thrill of the journey, but she needed a steadier paycheck.

Becky had heard about the job with *Premier Travel Magazine* in Winston-Salem, and convinced Kate that she should go after it. Now it was all on the line. She had to prove to Starner that she could handle the overseas assignments. True, this trip hadn't turned out as expected, but she was experienced enough to know that things didn't always go as planned. Maybe she would ask for something in the States, even a local assignment. She had to think. But residual effects from the flu, the overnight flights, and airport layovers had drained her mentally and physically.

The doors of the plane finally opened, and Kate was carried along in the line that spilled out into the jetway and on into the waiting area. She forced one foot in front of the other, pushing her way through the crowds and through the automatic doors to the outside.

She gulped in the fresh air made even sweeter by a cool mist. A couple of deep breaths cleared her head slightly and she looked up and down the lane for a cab. The next one in line pulled to the curb. Kate tossed her bag in ahead of her and slid into the backseat.

It was a long ride to the apartment near the historic district of Winston-Salem that she shared with her boyfriend, Mitch, and Kate tried to settle into the corner to rest. She pulled her cell phone out of her bag and punched in Mitch's number, the third time since the plane landed. There was still no answer. She had already left him a text and voicemail that she was coming home early. Finally, she told him not to meet her at the airport, that she would get a cab and go straight to the apartment.

The relationship with Mitch was not new. It began as a long-distance relationship because of her travel schedule but it had gotten more serious in recent months. When she told him that she wanted more stability in her life, a more permanent home base to come and go from in Winston-Salem, he had suggested that she move in with him. But she had sensed a change before this trip to Rome. He hadn't returned any of her calls, and it only added to her uneasiness. But she had enough on her plate at the moment, and she relegated the worry to the bottom of the list of her current problems.

The light mist continued to dampen the evening air, distorting the streetlights and headlights. The rhythmic beat of the windshield wipers soothed Kate. In the roomy back seat of the cab, she felt her tension subsiding, one muscle at a time, and she dozed off.

Kate was still groggy when the cab reached the apartment building. She paid the driver and hauled her bags up to the apartment. After fumbling with the lock, she dropped her bags on the floor inside. A faint light from the kitchen permeated the shadows of the apartment, sifting into the cozy living room. She searched the clutter on the bar that divided the two rooms for a note, but there was nothing. The sound of cars on the wet pavement came through an open window. She pushed back the dampened curtains and closed it tightly.

"Mitch, I'm back," she called out. There was no answer. She went down a narrow hallway towards the bedroom, peeling off her damp jacket and tee shirt as she went.

Kate switched on the light in the bedroom and skirted around the bed to the bathroom, tripping over clothes and towels as she went. She flicked on the light in the bathroom but then stopped—cold.

Something -- a flicker, barely within awareness -- caught her up short. Her mind tried to put it together, but couldn't, and Kate knew it wouldn't, not until she looked again. She grabbed the door frame as the entire scene slammed into her brain.

The remnant smell of perfume and sex permeated the air. An empty wine bottle stood on the nightstand on her side of the bed. Two wine glasses crowded the lamp on Mitch's side. A red negligee lay casually abandoned in the tangle of black satin sheets.

She turned and stumbled into the bathroom, her hands groping for the sink. She clamped down on the edge of it, her knuckles as white as the porcelain she clung to. It felt like the air had been sucked out of the room, out of her body. She rocked herself back and forth, trying to force air back into her lungs before she exploded. It came, finally, in wrenching sobs.

Her body stiffened as she heard the rattle of keys in the door and Mitch's voice tentatively calling her name. She tore herself away from the sink, wiping her eyes with her fists. She wanted to see his face when he realized that he could not fix this. He could not hide it or clean it up or make it go away. She went to the door of the bedroom.

Mitch stood at the end of the hall. He tossed his keys on the table next to the door and ran his hand through his hair and across the back of his neck. Kate stood, silent.

His hands moved self-consciously, his eyes focused on the floor, movements that pleaded for time. Desperate moments passed as the two of them stood, waiting in their unspoken pain. Finally, Kate stormed down the hallway and pushed past him.

"You're home early," he said. He picked up the tee shirt she had tossed on the floor, turning it over in his hands.

"I left you messages." Kate's throat was raspy, and it pained her to get the words out. "I guess you didn't get them in time."

She suddenly felt faint and weaved slightly. She reached for something to hold on to. Mitch moved toward her, but she shoved him back with one hand.

"Don't... touch... me!"

She spat out the words and sank down on the couch with her head in her hands, trying to stop the throbbing pain that was filling her head.

"Kate..." Mitch began. "I don't know what to say..." He stopped short of an apology as he looked at Kate, one hand pressed to her forehead, the other wiping the tears that washed down her face. "It's not enough with you, Kate. It's never enough."

Kate stiffened at his words and stared at him in disbelief. "What the hell are you talking about?"

"You don't want this. You don't want me." He stumbled over the words. "You want something else, something out there that you haven't found yet and you'll keep running until you find it. You're gone for weeks at a time. It's like a desert when you're gone and then a tidal wave when you come back! I got your messages. I know all about your problems with your trip and I'm sorry you got sick." He took a deep breath. "You've had plenty of chances and we've had our chance. And it's not going to work."

Kate drew herself up. His words drained the last shred of emotion from her. So, this was it. She suddenly understood everything, and her tears stopped cold. "You've got that wrong, Mitch. You never gave us a chance. You knew what I did for a living before you asked me to move in with you. You knew this and you wanted me anyway—that's what you said. You wanted me! But I guess it was all a lie." She ripped the shirt from his hands and defiantly put it on, covering herself.

"I know you're still not feeling good," Mitch said, picking up his keys. "You probably need to sleep. I'll go downstairs to Bob's place. I can crash there tonight."

"How many others were there?" Kate forced the words out. He put his hand out again to touch her, but she pulled away.

"Good-bye, Kate," he said and quietly left the apartment.

Kate sank down onto the couch, more pain rising with each breath until she had nothing more to purge from her heart. All feeling, emotion, and thoughts were drained away. She curled her long legs underneath her and lay silently, breathing slow, shuddering breaths, listening to her heartbeat.

Out of her fog, Kate heard her cell phone ring. In the hopes it was Becky, she grabbed it up, but the phone number was not familiar.

"Hello," she answered, and from the other end she heard a man's voice.

"I'm looking for a Kate Tyler. This is the Emergency Room at Wake Forest Hospital."

She sat up. "This is Kate Tyler."

"Ms. Tyler, this is Dr. Goodwin. We found your name and number in the wallet of a woman who was in a... a car accident this afternoon, a Rebecca Tyler."

"Is she all right? What's happened to her?" Kate's mind was suddenly clear, and she focused every ounce of strength she had on the man's voice.

"She's still in surgery. Are you a close relative?"

"Yes, I'm her sister, her twin sister... please is she going to be OK?"

"We think you should come as soon as you can. But we will know more when she gets out of surgery."

Kate grabbed her jacket and bag and ran down to the street.

The cabbie bullied his way through the evening traffic as if on a mission. Every car was in his path, every light against him, but he was honor-bound to move all obstacles to get his fare to the hospital. He was a big man, overflowing the driver's seat with his massive frame and bulky jacket. The radio crackled with the patter of cabbies and dispatchers. He hunched himself over the wheel with a singular purpose.

Kate gripped the edge of the back seat, her eyes closed tightly as they careened through the misty night. Fragments of childhood prayers rose from within her, desperate litanies of the unprepared. *If I should die before I wake...* she mouthed the words as her mind searched for the comforting rhymes and rhythms. *What comes after that? I pray... I pray...* The cab finally screeched to a halt in front of the Emergency Room entrance. The cabbie turned around.

"Ma'am, are you all right?"

Somewhere in the last ten blocks, Kate had become only a shadow of the person she had been leaving Mitch's apartment. The flood of adrenalin that had propelled her down to the street to hail the cab had vanished. She could feel the flush from her fever and the pallor of panic fight for rights to her skin, creating a peculiar pattern on her face. Her auburn curls hung wearily, barely able to contain the dampness that collected at the tips.

Kate stared at the man, puzzled, as if wondering how she had gotten to this place. He twisted around even further to look at her.

Kate saw his wide mouth moving to the wail of sirens, peaking and dissolving into the air. *If I pray for their souls... mommy, what comes next? I don't remember...* She dug some crumpled bills out of her bag and stuffed them into his hand without counting. She was barely out of the cab before he pulled away.

Kate turned around and found herself at the entrance to the Emergency Room. Wide glass doors opened and closed in front of her. But she was unable to stir herself. A trickle of tears mingling with salty sweat seeped into the corner of her mouth. Kate tipped her head, slowly, painfully, squinting as the light disintegrated before her. The sound of sirens faded as the roar in her head grew louder and louder. A chill coursed through her. Then everything was black.

2

THE AIR BUZZED AT FIRST, then voices drifted into her emerging consciousness. Kate tried to move her hands, but they tingled, and she lay them back down at her sides. She tried to place where she was and the voices that murmured her name.

"She's coming around," someone said.

Kate felt a cool damp cloth on her forehead, the gentle pressure of fingers on her wrist, and the squeeze of a blood pressure cuff on her arm.

A man in white leaned in and flicked a small light back and forth across her eyes. Kate could only focus on the ceiling, blinking, trying to remember how she got there. She lifted herself on her elbows but was too weak and dropped back down on the gurney.

"Don't try to get up yet," another person admonished, placing a pillow beneath her head. Kate heard a soft whir as the head of the gurney was raised.

The man in white asked what her name was, and Kate responded.

"Ms. Tyler, my name is Dr. Goodwin. You are at Wake Forest Hospital. You fainted outside of our Emergency Room. Do you remember coming here?"

Finally, Kate could focus. She remembered and nodded. "I want to see her," she whispered.

Dr. Goodwin sat on the edge of the gurney. "Do you remember that your sister was in an accident?" Kate nodded.

"She was very badly injured and was taken directly to surgery." He paused, his words leading her to the inevitable conclusion. She nodded again. "We did everything we possibly could, but we were unable to save her."

"I know she's gone," she whispered. "I knew... outside. Can I see her now?"

Dr. Goodwin nodded and helped Kate off the gurney. She regained her balance and held his arm as he led her through a maze of carts to a large room at the end of a long hallway. The doors opened as they approached. A bed was positioned in the center of the room.

He led her to the bed, his arm at her elbow. She took a deep breath and nodded. He drew back the crisp white sheet.

The face before her seemed oddly serene. Kate gently touched Becky's face. "You said she was very badly injured... I don't understand... she doesn't look hurt at all..." she said, searching for some outward proof of the trauma she must have suffered, anything to help her accept the devastating outcome of the accident.

"She suffered multiple internal injuries," the doctor explained. "By the time the emergency crews got to her, she was barely alive. She died shortly after arriving in the OR."

"Where was she when this happened? She was a careful driver. I don't understand."

He hesitated. "I guess I can give you details since you will probably hear about it on the news. The authorities told us that a passenger jet was headed to the airport when its engines failed. The only place they could even attempt a landing was on Route 40. The police were able to divert traffic except for the car your sister was driving. There were helicopters in the air trying to warn her. But she must have panicked and didn't get off the road in time. They say that the pilot did everything he could to avoid her, but the plane was out of control. It hit her from behind."

Kate had to repeat the words out loud, trying to make them real, trying to make sense of it. "She was in her car and got hit by a plane."

"Yes." A pager hooked to the doctor's pocket buzzed his attention. "I have to make a call. Would you like to be alone for a few minutes? Or I can call a nurse if you like."

"I would like to be alone with her." When he hesitated, Kate reassured him. "I'll be OK." The doctor nodded and left.

Kate didn't notice the tears streaming down her face until they traced Becky's pale cheek. Did Becky have time to cry? Or was she so afraid that she screamed? Did she even know what happened? Witnesses, police, doctors... none of them knew what Becky had gone through, how she felt. Kate knew, though. Becky had known fear. Uncontrollable, gut wrenching fear.

She wiped the dampness from Becky's cold skin and scrubbed the tears from her own face. She wove her finger through strands of Becky's hair and gently turned them over and over, like they would do as children, tucked together in their narrow bed, whispering secrets to each other in the dark. How many times had Becky come to her rescue? A spat with a boyfriend, and Becky told her to drop him and walk away, that Kate deserved better. A tough course in college, and Becky would study with her until she brought the grade up. Becky had taken care of everything when their parents died. Kate hadn't known the first thing about what to do. Now it was all up to her.

"Ms. Tyler?" Dr. Goodwin entered the room and approached Kate. "Is there anyone we can call?"

She shook her head. She pulled the sheet over Becky's face. "I will be in touch with the name of the funeral home. Thank you for all you've done, doctor."

Kate left the room, got her bearings, and found a side door of the hospital. The air was still misty, but it was fresh and cool and felt good on her skin. She made her way through the parking lot to the street. The movement gave her some strength and purpose, even though she hadn't yet formed a plan in her mind. There were people to call, arrangements to be made. She had to go back to the apartment, as distasteful as that was. She prayed that she wouldn't run into Mitch, but she had to pack her things.

Kate walked the ten blocks to the apartment, letting her thoughts wash over her. She was exhausted beyond words and prayed that she would be able to sleep. It seemed the only thing that would get her through the next day. She let herself in the front door, trying not to think about why she and Mitch had fought. She forced herself to walk past the bed they had shared and took a long hot shower. Soon she was curled up on the couch and falling into a deep, numbing sleep.

Thirst finally forced her to her feet and into the kitchen. She looked for a glass, but the cupboards were empty. The tap was on, the sink filling with water that was spilling out onto the floor. Kate looked around for something to hold on to as the water rose, lapping around her ankles and then up to her knees. The only life preserver in view was drifting away, just out of her reach. Seaweed tangled around her feet, pulling her down. The water rose higher and higher, covering her mouth as she screamed and screamed... until she awoke.

She was in a cold sweat, her clothes drenched. She forced her breathing to slow, tried to focus on the room and the familiar pieces around her. She glanced at the time on her cell phone. She had slept for three hours. She didn't know which nightmare was worse, the one in her dream or the one she was living.

Tears came again because of the hopelessness of it all, the loneliness and the burden. As much as their adoptive parents loved and cared for them, providing every advantage that they could, she and Becky had always felt a bond between them stronger than just sisters or twins. Rejection by their birth parents followed by the death of their adoptive parents had left its scars on them both. But Becky rose above it with a strength that Kate was never able to. Becky had put everything else aside after their parents' funeral to help Kate cope with the loss. And now there was no one for Kate to turn to.

Kate pulled a blanket off the back of the couch to dry herself and push off the chill. The fever that had resurfaced and set off her nightmares had finally broken. She pulled the blanket tight around her and drifted off to sleep.

The next morning, Kate awoke with the understanding that she needed to move forward. First, she needed to eat something, anything, though nothing appealed to her. Second in her mind was the desire to put some order in her life, even if it was just one hour at a time. She was alone—she could acknowledge that in the light of day, and she knew that accepting it was a good thing, for now. She had survived before, and she supposed she would survive this, though the way was not clear.

She would go to Becky's apartment. It would be difficult, but it would give her a place to stay until the end of the month and give her the space and time to plan what she would do next. She would meet with Becky's boss at the law firm. Before leaving for Rome, she was excited about her new job, new opportunities and happy to be traveling again. But now everything had changed. She would also have to explain matters to Starner, tell him that she needed time to attend to Becky's affairs, but that she could take another assignment as soon as he had one.

Kate found some yogurt in the refrigerator and a couple of garbage bags under the sink and ate while she threw her belongings into the bags. Her things had trickled into Mitch's apartment slowly, never in a suitcase, but usually as something she forgot to take out, rather than purposefully brought in. The remainder of the few things she owned were at a friend's apartment, where she used to crash between her trips, but it was nothing she needed.

She changed into a clean pair of khakis and a white shirt and checked herself in the mirror. The usual glow of her skin was gone but at least she wasn't seeing the gray pallor of the previous day. The freckles across her nose seemed wider and of a deeper color. The dark circles under her eyes were to be expected, she supposed. Her hair could at least be tamed by pulling it back. She hadn't the energy to fix anything. They would all have to take her as she was.

Kate gathered up her carry-on bag, still packed from her trip, her backpack, and the two garbage bags. She threw the apartment keys on the table and closed the door on yet another part of her life.

3

THE LAW FIRM OF TOWER, LIPFORD AND ASSOCIATES had
built what had come to be known as "The Power Tower." Its entire architecture, like the firm's rise to success, pointed skywards
and Kate easily picked the building out from the clutch of the
city in front of her. She resolutely pointed her car in the right
direction.

Soon she was stepping out of the elevator onto the
seventeenth floor of the Tower building. The lobby was carpeted
in a deep chocolate brown that seemed to have melted from
the dark paneling into a pool at her feet. The lighting was soft
and warm. Subdued voices drifted down the hall. Kate followed
the sounds. Paintings hung on either side of the hallway like a
gallery. A young woman in a dark blue suit soon greeted her. She
confirmed the appointment that Kate had made and ushered her
into a large conference room. "Mr. Tower will be with you in a
moment," she said.

Kate murmured her thanks and looked around the room.
A wall of windows covered one side, giving a view out over the
expanse of Winston-Salem. A long conference table was situated
in the center of the room with dark leather chairs neatly lined
up on either side. The wall facing the window contained a large
bookcase, filled with volumes of legal texts. She could picture
Becky here in this room, helping clients work through complex
legal issues and challenges. She could picture her happy and
fulfilled here. Now there would be a void.

More paintings hung in the room, and one in particular caught her eye. She studied it for a moment. It was a walled garden, and the colors of the springtime flowers seemed to burst through the canvas.

"That was Rebecca's favorite painting." Kate turned at hearing the voice behind her, to see a man whose appearance, elderly but tall and elegantly dressed, was fitting for his cultured tone. "Actually," he continued, "she was the one who found it in a gallery and insisted that I purchase it for this conference room. She had wonderful taste."

Mr. Tower turned his attention to Kate. "Ms. Tyler, I'm Robert Tower. Rebecca was a very special person. Her death is a tragedy for us, but for you... we are truly sorry." His eyes, rumpled with age and wisdom, revealed the sincerity of his words. Kate felt the sting of tears and fought to shake them off. "This can be a very overwhelming time," he continued. "Is there anyone helping with the arrangements?"

Kate shook her head. "No. Actually, I was hoping you could help me. I've never had to do this before. Becky was always the one..."

"Not to worry. I'll have our administrator, Mrs. Mims, make all the arrangements... with your approval, of course."

"Thank you." Kate took a deep breath and continued. "Mr. Tower, this is very difficult for me to ask, but I don't know... I don't have..." Kate faltered, not sure how to tell him that she had no money to pay for the funeral nor did she know if Becky had made provisions.

"I understand. Of course, you have concerns. But this should be the least of your worries. Please, we can go over everything in my office."

He guided her through a side door into his office, buzzed his assistant, and asked her to hold his calls. He motioned for Kate to sit in a large leather armchair and took his place in the chair beside her.

"Rebecca made quite a name for herself here at the firm. She was an excellent attorney. We were all very proud of the work she was doing." He hesitated for a moment. "I hope you will forgive me for asking such a personal question, but I understand that your parents are no longer living?"

"Yes. They were killed in a car accident several years ago. Becky and I were in college at the time."

"And you have no other living relatives?"

"No. We were adopted when we were infants by the Tylers. We never knew who our real parents were."

"I see." Mr. Tower moved to his chair behind his desk and arranged a file in front of him and began again. "Rebecca asked us to handle her Last Will and Testament. Are you prepared to go over this today?"

Kate was not, but then she would never be ready. "I think that's a good idea."

"Very well. Did Rebecca discuss any of her final wishes with you?"

"No. I mean, we were very close, but I guess neither of us ever thought...."

"I understand," Mr. Tower replied. "Rebecca named me as executor. I can only assume that her file is complete; however, as you go through her personal papers you may find that there are other assets that we were not aware of."

Kate agreed that she would, but the thought of invading Becky's privacy was a task that she was not ready to face.

Mr. Tower leafed through the papers and began to discuss the important points of the document. "Fortunately, she has no outstanding student loans from law school so that will not be a concern." Kate nodded her head as he ran through the list of Becky's assets: a checking and savings account, a 401K, and various other investments. She mentally catalogued the items as best she could. "She left everything, including her personal belongings and the house and property in Eden Springs, to you."

"Pardon me," Kate interrupted. "House and property? Where?"

"Eden Springs," Mr. Tower said. He set the papers down. "You didn't know?"

Kate shook her head. "I've been out of the country and she and I hadn't spoken in a couple of weeks. But she never mentioned anything about buying a house."

"I see." After a moment Mr. Tower rose and came around his desk to sit next to Kate. "She was on her way back from Eden Springs after the closing on the property when she... when the accident occurred."

Kate slumped in her chair. She hadn't thought about why Becky was on the highway or where she was coming from or going to. If she hadn't been in Eden Springs, if she hadn't had so much on her mind, perhaps... it was too much to take in. She shifted uncomfortably in her chair, suddenly feeling trapped.

"I'm sorry... this is too much... I can't do this right now."

"I understand." Mr. Tower's voice was soothing. "It will take a while to sink in. We can go over this some other time."

Kate needed to get out, get some air. She tried to stand but her body betrayed her.

"Are you feeling all right?" Mr. Tower asked as Kate reached for the chair to support herself.

"Yes, I'll be fine," she lied.

He took Kate by the arm and escorted her to the door. "Mrs. Mims will be in touch with you about the arrangements." He walked with her as far as the elevator, reassuring her again of the firm's support.

Kate managed a smile before the elevator doors closed. She punched "L" and grabbed the railing along the wall for support as the elevator slid downward. She squeezed her eyes shut so that she couldn't see the walls closing in on her. She had to remember to breathe. She found her way back to the car and crumpled into it. She flipped the air conditioning on high and gulped in the icy air. It seemed like an eternity before she felt her breathing return to normal.

She finally allowed Mr. Tower's words to re-enter her consciousness. This morning she was wondering where she would live, and now, suddenly, she owned a house, one that certainly had a mortgage. *How ironic,* she thought. *A place for me... and the two garbage bags stuffed with practically everything I own.*

Twenty minutes later, Kate drove up to the window at a McDonald's, bought the largest size drink on the menu, and downed three over-the-counter headache pills. She pulled into the far end of the parking lot, leaned back, and closed her eyes, letting the pills do their work.

Even curiosity would not make her go there, she vowed. She would call whoever it was that needed calling and tell them to sell the place. She wanted no part of it and doubted that she could afford it anyway. There would be some money, yes, but not enough to make her independently wealthy. Becky must have been out of her mind. And to not tell her? They shared everything... or so she thought.

Maybe there had been someone in Becky's life, someone she was building a future with. Becky had no lack of men in her life. But there were none that stood out in Kate's mind as "the one." No, Becky was too independent, too driven by success to settle down yet.

She tried to think of the last time that they spoke. It was before her trip to Italy, maybe a week or two. They had dinner at that new restaurant. No, Becky had to cancel plans at the last minute. Before that, a week before that, maybe. A sigh caught in her throat when she realized that she could not remember the last time they spoke or what they had talked about.

The sun was creeping down below the visor. Kate straightened up and put on her sunglasses. She needed her life back. She couldn't live someone else's life, in another town, in a house that she knew nothing about and had no desire to own. She was already late for her meeting with Starner. It was really the last thing she wanted to do but her job was too important, especially now, and she felt better for the decision.

The offices for *Premier Travel Magazine* were in a crowded, nondescript business park near the airport. Kate jacked up the volume on the radio to drown out the scream of a jet passing over her. She pulled into the parking lot, and sheer force of will carried her into the sprawling one-story building to Starner's office. She knocked and opened the door when he said, "Come in."

"Mr. Starner."

He swung around in his chair, glancing at his watch.

"Kate. You missed our appointment this morning."

"Yes, I'm sorry about that," she started again.

"Sit down, please." Kate swung her backpack into one chair and sat down in the one next to it. Starner was not one to mince words, so she waited for him to do the talking. "How are you feeling? Over that flu, I hope?" he asked.

"Yes, I am feeling better, thank you."

"I hated to pull you off this assignment, but I had no choice. You understand that, right?"

"Yes, of course. I am ready for another one though. Whatever you have."

After a moment of silence, Starner said, "I heard about your sister—through connections at the airlines and the news, of course. We are very sorry for your loss."

"Thank you. But really, I should be available for more work soon. I have to take care of some things for Becky..."

He held up his hand to stop her. "Kate, you are a very talented writer, and I'd love to have you do more work for us. But there really is nothing right now. Why don't you take some time, take care of what you need to, and then we can be in touch if we have something."

Kate realized that he was not giving her a choice. "Thank you. I'm sorry the trip didn't work out. I really appreciate the opportunity, though." She reached out her hand and he accepted the handshake.

"Good luck, Kate. And we'll be in touch."

Kate left quickly, winding her way through office cubicles to the building entrance. She felt weak and lightheaded. Her hand shook as she unlocked her car. She was afraid to drive, but the urge to flee was overwhelming. She forced herself to pull out of the parking lot.

Kate headed back into the city, this time to Becky's apartment. "One thing at a time," she told herself as she maneuvered through the rush hour traffic. She was still trying to process the events of the last two days, and her brain ached in the attempt.

The doorman of Becky's apartment building hesitated only slightly before recognizing Kate. He nodded and tipped his hat. She let herself into the apartment and threw her backpack down by the door. She checked the message on her phone from Mrs. Mims who had left her the details of the visitation and funeral, as well as the reception which would be held at a private club where the law firm held memberships. She had even offered to meet Kate for lunch the next day to go over the details of the service and help her select something to wear if she needed to. Kate texted her and agreed to the arrangements she had made and that she would meet her the next day.

Kate fixed herself a cup of tea, curled up in a bright floral print overstuffed chair, and looked around the living room. Becky had impeccable taste in furniture, art, and accessories. Every piece reflected her touch, from the fresh flowers on the dining room table to the framed prints artfully arranged on the walls. She had always made Kate feel at home, comfortable, and welcomed, as only a sister could. Now, Kate felt out of place.

Kate had never been alone in the apartment. Even knowing that everything was now hers, she felt she was intruding. There were still signs of Becky's life. Her scent still lingered in the bathroom, fresh vegetables waited in the refrigerator for the next meal, her favorite mug sat in the kitchen sink with her shade of lipstick on the rim and mail lay unopened on the kitchen counter. These small mementos held more life and breath in them than Kate herself felt at this moment.

Kate felt like she was at a crossroads. In the brief span of two days she had left her life behind and been suddenly thrown into someone else's, entirely against her will. She had wanted a change, but not this. Not a tastefully decorated apartment, not a house and property in Eden Springs, and certainly not a life without a family or Mitch. And now she was looking at a life without any immediate job prospects, or her hard-won position with *Premier Travel Magazine*.

Her eyes darted around the room, as if looking for answers. She tried to think of the future but had trouble getting past the next two days. Eden Springs kept coming to her mind. She had heard of it, a small town not far from Winston-Salem, but had never been there. She was sure that it was nowhere she wanted to live. The house did not sound like the tether she was searching for, the home base that would allow her to come and go as she pleased. At the moment, it struck her more as an anchor that would pull her down with it.

Eden Springs. She wouldn't have to go there. She could sell the property, maybe sell it back to the original owners. There was money from the insurance policy; she could make it last for a while, along with the little savings she had, until she got back on her feet. She could freelance again for another magazine, and maybe finish the book she had started. This small plan seemed to offer slight hope, and it mitigated her panic somewhat. However small, it was enough for now.

The light was fading, and a pastel hue permeated the room. Kate went to the French doors off the living room that opened onto a small balcony. The sunset was a soothing array of blues and violets with streaks of pink and red. Kate wondered if Becky had ever taken the time to stand on this balcony and watch the sunset. She watched the colors mutate into grays and darker blues as the sun disappeared behind the granite and glass of a city settling into itself. Even the clouds seemed more deliberate as they sailed across the sky.

Another day would be born tomorrow, then another and another.

That night, Kate awoke, her body buzzing as if electrified. Her feet tingled as they touched the floor and she stomped and shook her limbs to sever whatever connection had charged her. The burning dissipated with painful slowness. Her body had presented her with yet another torture. She wandered restlessly from room to room, finally escaping to the balcony. She let the cool night breeze wash over her. Bits and pieces of a disquieting dream, vague images of her childhood darting about in her memory, surfaced, and sank below her consciousness as if drowning. She could not rescue them.

4

THE NEXT DAY, MRS. MIMS WAS WAITING outside the restaurant, as planned, and introduced herself when Kate arrived. She was tall and slim with stylish white hair and impeccably dressed in a cream-colored business suit. Kate, who was wearing jeans and a sweater, wished she had made more of an effort in dressing that morning. But Mrs. Mims made her feel comfortable as she chatted about the weather and the restaurant.

"Mr. Tower spoke to me about your visit yesterday, Kate. I am sorry that you and I weren't able to meet then," Mrs. Mims said. "And I am so sorry about Rebecca. We will all miss her terribly. We are so grateful for her work on our annual charity to raise money for children with Cystic Fibrosis. When a cause was important to her, she was 100% behind it. I always admired her for that passion."

"Thank you. She did a lot of very good work for the community."

"So, tell me about yourself. Rebecca once told me that you are a journalist."

Kate was grateful for the way Mrs. Mims put her at ease; she found it easy to talk to her about herself and her memories of Rebecca, even humorous adventures that made them both smile.

"And how about you, dear? How are you doing? Mr. Tower was concerned about you yesterday."

When the topic of conversation turned back to herself, reality came crashing in. *I haven't slept well, I am still jetlagged and recovering from the flu, I haven't eaten much in the last week and I probably look as bad as that all sounds. Not to mention, well, everything else. Is that what she wants to hear?* Kate wondered.

Kate sat silently for a few moments, unable to put a voice to how she was really feeling. As she thought about the events of the last few days with Mitch and her job, they assumed little importance in light of Becky's death. So, she opened up to Mrs. Mims about her job, or lack of one, in passive terms. She shared Mitch's betrayal with a sense of resignation and described without passion the way in which she kicked aside the broken pieces of their life together. She immunized herself against the real pain with these tiny hurts. Loss was not a new word in her vocabulary. She had been there before. And she had thought that survival was part of her, too. But now she was not so sure. She needed to find a new word for where she was now and what she was feeling.

Suddenly she looked up at Mrs. Mims despairingly.

"What's happening to me?" she whispered. "This isn't me!"

Mrs. Mims reached across the table and took Kate's hands in hers. "Kate, listen to me. Mitch did something terrible to you and now, as if that was not enough, you have had the person dearest to you ripped away. These things were not in your control."

Kate closed her eyes. "I have depended on Becky my whole life," she said. "She would push me to the front of a line, ahead of her. She would pick me first to be on her team in school." Kate smiled vaguely as pleasant memories floated to the surface. "She beat up Tommy Morris in third grade, just because he teased me about my red hair."

She pressed a fisted hand to her forehead, ricocheting back to the present. "Why didn't she tell me about buying a house? Why wouldn't she share that with me? I don't understand what happened to us!" Guilt and remorse, unreasonable as they were, surfaced with a vengeance. "I wasn't a good sister. I must have done something wrong. Maybe I depended on her too much. She got tired of dragging me along behind her. Or maybe I wasn't there when she needed me the most?" Her shoulders heaved at the thought that she had somehow let down the most important person in her life. "I'm not going there. I am not going to Eden Springs."

"You don't have to go if you don't want to," Mrs. Mims responded. "And Mr. Tower and I will help you in any way we can."

Kate was surprised that Mrs. Mims agreed. "I don't have to go?"

Mrs. Mims took her hand again and squeezed it. "Listen to me, Kate. Rebecca was a strong, determined woman, and ambitious, but she never forgot you. She loved you. You must always remember that. You have been through a terrible ordeal these last few days. Your whole life has been turned inside out. So, you need to take care of yourself now. But," she continued gently, "you and Rebecca were so close. I am convinced that she wanted to share this with you. You can choose not to go to Eden Springs. No one can force you and no one would blame you. But I do know that this was something that Rebecca was very passionate about. Do you really want to leave this part of her a mystery?"

Kate had no answer for her. Deep in her heart, she was desperately torn. Should she simply walk away from it all? Or should she try to understand what Becky was doing on that highway in the wrong place at the wrong time?

"You must give yourself time, dear. Believe me. Time takes care of everything. It puts the pain where it belongs and leaves the good memories, the happy memories, where you can reach them and draw on them whenever you want. And there are many good memories that we both have of Rebecca. She left something of great importance in her life to you. She knew she could trust you to do the right thing. Just give yourself time."

Time, Kate thought. *We don't give ourselves enough time. It is sold to us at a price. We sacrifice loved ones, we sacrifice our dreams, we sacrifice ourselves just to live in the pain of the here and now. And then we squander what we have bought for such a dear price. We fight, we ignore, we cause pain. And we run.*

She had been here before. She had lost the two people who raised her and loved her and gave her a chance that she might never have had. They had been ripped away from her without warning, just like Becky. Why did she never get the chance to say good-bye to anyone? Why were they taken away from her when she needed them most?

"I don't know what to do next." Kate's moist eyes pleaded with Mrs. Mims. "I don't even know what to do when I walk out of here."

"Don't worry," Mrs. Mims assured her. "You are in good hands."

The server approached with their orders. After they ate, Mrs. Mims guided Kate to a boutique near the restaurant. The staff quickly helped Kate select two simple black dresses. As Kate looked at herself in the mirror of the dressing room, she thought it might as well have been a stranger looking back at her. The mourning clothes might have been for this person, this empty shell draped in black.

Something was missing. Kate searched in her backpack and pulled out a small jewelry box and took out a simple wooden cross. She rubbed her finger across the smooth surface, remembering the day she had bought it from an outdoor vendor in Israel. She had bought an identical one for Rebecca and suddenly remembered that her sister had been wearing it the last time she saw her. She clasped it around her neck, thankful for the connection she felt again.

Mrs. Mims nodded in approval as Kate shared this small detail with her. She gave her a warm hug. "You are going to be all right, dear. Just take one thing at a time."

The doorman swung open the etched glass doors to the apartment building with a flourish. "More flowers today, Ms. Tyler," he announced. He took the bags from Kate's hands as they made their way through the lobby. "They're in the office. I'll bring them by before I leave if that's OK. And I thought you should know that the building manager has been looking for you. Probably about the apartment. Don't you worry though. You come and go as you please." Kate thanked him. He pushed the elevator button and waited with her until the doors opened.

She entered the apartment, set her shopping bags down by the door, and curled up on the couch. Her fingers found the cross around her neck and she grasped it tightly. She slept soundly until morning.

On the day of the funeral, Kate awoke with some sense of restful sleep, a new sensation to her. The visitation of the previous evening left her with the knowledge that Becky's friends and colleagues truly cared for her and were just as much in shock of trying to accept her death as Kate was. This was a woman who had been full of life, ambitious, smart, who should have lived a long and happy life. But they had all lost her to a senseless accident, and now they had to find a way to go on without her presence in their lives.

The day passed by in a blur of shaking hands and accepting more condolences. Kate finally made her excuses, thanked Mr. Tower and Mrs. Mims, and left the gathering. The limousine dropped her off at the apartment building. She pulled more mail from the mailbox and she added it to the pile on the coffee table that had been growing over the past few days. She quickly changed into jeans and a tee shirt and returned to the living room.

Bills, advertisements, and sympathy cards were stacked high on the table. She found a letter opener in Becky's desk, a slim silver blade with a mother-of-pearl handle, and immersed herself in the task. She opened the sympathy cards first, making a promise to herself that she would reply to each one even though they were all strangers to her. Some were addressed to the "Family of Rebecca Tyler." Others brought tears to her eyes as she read about how Becky had helped them through difficult times in a court case or advised them on other legal matters. Kate felt very proud of her sister as she read the messages.

She tackled the advertisements next; credit card offers, fashion and house decorating catalogs, solicitations for donations to charities. They all went into the recycling. Then she sorted the official looking mail into piles—utilities, bank statements, and credit card bills to be given to Mr. Tower. There was a letter from an insurance company. The last one was from an attorney with a return address of Eden Springs, North Carolina.

It was postmarked Monday, the day of the accident. Kate opened it and slowly unfolded a personal handwritten note from a Mr. Wesley Carroll, an attorney, congratulating Rebecca on the purchase of the property and saying how he looked forward to working with her on the project to restore the gardens at Howard's Walk. Kate tried to recall if Mr. Tower had mentioned any gardens as part of the property, but nothing about it sounded familiar. A long-term project connected to the house did not make it sound any more appealing to her.

Kate thought back to her conversation with Mrs. Mims. No one would blame her for not dealing with this matter; she could easily have the attorneys and realtors handle it. But the letter had made her curious, and it was possible that the attorney did not know about the accident. Mrs. Mims was right. Kate decided that she didn't want this part of Becky's life to remain a mystery. No, this would be the right thing to do to honor Becky. She would go there, take care of it personally, and then move on.

5

BEN EVANS BACKED HIS TRACTOR into the potting shed, lowered the bucket loader, and shut off the engine. It was late afternoon and the employees of his business, the Eden Springs Garden Center, had all gone home for the day. The floodlights had not come on yet, so he still had enough daylight to do some work. He straightened up a lacy leaf maple and some potted perennials that had tipped over in the wind. He checked the rain gauge and tossed out the inch of water that had accumulated since the previous evening. No need to water tonight, he thought.

A load of potting soil had been delivered that morning and the bags needed straightening. He began to haul the bags into place, lifting the fifty pounds of weight easily, his arms and shoulders conditioned by years of outdoor work. He had always enjoyed the outdoors and working with plants. It was an interest that he shared with his Granddad Weatherly, and ever since he was a boy it had helped him escape from a difficult home life. This had led him to study horticulture in college and open his own garden center business shortly after graduation.

He took after his Granddad Weatherly in looks too. Ben remembered him as a tall, hard-working man with calloused hands, a man whose gaze could pierce through to your core. Ben had the same piercing blue eyes, and although he attracted women easily with his muscular build and sun-streaked blonde hair, he was oblivious to the stir he caused and usually paid no more attention to his looks than showering and shaving.

He had returned that morning from a trip to Charleston to visit his mother, Elizabeth. It was not a shock to him that she had finally decided to leave his father, Max Evans. She had discussed it with Ben before she made the move, and he wholeheartedly agreed with her decision. He had made the trip mainly to see for himself that she was all right.

It was difficult for him to picture her away from Eden Springs and the Woodlands, the family estate where he grew up. But he was relieved she had finally gotten away from his father and the control, cheating, and lying she had endured for so many years. She had tried to keep it quiet, but Eden Springs was a small town and the news of their separation had traveled fast.

"I'm happier now than I ever was with your father," she had said to him. "I have enough money to live on, and, more importantly, I feel safe here."

"But this isn't right," he said. Max had hired the best attorneys that money could buy, and both Ben and his mother knew that it would not be an amicable divorce. "You deserve something. You both worked to make the Woodlands a success."

"What I deserve," Elizabeth had responded, with a quiet confidence that was inspiring, "is respect, and no amount of money will give that to me. I don't want you to worry about me. You know, when you were little, you used to have this look on your face when you knew the world was wrong and you couldn't figure out how to make it right. I see that in your face now. I know your life growing up was hard. I bear responsibility for that, too, because I chose to stay. It wasn't for you to make things right. That was my job. I stayed for all the wrong reasons, but I wanted you to have a father and I made the mistake of thinking that things would change. I hope you can forgive me."

Her words had stayed with him for the rest of the day, churning up memories from his past that he would like to have kept buried. But he never blamed her for doing what she thought was best for him and for herself. It was not for him to judge.

So, in the end, when he saw her in the cozy apartment on a quiet street in Charleston, her hands steady and calm as she served him sweet tea, he knew she was content and ready for what was ahead. He vowed then and there to continue to do whatever he could to make her happy.

Floodlights soon lit the garden center, illuminating neat rows of burlapped trees and shrubs, and display benches of New Guinea impatiens and pink and red geraniums, all new stock for the coming season. Ben tossed one last bag on the pile with a satisfying thud and looked around at what he had built up, all on his own. His father had always expected him to take over the Woodlands business empire someday. But in the end, Ben had realized, just as his mother had, that he couldn't let his father control his life. He financed and opened the garden center on his own, without his father's help.

Ben and his father had a different definition of success and how to achieve it. Ben provided good service at a reasonable price, cared about his customers, and was satisfied only when they were happy with his work. He believed the community was a better place because of the work he chose to do.

Max Evans measured success in dollar signs and didn't care what he had to do to accumulate his wealth. In addition to the Woodlands, a successful farm on its own, he bought and sold businesses, always at a profit, and rarely with any consideration to the people employed there. He developed commercial properties in Winston-Salem but at the cost of losing many historic homes and buildings. His reach was long, and his name was associated with some of the most lucrative pieces of property in the area. His name had become infamous in Eden Springs when he built a textile plant and then moved it to Mexico when it profited him to do so, putting many local people out of work.

Ben grabbed the keys to the garden center gate and walked to the end of the drive to finish closing up for the night. He enjoyed his work but was also looking forward to the day when he would lock the gate for the last time, walk away from Eden Springs, and head into his future. He knew that he could continue to run the garden center successfully, but he had the sense that he needed to move on, away from the memories in Eden Springs. He had decided to put the garden center up for sale and go into a wholesale plant business with a college roommate in South Carolina. He had told his mother about his plans and was relieved that she supported his decision.

He secured the gate and walked back toward his house, a small yellow bungalow adjacent to the garden center. A breeze moved through the lot and stirred a set of brass wind chimes into a moody melody. Ben felt his life had been a case study in chaos theory in the last few months. Maybe now, everything would settle down. Maybe now, he would find peace.

6

KATE'S DECISION TO ARRIVE IN EDEN SPRINGS unannounced was simply self-preservation. She could leave as anonymously as she came, if no one expected her. She thought that the momentum of her decision would carry her through this, as if just deciding to do something made it happen. But the decision to come had to be made repeatedly in her mind.

It would have been much easier if her car hadn't started or if she had a recurrence of the flu... or if she simply did not wake up that morning. But she did, and, three days after the funeral, she got in her car and she drove, praying that nothing remained of the disaster along the interstate but keeping one wayward eye on the median, just in case.

She knew that sometimes small memorials would be left along the side of a road, crosses or signs to mark the spot where a tragedy occurred, where someone's personal loss was made public. She thought she might see something. But there was nothing. Maybe all traces of the wreckage had been erased already. Or maybe her mind chose not to see what was still there.

When Kate reached Eden Springs, she found a parking spot at the upper end of town. It was a warm day tempered by a light spring breeze. She shouldered her backpack, crossed at a cross walk and started walking down Main Street to get her bearings.

The street was picturesque with old-fashioned streetlamps and wide sidewalks; business names were displayed on colorful awnings above the doors and stenciled on storefront windows. The shops and businesses on Main Street appeared to be for necessary things, catering to the needs of the locals. Kate had passed some strip malls with grocery stores and other small businesses on the road into Eden Springs, but other than those few, farmland simply melted into the town limits. She soon realized that Main Street here was still a thriving business center, unlike so many other small rural towns across the south where box stores and fast food chains had replaced the heart of their communities. It reminded her of the coziness of so many of the villages in Europe where after a short stroll or bike ride you could be in the hub of daily life, where business was done and news was shared.

The Key Bank of Eden Springs, boasting the town's tallest building at three floors, anchored the street. Hubert Realty attached itself in a smaller building to the south side of the bank. Its front was still faced with old brick, solid, but clearly abraded by time and weather. Eve's Beauty Salon, Perkins Hardware, and Eden Springs News and Cigars were next in line with a quaint union of fronts and windows and doors. All showed some signs of wear but were tidy and freshly painted.

Slightly north of and on the opposite side of the street from the bank where Kate had parked her car was the First Baptist Church of Eden Springs. It stood on a hill with access granted only by climbing steps or trudging up the grassy slope, a daily reminder to the staunch membership that the work of the church began on the outside. The large brick building commanded a keen view of the town and its people. Kate heard the deep tones of the steeple bell pulsing through the air as it struck the hour.

The church shared a substantial parking lot with the Eden Springs Fire and Rescue building and municipal offices. A small brick courtyard had been designed between the two public areas. A wrought iron archway joined the buildings and served as an entrance to the courtyard garden and to the side doors of the fire station and the town offices.

Kate paused to read a small plaque on a bench in the courtyard memorializing veterans. The bench was one of several, set in new brickwork that flowed back in a circular pattern to a rear wall. Planters filled with bright purple and yellow pansies were placed throughout the area. Two elderly men sat on one of the benches, their conversation muffled by the sound of water flowing from a fountain set at the back of the garden.

After the firehouse, there was a narrow alley, then the Garden of Eden Florist, and finally Rosie's Café which took up the whole corner of Main Street and Columbia Avenue. The aroma of freshly brewed coffee from Rosie's mingled with the breeze and reminded Kate that she hadn't had a decent cup in days.

She paused slightly in front of the café, but resisted the urge to go inside and, instead, turned left and crossed Main Street. A display of old wicker chairs on the sidewalk outside of Orange Tabby Antiques caught her eye and she decided to take a closer look. She stepped over a large cat dozing in the sun and opened the door. A buzzer sounded from somewhere at the back of the store, but the only thing to greet her was the stuffy smell of old unwanted things. The room was long and cavernous, with high ceilings decorated in tin tiles.

There was only a narrow path to walk through, and Kate's minimalist tendencies felt under assault as she took in her surroundings. Shelves on either side of her were crammed floor to ceiling with glassware, plates, oil lamps, and figurines. Boxes of dishware, record albums, toys, and dolls blocked some of the side aisles, so she quickly retraced her steps to the front of the store. There was no sense of order to the place, and she wondered how anyone ever found what they wanted. A tall thin man finally approached her and politely asked if there was anything he could help her with. She said, "No, thank you," briefly feigned interest in a stack of old books near the door and then left, eager to be away from the confines of the store.

The small business district of the town seemed to end there, so she turned to walk back to the intersection. An ancient rust-red truck, its bed overflowing with bathtubs, sinks and radiators slowed to let her pass, but she waved him on. The driver nodded in her direction. After the truck passed, Kate looked up and saw a name stenciled on the window across the street. Law Office of Wesley Carroll. She clutched her backpack a little tighter. She needed a few minutes to prepare herself before going to the attorney's office and decided to try Rosie's Café. A bell jangled as she opened the door. She found a corner booth, slid across the red vinyl bench, and began to flip through the songs on the jukebox remote selector at her table.

"What can I get you to drink?" the waitress asked as she placed a menu, a clean paper place mat and silverware wrapped in a napkin on the table. She was uniformed in black slacks, a red apron, and a tee-shirt emblazoned with "Rosie's Café" done in an embroidered red script. Her voice was warm and southern and easy, tailor-made for the inviting surroundings of the café. Kate wondered if this was Rosie herself.

Kate ordered a cup of coffee and looked over the menu. Her appetite was practically non-existent lately. But after all she had been through in the last couple of weeks without time to recover or take care of herself, her naturally thin frame was showing more angles than usual. If it weren't for Mrs. Mims' parting words imploring her to "treat yourself well, dear," she wouldn't have bothered to eat at all. The waitress brought her a coffee mug and poured the coffee to the rim.

"Just visiting us today?" she inquired, pulling several non-dairy creamers out of her apron pocket and setting them on the table.

"Yes, but just for today. It's a lovely town."

The waitress smiled. "We like it just fine. Now what else can I get for you?" Kate ordered a blueberry muffin and a bowl of chicken noodle soup only because of her promise to Mrs. Mims.

Kate looked around the café. It was roomy enough with a row of booths along one side, a lunch counter on the other and several tables down the center of the room. A large red and gold jukebox stood by the checkout counter spilling out sad country tunes. The bell on the door jangled and she recognized the man from the red truck as he came in and hiked himself up on a stool at the counter. The waitress placed a cup of steaming coffee and a piece of apple pie in front of him without being asked. "How are you today, Snap?"

"Oh, good as any other day, I guess, Rosie," the man said.

A few moments later, Rosie brought the warm muffin and soup to Kate and went back behind the counter.

"Did you clear out the Jackson homestead yet, Snap?" Rosie asked. "I heard they were going to raze the place pretty soon."

"Yep, sure did. Got a few good pieces out of it. People like the old stuff these days. I can refurbish that clawfoot tub and sell it for a lot of money."

Kate ate slowly, pulling the muffin apart bit by bit, intrigued by the conversation. After seeing what she could only describe as junk at the antique store, she was surprised at the idea that people might want some of it and pay money for it, too.

"Lots of scrap metal in that place, too. That'll bring in a few bucks." He chuckled. "Enough to keep me in pie and coffee for a while!" When he finished eating, he pulled some money out of a pocket in his overalls and put it on the counter. "See you tomorrow, Rosie."

"See you, Snap." Rosie cleared away the dishes and wiped the counter, and after a few minutes she walked over to Kate's table and asked if she needed anything else.

"No, everything was really good," Kate said and realized that she meant it. "Can I ask you a question?"

"Sure."

"It looked like you knew what he wanted when he came in. Did you know what he was going to order? Did he call in ahead of time?"

Rosie laughed. "Heavens no! We do get some takeout orders here where people call in and pick up a plate of something, especially when we have a special on barbecue or fish or something like that. But Snap has been coming here just about every day for years, same time, same stool, same order. Just eats his pie, drinks his coffee, chats a little and goes back to work. One time," she lowered her voice a bit, "when he didn't show up for a few days, I had the sheriff go out to his house just to make sure nothing was wrong. Snap got a good laugh out of that! Turns out he'd just gone to his daughter's in Raleigh." She put the check on the table. "You want a to-go cup with some more coffee?"

Kate thanked her but said no and paid for her meal.

The diner wasn't busy, so she took the letter from the attorney out of her backpack and read it again. She tried to think about what she would say and what questions she needed to ask, but she really didn't even know where to begin and once again found herself wishing that she had asked Mr. Tower to send a letter instead of her making this foolish trip by herself. A knot formed in her stomach at the dread of rehashing the events that had brought her to Eden Springs. But she was here now, and it was time to get it over with.

Wesley Carroll hesitated, pressed the *end* button, and set the receiver down gently. His hand still rested on the phone, unwilling to break even the most fragile bond he had with Elizabeth Evans. Then he loosened the knot in his silk tie and ran his hand over his goatee, discouraged that he had not been able to speak to her.

"It's me, Wesley," he had said over the phone. "I have to believe that you left me your number for a reason, but I've left several messages and you haven't returned my calls."

His mind had raced ahead to what he wanted to say, needed to say, to her. He had never been at a loss for words before. Sentences came out fully formed, polished, and perfect, with little thought needed... until now. He rubbed the throbbing vein in his temple with the heel of his hand, frustrated with the unfamiliar feeling in the pit of his stomach.

He had stumbled again, wishing he could see her face in front of him. "I would like... I want to see you, but I won't come until I hear from you. I hope you are doing well. I hope you are happy." He paused for only a moment, afraid that her voicemail would cut him off. "Please call me."

Ever since he found out that Elizabeth had moved to Charleston he couldn't think, couldn't concentrate. He was used to seeing her in town, at a store, at committee meetings, or in church, to share a smile or brief conversation. Now there was a void.

He closed his eyes and tipped his face up to catch the breeze from the ceiling fan above his desk. The room was cool and dark, the early afternoon sun having passed the east windows that flanked the office. He was grateful for the solitude and allowed the memories to seep into his thoughts.

All those years, he could only watch from a distance, knowing that Elizabeth Evans suffered in a sham of a marriage, knowing that her husband was a cheat and a liar. When his own wife died fourteen years ago, Wesley never dreamed he would be able to love anyone else. But after a while, his feelings for Elizabeth began to grow stronger, and he sensed that she might feel the same for him. There was never anything concrete to hold on to, nothing more than a friendly word at church or a chance meeting in town where a sad smile might hold his gaze for a few treasured moments. He could have told her how he felt. He could have done it years ago. But she was still a married woman and that wasn't his style. It certainly wasn't hers. And he would have never done anything to stain her reputation.

He understood why she needed to leave. Elizabeth deserved to have a new start, away from the pain and the memories. But he needed her — like he needed air to breathe. "Just say the word, Lizzie," he said to the inert phone. "Just give me a sign."

A noise from the outer office startled him out of his thoughts. He stood and walked to the door of his office and looked into the small waiting room.

A young woman stood just inside the door. A battered leather backpack hung on her shoulder. Her pale angular face was set with dark serious eyes and framed with a mass of auburn curls. Her arms were clutched tightly around her as if pressing in on a mortal wound. Everything about her seemed ready to give way with only the slightest touch.

"Are you Wesley Carroll?" she asked.

"Yes, I am. How can I help you?"

She moved to hold out her hand but seemed reluctant to pull it away from herself and only halfway extended it. "I'm Kate Tyler. I'm Becky... I mean Rebecca Tyler's sister."

Yes, of course, Wesley thought. He hadn't expected her so soon. He moved closer and shook her outstretched hand.

"I need to talk to you about..." She wiped her eyes with her sleeve, first one, then the other, took a deep shuddering breath and pulled a folded letter out of her backpack. "I need to talk to you about this letter, about the property she bought..."

"Of course," Wesley said. "Please come in." He escorted her into his office. Kate sank into the chair Wesley offered while he took a seat behind his desk. He sensed her hesitation and took the lead. "I apologize for not getting in touch with you sooner, Ms. Tyler. We were notified Wednesday about your sister's death. Please accept our sincerest condolences to you and your family."

Kate thanked him and turned the letter over in her hands. "When I found this letter, I didn't know if you were aware of what had happened, what happened, I mean, to my sister."

"I am sorry you had to come all the way out here," Wesley said. "We were hoping, after an appropriate time, to contact you and discuss the situation as it now stands with the property. But since you are here, is there anything I can do for you?"

She moved to the edge of her seat. "Mr. Carroll, Becky had not discussed any of this with me, so I really have no idea what it's all about. I just learned about this from Mr. Tower—he was Becky's boss and he is handling her estate. But I don't understand your letter, about restoring the gardens. I really would rather put this off for as long as possible, but..." She took another deep breath. "If you have the time, I wish you would explain everything to me. I can't go through another day wondering why she bought this property. But, please understand, my real reason for being here is to put it back on the market. Becky left everything to me, but I have no desire to keep the house."

Wesley took stock again of the young woman before him. He had seen many grieving relatives in his time, but she was different. He sensed that she was only half there. Her hands shook as she unfolded and refolded the letter. She wiped her eyes again. He wondered what was hidden beneath the grief—there must be a smile or brighter eyes in this young woman somewhere. But they were not there now.

"I understand your concerns. Here it is, then," he began as Kate settled back in her chair. "The Howard property, or Howard's Walk as it is known, has been vacant for about fifteen years. It was the original home of the Howard family who made their money in tobacco. Enoch Howard refurbished it just after he returned from the war with his English bride, Bessie, around 1950. She was homesick for the gardens she had known as a young girl. So many of the gardens had been destroyed in the bombings that she and Enoch decided to start recreating them at Howard's Walk, as a tribute to their friends and loved ones. They started small but gradually added greenhouses and formal gardens and opened them to the public at peak seasons." The room had continued to darken, and Wesley switched on his desk lamp, then continued.

"They gained a good reputation and it gave the town quite a high profile in the fifties and sixties. Enoch Howard died around 1990 and Miss Bessie kept it up for a while, but she eventually moved back to England where she still had family. When she died, the family notified us that they would be willing to sell the property to the right buyer.

"That's when your sister happened along. She stumbled onto the property and when she inquired, of course, we were delighted that she was interested in it. After several meetings with Rebecca, the realtor, and myself, we began to see other possibilities. Tourism is a growing part of some local economies. Rebecca saw an opportunity to capitalize on that. Your sister was a visionary, and we agreed that this could be a great venture for our town. She would focus on restoring the house and a group of us from town would help restore the gardens."

Wesley waited for Kate's reaction. He had attempted to make it sound like a simple plan. But from the vacant look on her face, he could see that she was overwhelmed, and her first instinct would be to run from the whole idea. But he felt he had an obligation to the town and also to Rebecca. She had developed a true passion for the project and had convinced him that she had the determination to see it through to completion, despite some of the local lack of support that had been festering lately. But, for whatever reason, she had not shared it with her sister, so Wesley felt that Kate's loyalty to the idea would be tenuous at best. But if they gave her time, perhaps once she saw the place, she might change her mind.

Kate wiped her eyes as Wesley talked about Rebecca. She was quiet for a while as he gave her time to absorb his words. He sensed that she was torn up inside, trying to understand why her sister, whom she was probably close to, had not shared this with her.

Wesley brought Kate a glass of water from the cooler in the waiting room and placed it in her shaking hand. She took a small sip and it seemed to revive her.

"We were twins," Kate said quietly. "We shared everything. But she never said a word about this...." She finally straightened up in her chair and looked at Wesley. "I can't keep the house, Mr. Carroll. I know it might disrupt your plans, but I just can't. I'm sorry."

Wesley nodded. He thought for a moment and considered his options. He knew that it would not be wise to try to force her hand. And realistically, without any contract between Rebecca and Eden Springs or even a handshake agreement, their options were limited. Any discussions they had were still just that— discussions and some heated debates at Town Council meetings that revealed the concern of some of the citizens that this was a foolhardy venture without money to back the vision. But Howard's Walk, for some, was a symbol; a way to bring people to the area, grow the tourist business, revitalize Eden Springs, without losing farms and the families that worked them. He shook his head at the short sightedness of it all.

He turned his attention back to Kate. Her face told him everything he needed to know. She was not able, physically or emotionally, to take on a project of this magnitude right now. He needed to find out more about Kate Tyler, to fill in the blanks. And she needed to feel that she had some control over the situation. Otherwise, she would bolt.

"Well, then," Wesley said, "I think the next step is for you to meet John Hubert. Perhaps he could handle the sale as he did before. We can see if he is free now." He retrieved his suit coat from a rack near the door and guided Kate out to the street.

They walked up Main Street to Hubert Realty and found John Hubert at his desk. A sheen of perspiration covered his bald head. He pulled a worn handkerchief from his back pocket and swiped it across his head. The ceiling fan wobbled and clicked as it rotated over the warm, cluttered office. He rose from his chair as Wesley introduced Kate.

"Ms. Tyler," he said, shaking her hand. "Pleasure to meet you. I wish it were under better circumstances, of course. Our condolences to you and your family," he said as he motioned for them to have a seat. Kate thanked him and looked to Wesley to begin.

"Ms. Tyler is here about Howard's Walk, naturally. She was not aware that her sister had purchased the property. However, it has all been left to her and she came to me to fill her in on some of the details."

"I see," John said, rocking back in his chair.

"She has also expressed a desire to put the house back on the market."

John stopped rocking and rested his chin on clasped hands.

"I see," he said again. He and Wesley exchanged a brief look. The two men had known each other for years and Wesley hoped that nothing needed to be said for him to understand what the approach should be.

"Well, we would be happy to handle that for you, Ms. Tyler. Of course, there are some things to consider before that can happen."

Kate stiffened. "I don't understand. I am not obligated to anything here, am I?"

Wesley jumped in. "In cases like this, of course, when property is included in an estate, the best thing is to work through the details with the executor, first."

Kate quickly pulled out Mr. Tower's business card and said that they could contact him for any information they needed. "I do have one request, though," she said.

"Anything at all. What can we do for you?" John asked.

"I do want to see the house. I think Becky would have wanted that. Can that be arranged?"

"Certainly," he said. "Of course, we gave the only set of keys to... I don't suppose you have the keys?"

Kate shook her head slowly. "I'm afraid I don't have anything here that she had with her... that day."

"Not to worry," Wesley interrupted. "John, I'll ask Snap about it. He might still have keys from the house after he did some work for Miss Bessie."

They agreed to meet the next morning in front of Rosie's and leave from there. When Kate asked about accommodations for the night, Wesley was happy to suggest that she could find a room nearby at the Park Inn, a small bed and breakfast over Rosie's Café.

He wanted her to stay in town for as long as possible, to get a feel for it and its people. He wanted Rosie's opinion, too. Wesley realized that the two sisters were as different as night and day, but Kate must have something of Rebecca's courage. Otherwise, she would not have come here at all. But was she strong enough? What was she looking for? Did she have other family and job responsibilities? He didn't have any answers yet. But right now, she was grieving and at a total loss for what to do, of that he was sure.

So of course, her first instinct would be to sell. She had no stake in it. But, perhaps, given time, she might change her mind.

A few moments later, the three entered the café. Rosie greeted Kate with a smile. "Well, you are becoming a regular here, sweetie!"

"Rosie, this is Kate Tyler, Rebecca Tyler's sister," John introduced them. "She will be needing a place to stay tonight so we recommended the Park Inn. I hope you have a room for her?"

"We've already met, John. Well, sort of anyway! And, sure do, I've got just the right room. I'll take you up right now." Rosie led Kate through a door at the back of the café and up a narrow staircase to a hallway with rooms on either side. She unlocked the door to a room overlooking the street and showed Kate in. It was a cozy room, simply decorated with a dresser, a free-standing full-length mirror and writing table in the same dark wood, old but well-cared for. The bed had a metal frame and was covered in a quilt of geometric stars in faded shades of blue. Rosie pointed out the small bathroom and the closet space and television remote. "This is my nicest room, everything here you should need."

Rosie turned to go but hesitated at the door. "Kate, I was real sorry to hear about your sister. We all were. So, if there is anything we can do, just let us know. But since you are here, there is a town meeting tonight at the municipal building, right across the street. 7 o'clock. We will be talking about Howard's Walk and the garden renovations—you are welcome to come if you feel up to it. I'll be there, and Wesley and John, plus some others. I don't know what your plans are, but maybe you could come and meet some of the folks and get a better feel for Eden Springs."

"Thank you, Rosie, but the only reason I came is to talk to Mr. Carroll about Howard's Walk. He and Mr. Hubert will be taking me to see it in the morning but after that I'll be leaving."

"Well, if you change your mind, feel free to stop by."

At 6:45 that evening, Ben Evans parked his truck across from the municipal building and jogged across the street to catch up with Rosie and Reverend William Carpenter as they walked into the Community Meeting Room.

Rosie greeted him with a one-armed hug, balancing a box of warm cookies from the café in the other. "Hey there, Ben. Good to see you, dear."

"You, too, Rosie. Evening Reverend," he said, shaking the Reverend's hand. "I didn't want to miss this meeting. Sure is sad what happened to Ms. Tyler. Her family must be hurting right now. Has anyone heard from them?"

"I met Rebecca's sister Kate today," Rosie replied, setting the cookies on a table at the back of the room. "Twin sister, actually, but they don't look anything alike. She's in town and was talking to John and Wesley; she's taken a room for the night at the inn. She's real nice but seems pretty fragile right now. It's hard telling what will happen. She told me she was leaving tomorrow."

"Awful, just awful," said Reverend Carpenter. "It's discouraging but understandable considering what she's been through."

"We'll see what they have to say then," Ben said. "Will she be coming tonight?" He followed Rosie into a small kitchen off the community room.

"I invited her, but I doubt it," Rosie answered. "She looked pretty worn out to me. It might be too soon for her to be getting in the middle of everything."

Rosie carried an urn of coffee that she had started earlier out to the table and Ben grabbed a sleeve of Styrofoam cups and a basket of creamers and sugars from the cupboard.

"Rosie, you always think of everything," Reverend Carpenter noted. "Those cookies do smell good. You really are too good to this town."

"Well, I guess it's in my blood, Reverend. If there's people around, I just feel like I have to feed them," she chuckled. The room was filling up quickly as the meeting time approached. People began to take their seats, stopping at the refreshment table to pick up cookies and coffee.

Ben moved through the room, greeting his friends and neighbors. He knew each one personally, had grown up with many of them. Their stories were familiar and the troubles and concerns that brought them to this meeting were of no surprise to him. It was a tough time to be a farmer, and the lack of other employment in the area had not made it easy for them and their families. He realized that the opportunity presented with the Gardens at Howard's Walk was not a done deal for everyone. They didn't see Eden Springs as a prosperous town, and, just like their own budgets, worried about what the cost would be. Would it affect their taxes? Did other money need to be raised? And even though the plan was that the gardens would be open to the public, everybody knew that it would be Ms. Tyler's land value that would increase and not necessarily their own property values. It was a risky venture, and, for cautious people, this was not a climate to take risks in.

Ben suddenly sensed a change in the atmosphere. Eyes were focused at the back of the room and he turned to see what they were looking at.

Max Evans had entered the room. He was taller than Ben and fit for a man of his age. The likeness between the two men was undeniable but where the strength of the younger man was physical, Max Evans' strength was in his eyes and in his bearing.

"What are you doing here?" Ben demanded as he approached his father.

Max smiled, unfazed by his son's question. "This is a public building and a public meeting, isn't it? I have every right to be here. And I am very interested in the agenda tonight." He moved in front of the coffee pot, leaned against the table and folded his arms.

Ben knew his father was baiting him and he didn't want to fall for it, especially in a public place. He returned to his seat.

Wesley and John arrived and moved to the table at the front of the room that had been set up for the council members.

They were all present, so John, as mayor of Eden Springs, banged the gavel on the table and called the meeting to order.

"Now, let's get started. The reason I called this meeting was to update y'all on the status of this project we have been talking about, namely, the restoration of the Gardens at Howard's Walk. As most of you know, there have been changes— Ms. Rebecca Tyler, the new owner, was tragically killed in a car accident just a few days ago." There were murmurs among the people in the room. "I know, I know, this is a real tragedy and our thoughts and prayers go out to the family and friends. Now, her sister, Kate Tyler, has come to see us; she met with Wesley and me today, and she has made it clear she wants to sell."

"I'll buy it," Max Evans called out from the back of the room. "I'll make an offer to her tomorrow."

"I'm sure you will," Ben said under his breath.

John Hubert sighed. "Now, Max, let's not get ahead of ourselves. That's not what we are here to discuss tonight." He refocused on the people seated in front of him. "Now the reason I mention this is that we, that is the good citizens of Eden Springs, have not really made a firm decision on whether this project with the gardens would be a good idea or not. We've shared a lot of information, and we've been debating it—a lot. And I really think we need to come up with a decision one way or the other. Ms. Tyler might just be on the fence about selling so our support might help her decide. But if we are waffling about this, well, I'm not sure we could convince her otherwise."

"How do you feel about it, John?" asked a man in overalls in the second row.

"My feelings are not the issue here, Buzz," John said. "It's a matter for the Town Council to decide in the end, but this meeting is to get your input. I want to know your opinion."

Buzz Ender stood, his large hands twisting a faded John Deere hat. "Well, Maisie and me ain't getting any younger and the farm ain't doing what it used to. So, uh," he hesitated, "well, if we were to be made an offer on our farm, we just might consider it. And there are others that feel the same way. The kids are moving away, so no one wants to take over the farms. We've had developers sniffing around, talking a lot of money, more than we will ever make from farming in the next few years. I'm just saying that it's pretty tempting. So, if we sell, then what's to say that these gardens would even be worth the effort to fix them up? Who's to say this young lady would even stick around?"

Others chimed in with their agreement.

"And another thing, how much would this cost the town? What kind of agreement would we be getting ourselves into? Just sounds like pie in the sky to me, John. Maybe this town would be better off with some housing developments, maybe bring in some real businesses, not a bunch of tourists for Howard's Walk." Buzz sat down.

There were more murmurs of agreement from the group. Suddenly, Wesley stood and started toward the door. Ben turned around and saw a young woman standing there. His first impression of her was one of beauty out of place—an extraordinary presence among the dull and ordinary. She was the color of the tropics, with dark emerald eyes and soft auburn curls cascading around her shoulders, framing a delicate face. She held two bags, both well-worn and decorated with colorful travel stickers. But he could see those faraway places in her eyes, as if she had just stepped off a train from distant lands, and it made him want to know about where she had traveled to and hear her stories.

She set one bag down as Wesley approached.

"Ms. Tyler, please come in," Wesley said. "Everyone, I'd like to introduce Kate Tyler, Rebecca Tyler's sister."

"I didn't mean to interrupt," she said.

"It's no interruption at all," Ben said, stepping forward to shake her hand. It folded into his easily. "I'm Ben Evans. It's nice to meet you," he said. He introduced the group, leaving his father for last. "This is my father, Max Evans."

"Pleasure to meet you Ms. Tyler," Max said. "We are so sorry for your loss."

"Thank you, everyone. But I really can't stay," Kate said. "I am sorry for interrupting." She turned to go. The group began to reassemble for the remainder of the meeting, but Ben held back at the door. "Ms. Tyler, can I walk you out? Help you with your bags?" he asked, hoping to spend a few more minutes with her. He suddenly felt nervous in her presence, a sensation he was not used to. She turned to look back at him and he felt her eyes assessing him as if deciding whether to accept his offer. After a moment, she agreed, and Ben picked up the larger of her bags.

Once outside, she turned to him. "Can I ask you something?"

"Sure."

"Is this really as big a deal to Eden Springs as it sounds? Howard's Walk, I mean? From what I overheard, it sounds like people really aren't in favor of it."

"Not everyone is against it. There are some, sure, but they're just hesitant and still have questions. It's a small town and generally we agree about things. I guess this whole project would be different than what people are used to doing. I'm in favor of it, though, always have been."

"Well, it doesn't matter anyway," Kate said, firmly. "I won't be staying. The house will be put up for sale very soon. Maybe the new owners can discuss it with all of you."

"I'm sorry to hear that, Kate," he said.

They had walked as far as the Park Inn. "Well, good night... Ben, is it?" He nodded. "It was nice meeting you, Ben," she said, took her bag from his hand, and went inside. Ben walked back to the meeting with more than just Howard's Walk on his mind.

7

KATE UNLOCKED THE DOOR TO HER ROOM. Becky would have known what to do at that meeting. She probably would have been there to lead it, to make her case. But Kate was not Becky.

She shut the door, clicked the lock and began to unpack what she needed for the night. But something didn't feel right. She was not supposed to still be here—staying was not part of the plan, not even for one night. Suddenly, her hands were sweaty and trembling, her legs weak. This was not the first time; it had happened before and she instinctively sank to the floor, her throat slowly constricting with the panic.

Her eyes squeezed shut and she forced her surroundings from her vision, desperately willing a different scene to her mind, a scene of family and comfort and security, the only antidote she could ever draw on to defeat the attacks. But she could only bring the scene in waves now. Sweat burst from her skin. Her fingers grabbed at the floorboards but there was nothing to cling to.

Something inhuman had smelled her fear and attacked her in her weakness. The weight of terror that pressed down on her seemed determined to take the very air from her lungs. From somewhere in the depths of her panic she begged to be brought back whole or be utterly carried away. Finally, out of that depth she heard the sound of her own voice, giving her the smallest degree of strength to breathe again, then again. She called her own name, called herself back.

An eternity seemed to pass until the air began its return, layer by layer, relief settling into her brain one degree at a time. Her shirt lay on her like a second skin, her hair dripping down on to her face. She pushed it back and wiped away the sweat that lay heavy on her eyelids. She blinked them open and looked around her.

The room had not been ravaged by a beast. Bed and table were upright. Curtains blew gently at the open window. Kate had been visited by grief. It had finally clawed its way up through her, contorting the paths of simple sadness. Now, she knew, it would sit... and wait.

She crawled to the bed, pulled herself up and lay utterly still while the remnants of the episode left her body and her mind. Her muscles ached as if she had run a marathon and her head pounded from the utter terror she had just endured. Something had entered her unbidden. It had attacked her and trampled on her and left her for dead. Her hands felt raw from the battle, and she curled them under herself to stop the trembling. Sounds from the street slowly entered her consciousness and she finally realized where she was.

She wanted to flee but could not make her muscles obey any command to action. This room was a place of terror now and she prayed that it would not find her there again. She closed her eyes, content simply to breathe. She knew that this was not over. She knew she had just started down the path of heartache and pain. The last few days were just the beginning. But if the terror came again, could she endure it?

Kate finally fell asleep and spent another fitful night of bizarre dreams. Her work had conditioned her to sleeping in strange places and she usually adjusted easily to her surroundings. But an underlying restlessness and anxiety continued to plague her. Several times during the night she rose and paced the room. Several times she had her bags packed and her hand on the doorknob, ready to leave and not look back. But running away in the middle of the night was not the solution. She still had an obligation to Becky, and she intended to fulfill it.

A pale light filtered in through the curtains, urging Kate out of her sleep the next morning. What city was this? What country was she in? She forced her eyes open and looked around the room. She remembered. Eden Springs. She had an appointment. She had made a promise to herself to see Howard's Walk and she gathered her strength to get through the day. She forced herself out of bed and into the shower.

Thirty minutes later, Kate met Wesley and John outside of the café. She took the back seat of John's car while the two men sat in front. They took the right turn onto Columbia Avenue, then the left fork where the road bore off towards the interstate.

Kate took in the scenery with an experienced eye. She had traveled extensively in the United States and Europe and it was second nature for her to observe her surroundings through the lens of a writer, descriptive and full of imagery. Oddly, she had never been to Eden Springs before. The area had been in her own back yard since she and Becky had moved to Winston-Salem, but it had never drawn her as the rest of the world did.

She pulled a journal out of her backpack; it was already well used and one of several that she had filled with records of her trips and notes for her articles. Some of the pages were turned down to mark unique dates and events. She flipped to the first blank page and started making notes as they drove past fertile, flat farmland of tobacco and other crops. She wrote her observations of old sheds that stood in the tobacco fields, and the small white clapboard houses and brick ranch homes, the old cars parked next to them with long driveways leading in a straight line out to the main road.

Further along on opposite sides, larger farmhouses, barns and outbuildings stood as further testament to the orderly farming life inherent to Eden Springs. Long mounds of soil in newly plowed fields lay like plaited braids, hugging the ground. Kate sketched simple visual reminders of her surroundings in the margins of her journal, a long-standing habit that always served to trigger a special memory of a place that she had seen and experienced.

They turned right onto Chilton-Franklin Road. Kate caught John's voice from the front, explaining that the Franklin and Chilton farms, well known in the community, had been joined through the marriage of a son and a daughter, with the road named after them many years ago. Soon, John slowed the car. Kate sat up, sensing that they were closer to the house now. He pulled off onto the shoulder of the road, which was widened in one spot with enough room for a car to park.

Kate looked around for the reason that they stopped. Howard's Walk should be a large house, maybe a mansion, the way she had pictured it. But she saw nothing of the kind. The men got out of the car and John opened the door for her. She slowly emerged from the back seat and looked across the road.

The house before her was a low-slung wooden structure, fronted by a deep wide porch. The roof dipped at one end where a corner post had rotted away at the ground. Wide windows on either side of the centered door were visible but dark. A long shed attached to the right side gave the house the appearance of an old, injured dog, listless and waiting for its master.

The skeletal remains of a small stubborn barn sat to the left of the building and down a small incline. A variety of vines and branches had wrapped themselves around the remaining planks, and scraps of metal roofing clung precariously to the weathered bones of the barn. An assortment of reddish-brown farm tools peaked above the tall dense grass, their only usefulness now as contrast in color to the grays and greens that surrounded them.

The air was warm and still. Nothing moved now, nor appeared to want to move again. Kate could not overcome the inertia of the place and she stood motionless for several moments. The clouds were low and gray and seemed cemented above her.

"This is it?"

Wesley jumped in quickly to explain. "No, Kate, this is the caretaker's cottage. It is part of the property though, and we thought you'd want to see it. The main house is right around the corner." She breathed a sigh of relief and got back into the car. John and Wesley joined her and went into easy conversation about the crops and the weather. They rounded the curve and finally Howard's Walk was in front of them.

The road ended in a circular drive of gravel in front of the house, strewn with leaves and branches and sprouting weeds and misplaced grass. The center of the circle held a fountain, brimming with water from a recent storm. An impenetrable huddle of low shrubs encircled the fountain, new shoots sprawling awkwardly upwards.

She stepped out of the car and walked to the right to take in the full view of the front of the house. She had seen them before, the stately mansions of wealthy landowners, but not in this state of disrepair. A wide porch fronted the house, but it was crumbling at the corners. The shallow steps leading up to the porch were brick but uneven and worn. Trees and shrubs hugged the outer edge of the circular drive, hanging on to each other for support, draping branch over branch, their roots humping out of the ground and shrouded with moss and the clutter of wild undergrowth. Squirrels skittered in the shadows and birds called their pretty songs, oblivious to the decay around them.

Before starting up the steps she took in either side of the house. To the right, and shielded behind a tall hedge, was an attached greenhouse. The glass roof was littered with debris and one of the panels was impaled with the jagged end of a broken tree limb. To the left, a wing extended from the main part of the house, one and a half stories up, with banks of multipaned windows on the front, the brick green with moss.

She slowly walked up the steps. John fumbled in his pocket for the key, provided, as expected, by Snap. He inserted it into the lock, swung the door open and motioned Kate to go in.

She stepped into a large foyer punctuated with columns every few feet on either side extending all the way to the back of the room. Off to the right, French doors opened onto a flagstone walk that ran along the side of the greenhouse which she had noticed from the outside. On her left was another large room. Sliding pocket doors partially opened it to view. A stairway gracefully curved up along the left wall leading to a balcony on the second floor. Under that, at the back of the foyer, she noticed two doors—one on the left and then one on the back wall that stood ajar.

The foyer was empty of furniture except for a side table and another unidentifiable piece covered with a sheet and a thick film of dust. Ancient wallpaper peeled down the walls like bark on a white birch tree. One whole panel lay in a heap on the floor, exposing the bones of lath and plaster beneath. More broken pieces of plaster lay in dusty piles around the large room.

Kate toed the floor with her sneaker, then bent down to wipe it clean with her hand revealing a piece of the expanse of hardwood that led from the front door to the back of the foyer, except for what appeared to be rings of marble around each of the columns. A massive chandelier hung precariously just inside the front door, its crystals appearing to be held together only by cobwebs.

"Would you like to see the entire house first or go outside to the gardens?" Wesley asked as he came up behind her.

Kate was startled out of her silent sweep of the room. "I think I've seen enough," she said quietly. The two men looked at each other. John made another try.

"The gardens are just out here. Nothing has been done in years, but you can still see some of the attraction of them. They were quite beautiful in their day."

Kate shook her head. "I'd like to be alone for a little while, if you don't mind. Then I will be ready to go."

They nodded and left, closing the front door quietly behind them. Kate walked around the room slowly, trying to feel something, anything, of Becky. What did she see in this place? Had her ambition finally gotten the better of her? No, probably not, Kate thought. This was not too much for Becky, but it was too much for Kate. She decided that she had seen enough.

As she turned to leave, she took notice again of the table sitting in the foyer and saw that this one piece, free of dust or plaster, appeared oddly out of place in the neglected space. As Kate ran her fingers over the clean surface of the table, she noticed its front drawer was slightly open. She opened it and pulled out a white box.

Kate caught her breath as she realized that it was the box that had held a tablecloth given to her and Becky so many years before. She lifted the lid slowly and saw the familiar embroidered piece inside—crimson poppies, nestled among emerald green leaves; vines meandered along the edge of the tablecloth with artfully placed embroidered flowers across the center, the stitching giving them a beautiful depth and fullness. Her fingers trembled as she caressed it.

She lifted the tablecloth out of the box and brought the softness of it to her cheek. The slight movement unleashed memories of happier times—memories she had buried deep in her subconscious of Thanksgiving and Christmas dinners and daily family meals around the table, around the world, her mother preparing the meals, Kate and Becky setting the table, always with this tablecloth and the best china, their father serving the family. Laughter, stories, and even chastisements for teenage infractions—all were part of the traditions of the Tyler family.

Kate closed her eyes, recalling the last move that they made as a family. The moving truck had arrived late in the day and the men unloaded boxes and furniture. It was supper time and her father had just walked in with a bucket of fried chicken. A small table and chairs were arranged in the kitchen and their mother had instructed the girls to find the tablecloth while she searched for the dinner plates and utensils. Kate remembered groaning at the thought of going through all the boxes for a tablecloth. What was the point? They could eat supper without a tablecloth, couldn't they? When she posed the question to her mother, the look from her was answer enough, and Kate joined Becky in the search.

"What's the big deal anyway?" Kate had asked her sister when they were out of earshot of their mother.

"The big deal is that it's important to have something familiar when you move to a new house. Something that makes it feel like home, even when it isn't a home yet. And that's what this tablecloth is. Besides, it's an heirloom."

"An heirloom?" Kate had asked. "What's that?"

"It's something handed down from generation to generation. Something special that people want their kids and their kids' kids to have."

Kate had opened a large carton marked "Linens" and on top lay the white box that she instantly recognized as the tablecloth box. "I found it, mom!" she had called out.

"OK, then bring it here and we'll get the table set," her mother had replied. Kate did as she was told and soon they were all seated, saying a blessing, and diving into the bucket of crisp chicken.

Kate roused herself from the memory. She realized that she had not seen the tablecloth since her parents died. Becky must have kept it all these years and brought it here, to Howard's Walk. It was the most comforting feeling that Kate had felt since she learned of Becky's death, and once more she felt connected to her sister.

Kate suddenly realized that she needed more of this connection. She could not break it again, at least not yet. It was, at that moment, the only thing left of Becky and her family that she had to cling to. And everything that had happened in the last few days put her at this crossroads. She could start over in Winston-Salem. She could move on to another town, another city. But where? The only thing she had right at this moment was this house—this broken shell of a house that had probably seen happier days and days of sadness, just like she had.

Kate gently refolded the tablecloth back into the box, replaced the lid, and slid it into the drawer. She rejoined the men outside.

"I think I would like to take a tour after all," she announced. "And if it's possible, I'd like to stay here, at least until things are more settled. Is that possible?"

"Yes," John replied hesitantly. "It's certainly possible, but the house really is not livable yet."

"But, John, if you recall," Wesley interrupted, "Bessie Howard had arranged for Snap to keep up with some basic repairs at the house even after she moved away. And Rebecca had already contracted with several other local tradesmen to check on the electric and plumbing and I think had already paid a deposit." He turned to Kate. "I could get the work orders and look them over with you if you would like to."

Kate nodded. "Yes, I think I would like to do that."

The leaden sky interrupted their tour with a sudden downpour. But Kate had taken in enough for one day. With the appearance of the tablecloth, and the family memories that it had unleashed, Kate knew that Becky had meant for this place to be a home, a place where Kate would have been welcomed and wanted. She began to form a plan in her mind for a temporary stay in the house—for however long it might be.

The next morning, Kate called Mrs. Mims and asked if she could arrange for movers to go to Becky's apartment and pack her things to bring them out to Eden Springs. She ordered a mattress to be delivered to the house and found a vintage bedframe at Orange Tabby Antiques. Kate suddenly felt a new energy and a clearer head. After a quick inspection of the upstairs of Howard's Walk, Kate realized that the second floor was in worse shape than the first. But it simply wasn't in the budget to fix any more than was necessary right now. The space in the large foyer would suit her well for now as a place to sleep and the French doors off the foyer offered a breeze that was refreshing.

A couple of hours later, Wesley brought the work orders as promised and helped her review them. She made some modifications and Wesley agreed to call the contractors to let them know what she had decided. The next day, troops of men and women with hammers, nails, pipes and wires began their assault on the house.

Plumbers attacked the downstairs bathroom off the kitchen, making it serviceable once again with a new toilet, vanity and shower. Electricians sparked the house to life, checking the outlets and wiring on the first floor. Snap brought new appliances for the kitchen, and the carpenters that were working on the walls of the foyer confirmed that the roof was, at least for the time being, solid and would keep her dry here on the first floor.

Kate overheard the contractors speaking among themselves of past work that had been done on the house. This was John Burnie's plastering. That was Bim Archer's handiwork in the foyer. This was Snap's plumbing in the bathroom and kitchen. They would have spread through the entire house like ants, gutting and rebuilding as Becky had ordered, if Kate had given them half a chance. But, true to her decision, she halted their work once the necessities had been taken care of.

Kate was caught up in the energy, too. She scrubbed the hardwood floors and made the windows sparkle. She dusted the wide baseboards and raked the debris from the drive. She fell exhausted into bed each night. Dreamless and heavy sleep saved her from thinking, from remembering.

Until everyone was gone.

Kate could have gone to town, but the weather was rainy and forced her seclusion in the house. She could have called Mrs. Mims, or her friends. But once the hustle and bustle of the work was over, she lost any desire to make the connection again.

The next two days passed slowly, with no letup in the rain or dreariness of the overcast sky. Finally, the moving van arrived with all of Becky's belongings. Kate signed the papers handed to her to confirm the delivery and watched as they raised up the door on the back of the truck.

Kate gasped as Becky's life appeared before her, bubble-wrapped and boxed, taped and neatly labeled. She clutched at her stomach, suddenly regretting that she had asked Mrs. Mims to have everything delivered here, to this house. She should have sent them to storage, somewhere else, anywhere but here. Kate stood, frozen, as she stared into the truck.

"Ma'am are you OK?" the driver asked.

"I'm... I'm fine. I've changed my mind. Just take everything to the house you passed on the way in. Wait, I'll get the key."

When she returned, the driver asked, "You mean that building just down the road from here?"

"Yes, it should all fit."

He shook his head. "All due respect, ma'am, that building won't work. The roof on that place is all falling in and this nice furniture and all would just get ruined. We can move it in here, though, no problem. We can even set everything up for you— that's our job."

Kate shook her head. "No! It all goes into storage. All of it." Then she thought for a moment and resigned herself to the fact that everything had to be moved into the house. There was no other option. "Wait. There's a room on the first floor in the house you can put it in. Follow me."

She led them inside and slid open the pocket doors to the room on the left side of the foyer. It was the size of a small ballroom and the movers agreed that it should hold everything that was in the truck.

After the last box was unloaded, the movers left, and Kate was alone to look at everything from Becky's life. This was not how it should have been. Moving day for Becky should have been a happy one, full of excitement and anticipation. Becky would have furnished the house in her signature style, finding pieces that she loved and decorating in a way reminiscent of the grandeur and history of the home.

Kate slammed the doors shut. She couldn't look at it any longer and she wasn't sure when she might be able to tackle it. She knew it wouldn't be today.

8

IT WAS MORE LIKE HIBERNATION THAN SLEEP, that subconscious depth in which Kate languished that night. And, like an animal crawling out from its winter bed the next morning, she squinted at the sun that pricked at her eyes. She was finally aware of a sound—first a squeak and then the resonance of metal on metal—rapidly—then it stopped. Then again.

Kate wedged herself up on her elbows and pinpointed the origin of the sound as the brass knocker on the front door. She almost shouted for whomever it was to go away, to leave her in her misery. But the words tangled in her dry throat. The banging continued and she saw someone peering in unabashedly through a window that flanked the door.

Kate threw back the covers, grabbed her robe and strode to the door, suddenly very awake. The face was still hovering on the right side of the door so she sidled up to the one on the left, praying that she would not come face to face with anyone else trying to have a look.

There were two of them standing on the porch, one lanky and lean with beard and hair trimmed to the same neat length, and wire rimmed glasses perched on a rather long nose. He was fumbling with car keys. The other, the Peeping Tom, stood about half a foot shorter and pudgier, with hair that seemed to be thinning in odd ways. A pair of sunglasses pushed it up in a peak on his head.

The tall one banged the knocker again. They looked harmless enough, so Kate found her voice and yanked open the door, ready to turn them away. She didn't want what they were selling.

"Can I help you?"

"Hey there!" It was the short one, now with a big smile and not in the least bit embarrassed about being caught looking through her window. "We're looking for Becky. Is she here?"

Kate gripped the door.

"She's not here," she replied tersely. Then slowly, in a tone no less conciliatory, she asked, "Are you friends of hers?"

They laughed, unfazed by her tone. "Oh, we're old friends," the short one said. "You must be Kate. Becky has told us so much about you!"

The other man chimed in. "We're Sam and Martin. Sammy and Martini?" Sam, the tall one, said, as if this would jog a memory of their existence.

"Becky's expecting us," he continued. "Well, not this soon, but we just got back from vacation and, well, here we are! We're here to help with the gardens, as promised. Is Becky around?" he asked, trying to see into the house.

Kate regained some steadiness, drew her robe around her, cinched the belt and stepped out onto the porch. She could have told them just to go away, to pretend that she didn't know what they were talking about. But they knew her sister as Becky. Only Becky's closest friends were allowed to call her that. She couldn't turn them away and steeled herself to say the words.

"I am sorry to have to tell you this, but Becky was killed in a car accident two weeks ago."

Keys clattered to the floor; the two men stood in devastated silence. Martin finally found his voice. "How... what happened?"

Kate desperately needed to sit down.

"Why don't you come in," she offered and led them back to the kitchen. She motioned for them to sit at the large kitchen table while she busied herself making coffee. She gave them a few moments of privacy to compose themselves.

The tall one, Sam, wiped his eyes silently while Martin began to sob, his cheeks wet with an unstoppable flow of tears.

After the initial shock wore off, Kate explained, as much as she understood herself, what had happened to her sister.

"You haven't told me how you knew Becky," Kate reminded them when she had finished.

Martin asked for another cup of coffee, composed himself, and began. "Sam and I have a business in Lakeville. There was a client that we did a really big job for in Winston-Salem, but he never paid us, so we took him to court. That's when we met Becky. She represented us." He smiled. "She sued the pants off the bast... pardon me, off the man... anyway, we owe her everything. She saved us and we just adore—adored her," he said, correcting himself again.

"When she decided to buy this place, she called us and insisted that we help with the gardens—that's what we do, design ornamental sculptures for gardens. But she wanted us to help with the design and all, too. We were really looking forward to it. But now..." Martin hesitated as a thought came to him. "You are going ahead with the plans, aren't you?"

"I'm sorry," Kate apologized. "I'm not in the same situation that Becky was in and I just don't have the funds. She left it all to me, but the house will need to be put back on the market again. As soon as it sells, I will be leaving."

For some reason, she was almost sorry to tell them that, although it was the truth. She felt like she was letting them down, even though she had just met them.

"Well," Martin nodded, "we're sorry to hear that but we understand you have to do what is right for you."

The two men exchanged a glance and they both got up from the table.

"We won't take up any more of your time, then. Thank you for the coffee," Sam said.

They walked to the front door where they each gave Kate a hug.

"We are so sorry about all of this," Sam said. "She was a great person and a dear, dear friend. We will miss her very much."

Kate felt her eyes tearing up at his words. Sam held her at arm's length for a moment. "And how are you holding up?" he asked.

Kate suddenly burst into tears. "I'm fine," she mumbled.

"Fine? You are not fine, dearie." Martin joked. Kate looked at him and they all laughed. "You look like hell and I don't mind saying that even though we just met because you're Becky's sister and she would tell you the same thing!"

"He's so bad, Kate, just ignore him," Sam sighed. "He can't help himself sometimes. Anyway, maybe we've cheered you up a bit."

They said their good-byes and Kate walked them out to their RV. *Martini's Marvels* was written on the side of it in colorful fluid letters, wrapped around images of plants and sculptures. Kate was almost sad to see them go. *They would have done wonders for the place*, she thought.

She waved as they drove away, honking and waving back at her. She went back inside and curled up in her bed and stayed there the rest of the day with fresh, stinging memories darting in and out of her consciousness.

The rain returned. Kate had been alone for too long now. Except for the visit from Sam and Martin she saw no one. As the days passed, she ate from a stockpile of soups and ice cream until it was all gone, and after a while, even stopped checking her social media sites and the news outlets. She could not bring herself to take out her journal. Putting words to paper about what she was feeling would bring a reality to it that she did not want to face.

A mist drew over the house, ebbing and flowing like the tide. Sometimes it was like a blanket, enveloping the trees, and sometimes it was just heavy enough to soften the edges of everything, to make you want to peer a little harder, to walk forward toward things to get a clearer look, where on any other day, you could easily take everything for granted.

She felt removed from the world. There was no garden outside her door, no Eden Springs, no countryside nor interstate linking her to anyone or anywhere. She was alone with whatever the house kept within its walls—its secrets, its memories, its hopes and dreams, even the ones so recently imprinted upon it through Becky's eyes.

She knew that the house would never have owned Becky. It would have submitted to her wishes and allowed her to tear down its walls and rip up its floors if that was her bidding. But it could easily own Kate.

She curled up in her bed and dozed off and on through another misty day. She opened the French doors and let in the mist so that the outside was inside, and she dreamed and listened to her heartbeat and the distant rumble of thunder and the sound of water dripping from the eaves onto the slate below. She smelled the damp bark and the soil that was constantly grinding the leaves back into itself. She could almost hear it.

She could lie like this forever. Maybe the soil would claim her, too, and the dripping water would wear her away like the rocks. She would be altered, disintegrating into molecules and blow around with the mist.

It was the closest she could get to dying that day, to go so deeply into herself and yet so far away as to be nowhere at all. *That must be what death is like,* she thought. *Like mist.* Becky— Becky. Becky was slowly fading into the mist and Kate fought the war within herself to keep her and to let her go. But to let her go meant filling her heart and her mind with something else. And except for the shell around her, this house, she was becoming unable to think of anything else. If she had made plans, they were gone. If she had met people in the last few weeks, she could not place their faces. If someone had stopped by to see her, she did not know it.

The fog took away night and day and left her with a sameness that became her world.

Kate finally woke to bright light streaming in through the windows. She shielded her eyes against it and checked her phone. She had slept for a full day. She felt weak but made her way to the kitchen and sat at the table. Her hands were shaking. She pushed the mass of curls back from her face, but she could not run her fingers through her hair without meeting a snarl of knots. Her nightshirt felt clammy and she was desperately thirsty.

The kitchen was a mess. A brand-new box of tea bags sat on the counter along with other unopened packages—a box of crackers, ten packs of instant noodles and a tomato that was days past its prime. A mound of plastic grocery bags lay on the floor right where she had left them after emptying the contents on to the counter. Dirty dishes sat in the sink.

She steadied herself on chairs and the wall and found her way to the bathroom. A corroded mirror hung unevenly over the sink, and Kate squinted into it. A stranger was reflected back at her, the face of an alien. Displaced from another planet, escapee from a disintegrating world and abandoned in a new one. She sighed. *But this is where you are, Kate. A new world, maybe. But this is where you are.*

She knew she had been in a bad place since Sam and Martin left. And it frightened her. She needed to shake herself out of it, so she showered and dressed and busied herself in the kitchen. She was ravenous and ate two sandwiches while she organized her cupboards with some random dishes she had picked up at the antique store.

She heard a banging on the front door and recognized Martin's voice calling her name.

"What are you guys doing here?" Kate asked as she opened the door. "I thought you were going back home."

"We didn't go back home to Lakeville at first, Kate," Martin replied. "We went to Winston-Salem, to say good-bye to Becky."

"And then we started thinking about what we had promised to do for her and considering all she did for us when we needed help...."

"And we were worried about you..."

"So, we decided to stop by again and see how you were doing," Sam finished.

She invited them in. It was a warm morning and they settled themselves on the stone wall that edged the patio on the back of the house.

"We took some flowers to the cemetery, Kate. We didn't think you'd mind."

Kate assured them that it was a lovely gesture, and she thanked them. After a few moments, she asked, "I've been wondering about the last time you spoke to Becky?" she asked. "Do you remember the date?"

Kate wasn't sure why the date was important to her, but she had been thinking again about the fact that Becky hadn't shared her news of the house with her. She wondered more and more about where she herself had been during the time leading up to the tragedy, still trying to make some sense out of it.

"Well, Sam, you are the detail man—do you remember?" Martin asked, trying to keep the mood light.

Sam thought for a moment. "April 1st. I remember because it was April Fool's day and we were on our way back from Cedar Village, where we were doing that courtyard landscaping job."

Martin turned to Kate to explain. "That's a retirement home. And the activities coordinator thought it would be a great idea for the people to help out, you know, like therapy? Well, I want to tell you, I hope it was therapeutic for them because it was definitely not therapeutic for us. Took us twice as long as it should have. Everywhere you turned there were old ladies trying to tell us how to do our jobs. It was like they hadn't had anyone to boss around in years and were taking advantage of the opportunity."

"But what did you talk about? What did she say to you?" Martin had gotten off track and Kate really wanted to hear about Becky.

"That was when she said everything was in place, that she was going ahead and buying Howard's Walk. She had already talked to us about helping with the gardens, but I guess she was trying to seal the deal, so to speak. She asked if our schedule was still open in about a month and we said we'd be there with bells on."

"Was she happy?"

"She was excited," Martin said. "And yes, very happy."

Kate was silent for a moment. "I didn't know about this house. She never told me."

"You really didn't know?" Martin asked. "We assumed you knew."

"She and I used to share everything. I don't know why she never mentioned this though. Did she ever say anything about telling me?"

"I remember that conversation very well, don't you, Sam? And the last thing she said to us was that she couldn't wait to tell you. But you were planning a trip and she knew you wouldn't be able to get together before that. She wanted to tell you in person."

"I was going to Italy, an assignment for *Premier Travel Magazine.* But all that time that she was coming here and thinking about it? She could have asked my opinion or brought me along."

"She was very independent," Sam reminded her. "She probably didn't want to say anything until she was absolutely sure herself. No wonder you were thrown for a loop on this one. You've had a lot to absorb lately."

"You don't know the half of it." So, Kate revealed everything she had gone through in the days before and after Becky's death. It was the first time she could speak of it without crying and it was a relief to share it.

When she finished, Martin moved to sit next to Sam, and they nodded to each other, a look of agreement passing between them. "Kate," Martin began, "Sam and I have been thinking and we have a proposal for you."

"OK, what is it?" Kate said.

"We told you Becky helped us a while ago with that client that didn't pay us," Martin said. "Well, actually, she did the work pro bono for us—the guy had really put us in a bind and that money made the difference between us staying in business or closing down. So, the reality is that we promised to do this work for her as a way to pay her back."

"Kate, we really want to honor that promise to Becky," Sam said. "We know you can't pay us, and we know you might not stay here but there is a lot we can do to help clean things up..."

"That would help a lot for resale value," Martin finished.

"That's very nice of you," Kate said, "and I appreciate it, but I wouldn't want to take you away from your business."

"No problem," Martin quickly answered. "We have a job not far from here so we will be in the area. We can work here in the mornings when it's cooler and then go there in the afternoons."

"And there is a lot more room here to park the RV overnight if you wouldn't mind. We could park it down the road. You won't even know we're here."

"What do you think, Kate?"

Kate thought for a moment. The last few days without anyone around had not been good for her at all. She knew she needed to get back on track with deciding what to do about the house, so she smiled and said, "Yes, I think that would be fine. And thank you both. I know Becky would have been happy to have you here, too."

True to their word, Sam and Martin began working over the next few days to clean up the property, starting with the back lawn. They parked the RV just down the road from the house and would often stop by for dinner with Kate.

"The best gardens invite you in," Sam said late one afternoon as the two men prepared dinner. They had all decided to take turns for the evening meal while they were there. Tonight, they cooked, and it was Kate's job to open the wine. After discussing its virtues, or lack thereof, and decrying the meager offering of labels at the local grocery store in Eden Springs, she poured three glasses of the California red blend that had become a favorite.

"Like an old friend you haven't seen in a while, who may seem different, but deep down is the same friend you knew long ago," he continued.

"Look out," Martin said in a stage whisper to Kate. "He's starting on the 'gardens are old friends' philosophy. He'll go on for hours."

Sam waved a spoon at him.

"At least I have a philosophy. Nothing is ever the same with you. Something new every time. I like a little familiarity, that's all."

"Can I help it if I am the creative one?" Martin snapped. "Creativity is not 'sameness,' Sam. By definition, it is 'newness.' So, you do what you do, and I'll do what I do."

Kate was getting used to their banter. She knew they meant nothing by it and would get over the spat quickly. "Well, I can speak to both philosophies," she said softly. She hadn't offered a single opinion since they had arrived, and this extraordinary comment made them sit down for more.

"And..." Sam prompted.

"And they both have their merits," she replied. "Martin, Sam's philosophy is just an attitude, a way of thinking about something. Sam thinks about gardens as old friends because they are a constant; if you have planted roses one year, you will have roses the next year. Tulip bulbs one season will produce tulips in the next. But with your talent of adding to the beauty of the gardens, creating statuary, for instance, which can be new as often as you want, you bring 'newness' to a garden."

"Kate, that was brilliant! You really get us! Thank you." Sam grinned.

"You're welcome. But I'd like to hear more about your philosophy."

He looked back over his shoulder at her, talking while he worked. "Well, OK, then. A garden should be inviting. Gates are a prerequisite, of course. Some think gates are there to keep people out. But I look at them as an invitation. On one side of the gate, you are in one world, but on the other side, you are in a new one, in a new space and time."

He sat down at the table. "It should be private, almost intimate. It should surround you. It should feed your soul with its scents and its sounds. Everywhere you look, it should fill you with the wonder of color and shapes and movement. It should bring all of your senses alive."

Sam suddenly set down his spoon, took Kate's hand and led her out the kitchen door to the wide stone patio that spread across the back of the house. It looked out over a broad expanse of what used to be a well-kept lawn. He turned her towards the old gardens off to the right.

"Close your eyes, Kate." She obliged. "It's early in the morning. Picture your hand on the gate. You are lifting the latch. You want to see what the morning has brought you in the garden. There is always something new to see, to taste, to smell. You walk barefooted on the cool, damp flagstones. The sun is filtering through the trees and shimmering through the drops of water that are lifted off the leaves on the light breeze. You come to the fountain and dip your toe into the cool water, creating a ripple that sends the goldfish scurrying away. You breathe in deeply, a mixture of earth and fragrant flowers at every turn. A carpet of sweet alyssum and Lily of the Valley hugging the ground and sending their fragrance upward with the breeze. A splash of lavish colors greets you—impatiens, lobelias, marigolds, and begonias. The irises nod their bearded heads as you pass. The tulips draw you into their cups of color and scent like sipping a tropical drink. A chipmunk scrambles through the trees above you, bringing your eye up a majestic magnolia. You sit on the bench where the morning sun washes over you and you have never felt so alive. Not ever."

Sam turned her to him. "It can be like that," Sam said. "It could all be just like that, if you want it to be."

Sam's description of the gardens had moved Kate with its imagery. But it was a vision out of her reach. She felt tears well up in her eyes. "Can it, Sam? Exactly how can it be like that? Don't you get it? I am not Becky! I can't do what she does... did... I never could! So, what makes you think I can start now?"

But she had almost pictured it. She almost had it in her mind—almost.

Sam took a step back. "Kate, I am so sorry. I didn't mean to. I'm sorry."

"I know you didn't mean anything by it," she said. "It's just that... I have thought about it. And you guys make it sound so possible and so wonderful... but... I just don't know how..."

Martin shook his head. "Don't give it another thought. We mean well, you know that. But sometimes we just get carried away and don't think first before we open our mouths."

Kate stared out across the darkening lawn. "No matter how I try to work it out in my head, I always come to the same conclusion. I don't have the money or the energy to do what Becky must have wanted for this place. I wouldn't even know where to begin. And besides, I have a life, too, you know," declaring this out loud as if to convince herself as much as for their benefit.

"I get it, I really do," Martin said. "I mean, we aren't even sure what Becky did want. She never really finalized plans with us."

After a moment, Sam said, "I think supper is ready."

Kate turned to him and smiled. "Thank you, Sam. Martin, you go on in. I'll be there in a minute."

Martin joined Sam in the kitchen. Kate sat on the wall of the patio and faced the house. A soft light filtered through the curtains in the kitchen windows. Her gaze went upwards to the roof of the house and the windows of the second story, dark and empty. Howard's Walk seemed to tower above her, and, in that moment, she again felt small and powerless. She had overreached before when she thought she wanted something, when she had a vision of where she thought she wanted to be and tried to grab it. Her job at *Premier Travel Magazine*—her trip to Italy—her relationship with Mitch. But Sam's words pushed back. *You have never felt so alive... not ever.* No, she decided, if she attempted this, it was bound to fail. And she knew she could not endure another loss of that magnitude.

9

KATE JOINED HER FRIENDS IN THE KITCHEN. Sam and Martin chattered on through the meal. She pushed her food around on her plate and sipped her wine while they cleaned up. A few minutes later Sam finally took her plate and refilled her glass. He put his hand on her shoulder.

"Kate, we're going."

"What?" She looked up at him.

"We're going out to the RV now. Will you be OK?"

"I'm fine. Just a little tired," she said, rubbing her forehead.

"Get some rest then. And, Kate, we're so sorry."

Kate got up and hugged them both. "No, I'm sorry for being such lousy company tonight. Really, I'm OK."

After they were gone, Kate ventured back out onto the patio. A warm breeze skated across her face and stirred a wind chime to its song. She closed her eyes and let the sounds and warmth envelop her. Sam's words surfaced again. *You have never felt so alive... not ever.*

Alive. She felt a tugging at her heart. *Am I even living? With everything I have lost, do I even know how to live anymore? Do I really have a life?*

Suddenly, she shook herself out of her trance. *Stop feeling sorry for yourself, Kate.*

She went back inside. She needed to be busy, anything to get her mind off everything that had happened in the past few weeks. Sam's words had reached a part of her that she had been neglecting. The beauty of the garden he described was authentic and tangible; it could have existed just as he portrayed it. The image he evoked reminded her of the power of words and how they can open up new worlds for people, which was the reason she loved her job as a travel writer. She found her journal and began to write, jotting down notes of Sam's description of a garden and memories of the gardens she had visited in her travels, finding words that prompted images of neatly manicured gardens in Germany and steamy tropical gardens in Hawaii, home vegetable gardens and simple window boxes. The words flowed easily onto the page.

Kate heard a knock at the front door and groaned. "I thought you were going to leave me alone tonight, guys." She strode to the door and pulled it open.

"Oh," she said when she saw a man standing there with a bakery box in his hands. He flashed her a smile.

"I know this is unexpected, Kate," he began. "May I call you Kate?" She nodded. "We met at the town hall meeting. I'm Max Evans, Ben's father. I would have called but, unfortunately, I didn't have your number. I wanted to properly welcome you to Eden Springs, and I couldn't come empty handed, so I brought the best apple pie in town. Would it be an imposition to come in?"

His seductive southern drawl, easy smile and the aroma of fresh apple pie quelled any hesitation to invite him in.

"Of course not." She stepped back to let Max enter and suggested that they go to the kitchen. "That pie smells delicious. Coffee?"

"That would be perfect," Max said.

Kate set up the coffeemaker to brew and looked in the cupboard for plates. She moved aside a stack of chipped floral-patterned castoffs from the antique store and instead chose two platinum rimmed dessert plates that Sam and Martin had brought from their RV, teasing that they would class the place up. They certainly had the same exquisite taste as Becky. But, looking at the plates now, she realized that they were like diamond earrings on a pig. Chinette might have been a better choice, she thought. But it was too late. She carefully centered the two exquisite pieces of china on the faded plastic placemats and added two mismatched forks to the display.

She smiled nervously at Max who didn't seem to notice the incongruity of her table setting. She hadn't seen anyone except Sam and Martin for days and she felt awkward. But Max had been pleasant to her at the meeting in town. And he had come bearing pie. She decided to give it her best shot.

"To what do I owe the pleasure?" Kate asked, forcing a brighter smile on her face. Max held out her chair for her and then also sat down at the table.

"I'm sorry we didn't get a chance to talk more when we first met."

"It was a long day, Mr. Evans; I had just gotten into town, so I really wasn't ready to get to know everyone," she explained. He was an attractive man, she thought. And a gentleman. A hint of gray at the temples set off nicely tanned features. Denim shirt and jeans on another man his age might have come off as trying too hard. But on him, it worked very well. *So, this is where the son gets his looks,* she thought.

"Please, call me Max. And again, I want to extend my condolences. I know you have been through a very difficult time and if there is anything you need during your stay here, please don't hesitate to ask. After all, we are practically neighbors. The Woodlands, my family home, is on property that borders yours to the west."

He pulled a business card out of his shirt pocket and slid it across the table. "My contact information is all there. You can call me at any time."

Kate picked up the card. "Thank you. That's very kind of you."

Max looked around the kitchen. "I see you have made some improvements here. I hope you have been comfortable?"

"Yes, I have." Kate saw that the coffee had finished brewing. She got up and pulled two mugs out of the dish rack by the sink and poured them both a cup. "I just needed the bare minimum to make it livable, until I decided what... well, until things are settled."

She cut them both a slice of the warm pie and plated them.

"Good. I am glad to hear that. And a wise choice, too, staying here, keeping an eye on things." Max sectioned off a small piece of apple from the pie and then took a sip of the coffee. "What kind of work do you do, Kate?"

"I'm a travel writer, mostly freelance. I just got back from Italy ... but... I was able to take some time off."

"Italy?" Max smiled. "Some of my best memories are of traveling in Italy and France. Mostly it has been business, but I always tried to take in some of the sights. The countryside of southern France—paradise, if you ask me. Have you been there?"

"I lived in Paris for two years when I was growing up. My father was stationed there," Kate replied. They began to talk about their travels, comparing notes on the best places to stay and to eat. He asked her if she could recommend any places in Lisbon, since he was planning a trip there soon. She mentioned a boutique hotel that should suit him and recommended a few restaurants that he could try. The time passed quickly.

"I'm sorry for rambling on," Kate finally apologized.

"No, please. I am enjoying it immensely." Max pushed his plate away and looked intently across the table at her. "May I ask you a personal question?"

"Sure."

"You have the wanderlust in you, I can tell. Are you really ready to settle down... to take on this house... this project?"

Kate was silent for a moment. "This has been a very difficult time for me, and I've been lucky to have the time and space to spend making some important decisions." As she said the words, she realized that this was only partially true. She wondered what he would think of her if she told him that had he stopped by a mere four days ago she probably would not have answered the door, that she had barely been able to make it through each day and that she already knew the task of reviving the house and the gardens would be a failure.

Max leaned forward. "I could be wrong, but it seems to me that once a person is a wanderer, they always have it in their blood. Sooner or later the road will beckon you again."

Kate wondered how he had come to assess her so easily. He had echoed her thoughts from earlier. *Am I that transparent?* she thought. But Becky had told her more than once, "With you Kate, what you see is what you get." It was in her eyes and her movements. It was part of her. It was true that she had only moved into the house on a temporary basis, and Max had picked up on it.

"Don't get me wrong," he continued. "This is a great place to settle down, a great base of operations for a freelancer. I had the pleasure of meeting Rebecca, just once, and she impressed me as a very determined and capable young woman. But... this project, with the gardens and all... lots of responsibility, if you ask me."

Kate set down her mug, nodding her head in agreement. "To be honest, it is pretty overwhelming," she finally confessed. "I wouldn't know where to begin. So, the house will be put on the market."

"I see," Max said. "I didn't notice a For Sale sign outside yet?"

"No, I guess it has taken a while. But I am sure it will be up soon."

"Who is your realtor if you don't mind me asking?"

"John Hubert. He handled it when Becky bought it, so..."

Max chuckled. "Kate, if you really want the best price, going with John Hubert is a big mistake. You don't know the town like I do. In fact, I doubt that John Hubert wants you to sell at all. Looks to me like he is dragging his feet."

"I see," Kate said. The question had crossed her mind over the past week as to why she hadn't heard from John about getting the house on the market. But she had dismissed it as just how things were done.

"Kate," Max said, "I am a businessman. When an opportunity comes my way, I know to trust my gut when it tells me whether it is right for me. This place is a good investment so I'm going to make you an offer. Your asking price, whatever it is, plus an additional ten thousand dollars."

Kate repeated the sum to herself. Ten thousand dollars over asking price sounded generous to her. Maybe Max was right. Maybe John was delaying on purpose. She was suddenly a little concerned about John's abilities to do a good job for her. "You don't even know what I am asking for it and you are willing to go higher?" she questioned him. "That doesn't sound like good business to me."

"Well, I'm guessing that because you might want to make a quick sale, your asking price, once you have an idea of what it is, probably isn't any higher than what your sister paid for it... and ten thousand would be a little help to cover the cost of the improvements you've done, of course." Max leaned in across the table. "You might not get a better deal than this, Kate. What do you say? Are you interested?"

Interested? It was a lifeline. "Yes, I might be interested," she said. "But..."

It was a lot to take in, and Kate hesitated a moment. She moved to clear the table and touched the platinum rim of the dessert plate. It was perfect and fine, and she suddenly remembered sitting cross legged in front of a Christmas tree with

Becky, with china plates piled high with homemade cookies and fudge and sipping steaming hot chocolate from mugs with Santa faces on them. Perfectly mismatched... and a perfect evening.

"There are other options, of course," Max interjected, sensing her hesitancy. "I know an excellent realtor who will really have your best interest at heart. She's young, and a real go-getter. She'd have this place sold in no time, probably multiple offers."

She looked at Max. "It's a lot to think about. I really need more time."

"I see." Max nodded, pushed back his chair and stood. "Well, I have taken up enough of your evening. Thank you for the coffee. I'll say good night then." They walked to the front door where he shook her hand. "I'll be in touch in the next few days after you have had some time to think over my offer. Remember, Kate, this is a great opportunity for you."

Kate sat on the front steps as Max drove away. The air was cool, and dampness was settling in. *What were you thinking, Becky? I wish you were here to talk to.* Kate cleared the gathering tears from her eyes with her sleeve. It might be foolish to refuse his offer. But her intuition told her that she should not be pushed into accepting an offer out of the blue from a man who just showed up at her door.

Max Evans pulled his Escalade in behind a Mercedes parked in the circular brick paving in front of the Woodlands. His butler, Angus, greeted him in a heavy Scottish brogue as he strode up the front steps of his mansion. "Ms. Carroll is waiting for you in the library, sir."

"Thank you, Angus. And bring us a bottle of champagne — the Alfred Gratien will be nice."

"Very good, sir."

Max entered the library. It was a man's room and yet intimate with rich red leather seating throughout. A marble fireplace anchored the space, flanked by bookshelves that extended from floor to ceiling, filled with classic literature, many first editions, and several small French Art Deco pieces discreetly placed throughout. A massive carved writing desk occupied one end of the room, with a well-stocked bar in an alcove at the other. A fire had been set in the fireplace. An attractive young woman stood at the mantle.

"Colleen, dear. I see you got my message."

"Of course, and when you call, I come running." She smiled. "Really a bad habit I have. I must do something about it."

She was tall and willowy, her shoulder length black hair a contrast to the form fitting white dress she wore.

"Not at all," Max replied. "I rather like your attentiveness to my demands."

Colleen frowned. "Speaking of demands, then, what exactly do you want?"

Angus entered with the champagne and two glasses. He popped the cork and poured for each of them, then left as silently as he had come.

Max gave Colleen her glass and took one for himself. He sat down in one of the leather armchairs and motioned for Colleen to do the same. "You look amazing."

"Don't change the subject. I am not staying, if that's what you had in mind. We've had that discussion already. Besides, I have plans with Simon tonight."

"And how are things going with Mr. Barclay?"

"It's not really your business, but it's going fine."

"Good. I thought you two would be a good match."

"Max, thank you for introducing us, but this relationship will be what Simon and I make it. Your interference at this point is really not necessary."

"Very well. He is a promising young entrepreneur though. You could do much worse. I may decide to take him under my wing."

Colleen's eyes flashed at the smug look on his face. "So why did you ask me here?" she asked, changing the subject.

"I met with Kate Tyler earlier. She inherited Howard's Walk from her sister and just moved in. I made her an offer on the property."

"Really? I'd heard that someone had inherited it. But I didn't know it was on the market yet."

"It's not. She said she was thinking of going with John Hubert. Of course, I tried to dissuade her of that notion and go with another, better, realtor. If you are up for the job, of course."

Colleen sipped her champagne, tapping a brightly manicured nail against the glass. "I certainly would be up for it. What is she asking?"

"We didn't get that far. I just told her ten thousand over asking price, whatever that was."

"Ten thousand, Max? Are you kidding me? That's pocket change for you. You really don't know how to use your money wisely."

Max laughed. "This girl is not sophisticated. Sure, I could have gone a lot higher. But her eyes got big even at that number."

"So why didn't she say yes, right on the spot?" Colleen leaned in closer. "Why didn't you close the deal, Max?"

Max smiled thinly. "I didn't really want to close the deal, Colleen. I wanted to show my interest, that's all. And that's not how I want it done. I want you to get the sale. It will be good for your reputation. You've done quite well so far, with my help, but I want you to be at the top in this business. Big things are about to happen and there is too much at stake."

"And, I suppose it wouldn't hurt that you were the one that recommended me, right?"

"Yes, that is very right."

"So, you think I will owe you for this favor, right?"

"Right again, my dear. So, what you are going to do is meet her, endear yourself to her as only you can; friend, girlfriend, whatever, I really don't care, just make sure you get me that property. And I don't care what shape it's in. Am I making myself clear?"

"Perfectly." Colleen drained her glass. "You've met her. What do I target? What's her weakness?"

"She had this dumped in her lap, she does not want to be tied down—really the wandering sort I think—a lot of bad memories for her because it reminds her of her sister, Rebecca. I met Rebecca when she was here, and found her to be a very ambitious woman. But it really is too much for the sister to take on. She doesn't have any of Rebecca's drive. I have some people checking into Kate's background, too. I'll let you know if they pick up on anything."

Colleen stood and picked up her bag. "Good. I'll be in touch then. And, Max?"

"Yes?"

"If I am as good as you claim me to be—which I am— then you and I won't be joined at the hip forever. I might even have my own company someday. Who knows? We might be competitors."

"I look forward to it."

Max escorted Colleen to her car and then went back into the house to the bar and poured himself another glass of champagne. He had played Colleen before and he knew he could do it again. She was ambitious, smart, gorgeous, and willing to do whatever was needed to get ahead in the real estate business. He had helped her get her real estate license and when she showed promise, he brought her a few minor sales to get her started and she had followed with a few more lucrative on her own. She was good enough for the big leagues and he intended to get her there. And she was right, she would owe him—but he knew that with her ruthless ambition, he would have to be careful of her in the future.

His thoughts went back to the plans he was putting into place. Eden Springs was ripe for the taking. The nearby city of Winston-Salem was growing. The suburbs were creeping out into the countryside as people looked for less crowding, less traffic, good schools, and new homes. The farms surrounding Eden Springs would not be sustainable for many more years. A few might be able to still turn a profit, maybe find agritourism options for some of the old homesteads. But that took money, which Max made sure was in short supply. No, the best option for them would be to sell to developers. And Woodlands Real Estate and Development Company, a subsidiary of Woodlands, Inc., was poised to be the one on their doorsteps, ready to buy. He knew that when the first one went, the others would fall in line. Any holdouts—well, there were ways to encourage them which Max was not afraid to employ. No, the time was here, now, and Max was not going to let this opportunity slip by.

Max seated himself in front of the fireplace and looked up at the portrait of his father and mother, Harley and Pearl Evans. It was thirty-three years ago that month that his father had died. And thirty-three years since Max returned to the Woodlands. He had been a young man of twenty-two, traveling in Europe, ready to take on the world. He loved his father, and while Harley Evans could not understand his son's need to break out on his own, to leave behind what he had tried to build for his only son, he gave his blessing to Max to find his own way.

But news of his father's death pulled him back into an existence he had tried to escape. On receiving the devastating news, Max immediately returned from Europe with his fiancée, Chloe, a beautiful young French woman. He buried his father and got down to the business of the Woodlands. He quickly discovered that his family was almost bankrupt. There was nothing left except the house and the land. The stable, which had once been filled with thoroughbreds, was empty. The remaining livestock were there only because no one would buy them.

But Max had not been content to always wonder why the situation had gotten so bad so quickly. Something devastating must have happened while he was in Europe. He reviewed the books. He talked to the bank and to their attorney. But he learned the most from his mother.

She believed that the demise of the Woodlands was all because of one man. A man who could have helped Harley Evans if he had wanted to but didn't. A neighbor, and so-called friend, Enoch Howard, owner of Howard's Walk, had convinced Evans to join him in an investment. When the deal went bad, Howard got out just in time, but Evans lost almost everything. And, as his mother relayed it to Max, Howard never warned his friend, nor did he lift a finger to help him after that. She was sure that it was the financial losses and betrayal by a close friend that had killed her husband.

It wasn't long before Max's plans to marry were shattered by an ugly and humiliating conflict between Chloe and his mother, whose grief had driven her deeper into her alcohol addiction. She was a weak woman when sober, and savage when drunk. Chloe soon returned to France. Max never heard from her again.

But the anger Max felt after his father's death, the loss of his fiancée, and the responsibilities left to him fueled his ambitions, and he drove himself to succeed. He soon met and married Elizabeth Weatherly, a southern debutante, in what was, for both, a marriage of convenience. She was beautiful, smart, and polished, and her family's money helped get them through some hard times. And the Woodlands began to flourish from the disaster his father had left to its current success.

But Max swore that he would get revenge for his father by owning Howard's Walk one day. He had tried to buy the estate for years without success. And when he went to visit Kate Tyler, being in the house after so many years, the desire returned with a vengeance.

He turned out the lights in the library and walked up the wide staircase to his bedroom.

Max Evans wanted to own Howard's Walk. He wanted it. And he wanted to destroy it. He wanted to bring it down brick by brick, burn it down, bulldoze it—it really didn't matter how. He wanted to destroy Howard's Walk so that no memory of it remained.

10

EARLY THE NEXT MORNING, on strict instructions from Sam and Martin before they left for Lakeville for a few days, Kate was pulling weeds in an overgrown area of the back yard that bordered the patio. At least she hoped that was what she was pulling. One green blade looked the same as another. *Therapy,* Martin had told her. *It will be good for you,* he told her.

"Right, Martin," she said, yanking up another random clump.

"Hey." A sudden voice rumbled behind her like a roll of thunder. She turned to see who it was. She sat back on the ground as she first took in the giant boots, clumped with mud and grass, at eye level. Her eyes traveled up past calves and knees, then thighs, on up past a belt buckle the size of Montana and a chest that could stop a train. On and on, further up to a face with a grin as wide as the Grand Canyon.

"Hey, yourself," she croaked. She sat frozen to the ground, trying to get a sense of who this young man was and why he had suddenly showed up on her property.

"Hey," he repeated. "I'm Billy. Mama sent me to help."

Help me move my house from one side of the yard to the other? she wondered.

Billy was a force of nature.

"Well, Billy, I don't know if I need any help right now..." she started.

"I'll help you move stuff," he persisted. "Whatever you got, I'll move."

"I'll bet you can, Billy." Kate finally relaxed, reassured somewhat by his easy smile.

She stood up, taking a step back to get the full effect of her visitor. His arms were bowed out as they hung down at his sides like they could easily reach around a small horse or bale of hay. He wore a safari hat that appeared to be pieced together from two separate hats, with material added to make it fit his large head. His hands were broad with fingers like sausages and his thumbs were tucked inside his fists.

Billy blocked the sun like a moving mountain. He looked at her with eyes that were as bright and blue and as big and clear as twin lakes, fringed in long lashes and tipped with sandy eyebrows. His hair was blonde and untamed. He struck Kate as beautiful.

"Are you sure you are in the right place, Billy?" she asked. "Do you live near here? Is your mama coming, too?"

"Mama's coming in the car. I came through the woods," he said pointing behind him. "We live over there."

Just then, Kate heard a car drive up. From around the corner of the greenhouse, a woman hurried toward them. She was aproned and flour-dusted with wisps of gray slipping from the bonds of a tight bun on the top of her head. When she reached them, she was out of breath, her pale lips pursed to better control her breathing. She held a basket covered with a checkered towel.

"Billy, you were to wait for me—we could have driven over together," she chastised.

"That's OK, mama, I took the short cut. I beat you here!" He looked delighted.

The woman turned a worried face towards Kate. "I'm sorry, Ms. Tyler, we were to come together so that I could introduce you properly, but I see you've already met. I'm Mimi Zink. This is my son, Billy. Billy, shake Ms. Tyler's hand... and be careful."

Billy held out his hand. Kate grabbed one finger and held on as he shook his hand up and down.

"We're your neighbors, just on the other side of the woods there. I heard you moved in about a week ago and I'm sorry I haven't been by to introduce myself earlier. But I brought you some chicken and dumplings," she said, handing the basket to Kate. "I hope you like it. It's one of our favorites."

Kate thanked her.

"I thought maybe Billy could help you with some heavy lifting, right Billy?" Mrs. Zink continued.

"Right, mama."

"Well," Kate said, "I'm not doing a lot of work around here right now." She glanced around the yard, her gaze landing on a stack of flagstone. The company might be good for her, and she was won over by the eagerness in Billy's face. "But I do have some flagstone that maybe he could help with. Would you like to do that tomorrow, Billy?"

"That sounds fine." Mrs. Zink replied.

"OK, Miss Kate. I'll be here tomorrow!"

Billy turned abruptly and lumbered off across the wide lawn and into the woods.

"I hope he won't be a bother to you," Mrs. Zink started. "He loves to help, and he has always loved this house. I know it's trespassing, but he knows these woods better than anyone. And, well, I was good friends with Miss Bessie Howard for many years, so I didn't think she would mind."

She placed her hand lightly on her chest as if to still her heart from its pounding. Kate noticed the gesture and invited Mrs. Zink in for coffee. They sat together at the kitchen table while the coffee brewed.

"And don't you worry, I'll tell him only to come when he's invited from now on."

Kate said, no, she did not think it would be a problem at all. "I honestly don't know how long I'll be here, but we are cleaning up the yard and gardens a little." She poured the coffee and offered cream and sugar to Mrs. Zink. "You said he was your son?" The question came out before she realized what she was asking. The woman looked old enough to be Billy's grandmother. His age was hard to determine, but Kate guessed he was at least in his twenties.

"He's our adopted son. Calvin, my late husband, and I, we could never have children of our own, so when we heard about Billy, well, we couldn't turn him away. Of course, we didn't know about his problems at the time, but it would have made no difference to us. We loved him from the start. He was our son, and that was all there was to it."

"He's big." Kate smiled at the understatement.

Mrs. Zink chuckled, too. "That boy was so small when we first got him, Cal could fit him in the palm of his hand. We were worried at first, but when he started eating, he just never stopped. It sure was comical to see Cal, that old string bean, and Billy walking side by side across the fields. They were inseparable." She sighed. "I don't know what I would do without him. Now that Calvin is gone." Mrs. Zink suddenly grew quiet. She pulled an embroidered handkerchief from the sleeve of her dress, sniffled and dabbed at her eyes.

"Are you all right, Mrs. Zink?" Kate asked.

"Oh, I'm fine. I don't want to bother you with an old woman's worries."

"But I think something is bothering you. Is it about Billy? We're neighbors now, and if Billy is going to be helping me here for a while, if there is something I need to know...."

"Well, you are right, of course," Mrs. Zink admitted. "It's just that with Cal gone it's been a hard road. I'm not getting any younger, and Billy is going to need a lot of help all his life. But," she said, taking another sip of her coffee, "I'll just trust the good Lord to provide. He's always shown the way before and I trust He will continue to do just that." She smiled weakly at Kate. "I just wish sometimes He'd let me in on the plan, you know?"

Kate knew exactly what she was talking about. "Do you have any relatives? Someone that could help out?"

Mrs. Zink shook her head. "No. I was an only child and Cal's two sisters want nothing to do with him. Their kids are all older than Billy and I think they are all afraid of him. Nonsense, if you ask me." She stood and looked out the kitchen window across the expanse of lawn that Billy had just crossed.

"Well," she said. "Enough of that. Like I said, some way will show itself when the time is right. I've no right to complain. We are very blessed."

She smiled at Kate and took her hand. "It was nice meeting you, Ms. Tyler. And thank you for letting Billy help. He loves to work outside, and it will keep him busy. He'll be by again to see what you need."

Kate walked her to her car and watched as Mrs. Zink drove off. She was suddenly struck with the thought that she had spent her whole life traveling the world, seeking out other people and places, and yet here, in the middle of nowhere, people were somehow finding her.

Two days later, Kate was outside again, in the same spot, pulling what she thought were the same weeds, or whatever they were. She looked up to see Billy lumbering across the yard with Ben Evans in tow. Billy had him by the arm, practically dragging him towards the spot where Kate was working.

"Hey, Miss Kate! Look who I brought! This is Ben!"

Ben gently pulled his arm from Billy's vice-like grip and rubbed and stretched it.

Kate couldn't help but smile when she saw Billy. He radiated a simple happiness and contentment that was contagious.

"Hi, Billy," she smiled back at him. "And, yes, I have met Ben already. Hello, Ben."

"Hello, Kate," he said.

"Whatcha doin' Miss Kate?" Billy bent inquisitively over the spot she was weeding, hands on his thighs, looking at the ground intently.

"I think I'm pulling weeds," she answered. "Although I am never quite sure," she said, directing the comment to Ben.

Ben surveyed the pile of refuse stacked neatly on the ground next to her.

"Well, you're about half and half, I would say."

Kate sighed and pulled off her gloves.

"That does it then. It's time for a break. Come on inside and I'll get us something to drink."

They went into the kitchen and Kate retrieved three tall glasses from the cupboard and a pitcher of cold lemonade from the refrigerator. Billy stood waiting, and smiling, as Ben hovered near the door.

Kate remembered her first encounter with Ben and wondered if he did, too. His face had lingered in her mind a little more vividly than she had expected, and she realized she was curious about him.

Billy broke the silence. "I told Mister Ben I was helping you move stuff, Miss Kate. He said he'd like to see what I was moving, so I brought him." Kate gave a sideways glance at Ben.

"It wasn't quite like that, Kate. What I said was..."

"It's OK. You don't have to explain."

He took another step inside as she handed him the glass.

He glanced around the kitchen. "I haven't been inside this house in years. When I was little, I used to come here all the time. I would come in the kitchen door, just like this, and Miss Bessie would make me stand right here while she checked my shoes for mud. Then, if they were clean, she would let me come to the table. She always had fresh bread ready to give me, right from the oven with butter and jam, or sometimes chocolate chip cookies. And always a big cold glass of milk." He took a gulp of the lemonade. "Not much has changed, I see."

"I didn't have much work done, just the essentials. I was told that Miss Bessie had been keeping it up over the years, even though she had moved back to England. I won't be here long, though."

"So, a temporary stay." He smiled and leaned up against the sink, draining his glass. Kate took in the line of his body as he finally relaxed. Yes, she could see the father in the son. But Ben was not as aware of his looks as his father was and didn't seem inclined to use them to persuade or charm. She would need to watch out for those two.

Billy was holding out his glass for a refill and Kate obliged.

"So how did Billy happen to bring you along, then?" Kate asked.

"I saw him on Chilton-Franklin headed home and gave him a lift, but then he said he wanted to come help you 'move stuff,' and he made me drive here, dragged me out of the truck and here I am."

"I moved rocks, Mister Ben, and brush and trees. And the stuff that Miss Kate piles up, I move that, too. She let me use a wheel-barrel yesterday, too."

"And you did a great job, Billy. Can you help again this afternoon? There are more flagstones to set out, so we can do that today, if you want to."

He became so serious at hearing this, it made her want to cry. "Yes, ma'am," he said, gulping down the rest of his lemonade. Kate told him to get the wheelbarrow out of the shed, like he did yesterday, and wait for her in the garden. Billy ran out the door, slamming the screen door behind him.

"Have you known him long?" she asked.

"All my life," Ben replied. "He's about two years younger than me. Everybody knows Billy. And we all watch out for him, and Mimi, now that Calvin is gone. They are good people and have taken good care of Billy all these years."

"Do you know why he is the way he is?"

"Not really. He was adopted so they really didn't know anything about his family. Young, unwed mother—that's all I know. Handled through the pastor at their church, I think."

Kate knew what it was like not to know who your parents were, but Billy probably didn't grasp the concept. The Zinks were his parents and that was all there was to it. She doubted that Billy even knew he was adopted or what that meant.

"Becky and I were adopted." Kate surprised herself at voicing her thoughts out loud, especially to Ben, whom she hardly knew. Other than a slightly raised eyebrow, he didn't respond. Kate could have given him a long explanation but decided to leave it well enough alone. She took his glass and set it in the sink.

"I guess we'd better go find Billy and keep him busy. He'll have the greenhouse moved if we're not careful."

They found Billy picking up the weeds Kate had pulled. A length of twine had been stretched from the corner of the back patio to the greenhouse in two rows and staked at several points creating a marked spacing for the flagstones.

"This is impressive," Ben said, looking at what appeared to be preparation for a walkway. "I was under the impression you didn't know much about gardening?"

"Oh, I don't, trust me. This was all Martin's doing," Kate replied, and she told Ben about the two friends that had been there helping her over the last few days. "They've been amazing since I've been here. But they have a business in Lakeville and had to go back to check on things there."

"Well, it looks like they know what they are doing. Hey, Billy," he called. "Help me get these set out for Miss Kate."

Billy lifted the stones easily, following Ben's lead and with Kate encouraging him at each step. When they were done, Kate asked Billy to take the wheelbarrow back to the shed and reminded him to lock the door on his way out. He completed the task eagerly and clicked the padlock shut as he had seen Kate do, then pumping the air with his fist. "All done, Miss Kate!"

"Good job, Billy!" Kate called to him as he plodded off, his boots imprinting the loose soil around the newly laid stone walk.

Now that the work was done, an uncomfortable silence settled in. Ben spoke first.

"So, you are still thinking of selling?"

Kate poked at the ground with a shovel. "I think so. What difference does it make? It's a drafty old house with overgrown weeds and broken-down buildings that need repair."

"Is that all you see?" Ben asked. "I think you are missing the best part. But you weren't here when Bessie Howard was here. It was peaceful, almost magical in the gardens. Eden Springs was a great place to grow up and Miss Bessie always made me feel welcomed here at Howard's Walk. She once told me that she was born English, but because she loved an American and loved a Southerner, that meant that she lived American and lived Southern." He leaned down to gather up a handful of soil and let it fall back through his fingers. "This was where her roots took hold. I was only about ten when she said that to me, but I will never forget it. Howard's Walk was part of the reason I am in the plant business. I love plants and gardening and opened a garden center a few years ago."

"I don't understand roots," Kate admitted. "We moved around so much growing up that I never grew attached to any friends or to any place. I don't see how anyone could stay in one place their entire lives."

"Maybe you're right," Ben half-heartedly admitted. "I'll be selling the garden center soon and moving to South Carolina."

"Really?" Kate asked, surprised. "Why? You sound like you love it here."

Ben shook his head. "I'm not sure I even understand why. It's beginning to seem a little unreal to me lately. I'm going into business with my college roommate."

"So why do you want to move away from here?"

"Well, my mother moved to Charleston. My father and I aren't close. I have some friends here but other than that, there's really no future for me in Eden Springs."

Kate thought for a moment. Maybe the solution to her problems was right here in front of her. "Make me an offer," she demanded.

"What?"

"Make me an offer on this place. You seem to love it. You will have the money if you sell your business. You could buy it and restore the gardens."

Ben shook his head and looked out across the property.

"I used to think about owning it. And you are right. I could afford it if I changed my plans and stayed here." He turned to face her then. Kate was suddenly lost in the sea blue of his eyes and the closeness of him. She hadn't noticed the curve of his mouth before, or the slight stubble of his beard. "I can't be sure about your sister's plans," he said quietly, "but if she meant for it to be her home, I wouldn't want to be the one to take that away from you. She entrusted it to you, and I think that means a lot."

"I don't know if I belong here," she whispered. "I just don't know."

"Well," Ben said, smiling. "It's always worth a try, right?" He searched across the lawn for Billy. "Time to go, Billy!" he called when he spied him pulling brush out of a riot of overgrown shrubs. "Gotta take you home before your mama gets after me!"

Billy waved and lumbered towards them. "OK, Mister Ben, let's go home!" He ran past them to the truck and hauled himself inside. Ben joined him and started the engine. Kate knocked on the window of the truck and Ben rolled it down.

"Ben, thank you. Maybe I needed to hear someone say that."

"You are very welcome, Kate. I'll see you around, OK? And thanks for the lemonade."

11

BEN'S WORDS LINGERED WITH KATE throughout the day. What she realized though was that she knew more about Howard's Walk itself than about Becky's reasons for buying it or what she planned to do with it. And now it was all hers. She felt as if the past was trying to speak to her through all she had learned but she couldn't manage to catch it up to the present.

Kate picked up a wine bottle and glass from a stand beside her bed and resolutely made her way up the curved staircase to the second floor. Once there, she turned towards the balcony railing overlooking the foyer and closed her eyes.

First, a musty smell came to her, much stronger than she had noticed on the first floor. The air on the second floor was stagnant and uncomfortable. In the distance, she heard the motor of a tractor on one of the nearby farms. A lone bird chirped. The refrigerator clicked and ran with a humming sound. The sparseness of the sounds surprised her.

She opened her eyes and walked to the nearest door. It probably had served as a bedroom, but was now completely empty, as was the next room. She turned back down the hall and crossed the balcony to the other rooms that faced the back of the house.

Kate had made only one trip to the second floor since her arrival. A trunk and some miscellaneous furniture were the only things stored there. But she couldn't bring herself to explore the contents of the trunk at that first exploration. The trunk definitely did not belong to Becky. It held something from another world, and Kate wasn't even able to deal with the one she was in at the moment. But now, maybe now, she was ready.

She went into the room where she had seen the trunk. A bank of windows and French doors stretched across the back of the room and opened to a small balcony that overlooked the gardens. Kate set down the bottle of wine and her glass and tried to open the doors to the balcony, but they wouldn't budge. She turned her attention to the trunk, pushing and pulling until it was finally situated in front of the doors and sat on the floor in the afternoon light.

The trunk was flat topped with leather handles and brass plated hardware. Kate wiped the layers of dust with her hand until the wood beneath was uncovered, revealing a stunning grain in the wood. She unlatched the round brass lock on the front and slowly lifted the lid. The lingering scent from the cedar lining permeated the room. Kate inhaled the aroma of a bygone era, closed her eyes and let it fill her.

After a few moments, she opened her eyes and looked in at the contents. It was full and appeared to be neatly packed for moving. Kate wondered if it had simply been missed in the hustle and bustle of moving day. But as she looked through it all, she couldn't help but wonder how anyone could have left this behind when she saw the mementos, personal items, forgotten pieces of their lives.

Kate started sorting through the contents. First, she pulled out a packet of what appeared to be newsletters tied with twine. She untied the first bundle and gently unfolded the brittle paper. They were entitled *The Market Bulletins* and seemed to be newsletters distributed throughout the South among people with an interest in plants, flowers, and seed exchange. In more than one issue, Bessie Howard had written articles about gardening and flower propagation, one on how to take stem cuttings or divide perennials and another on how to collect heirloom plants. And her articles always ended with a thought about her love of gardening.

One in particular caught Kate's attention. She began to read.

I walked barefoot in the garden today on the sun-
warmed bricks and rocks, through the dewy grass.
I got mud between my toes and rinsed them in the
cool, refreshing water of the pond. I smelled, I tasted,
I let the beauty fill me. This is my bit of heaven. This
is my memory, my present, and my future. Good-bye.
Until next time.

It was dated May 11, 1955 and was the last edition in the collection of newsletters. Kate was intrigued about the rest. It was becoming clear that Bessie Howard had an impact on people, both through her writings in the newsletters and personally, as she must have with Ben. Kate would go through all of them, she decided, and laid them aside for later.

Next, she found two photo albums filled with black and white photographs of a couple who she took to be Bessie and Enoch Howard standing in front of the house at Howard's Walk as it was being remodeled, labeled 1951. She turned page after page of the black and white photographs—the renovation of the house and then the creation of the gardens; Bessie digging and planting; Enoch on the tractor or using horses to pull stumps to clear the grounds. They were always smiling and laughing. Further on in the album the photographs were in color—pictures of a baby in a stroller, then later a toddler, then a young girl looked back at her from the page—sullen and sad. She turned over the photograph. *Jenny Howard, 13 years old, 1986.* Kate set them aside, eager to show them to Sam and Martin.

In the next layer were three small baby blankets in yellowed tissue paper. Kate carefully pulled them out. The rest of the trunk was filled with shawls and books and one in particular caught her eye—*Fried Green Tomatoes at the Whistle Stop Café.*

She opened it, and written on the inside cover was a note: "To My Daughter Jenny on her birthday, 1987." Each of the other books were inscribed in the same way, with varying years that stopped at 1989. There were other odds and ends; it appeared to be a catchall of the things that would not fit anywhere else in the packing but had seemingly been left untouched for all these years.

Kate looked back through the photo albums. How happy they looked together, this young couple, Bessie and Enoch. Bessie must have expected to spend the rest of her life here with her husband. But no place is guaranteed to hold a future, as Kate knew too well. Becky had made plans and they were torn away from her in a split second. She would never get another chance.

Kate felt tears well up in her eyes, and she quickly downed a glass of wine to blur the edges. Death had cheated Bessie and Becky out of the futures they had dreamed of. It hardly mattered, Kate thought, if it was your own future, or if it was that of someone close to you. Death was the common denominator.

Kate threw the papers and the albums and the blankets back into the trunk and slammed the lid closed. She ran downstairs and out onto the patio, tears streaming down her face. *Not again,* she thought. *I just wanted to look in the trunk. I didn't want to think about this all over again.*

She sat on the steps, her head in her hands, rocking back and forth. Words came to her quickly, voicing her hurt, begging to be let out. She wiped her eyes and went back inside and curled up on the bed. She picked up her journal.

The writing came like a dam bursting.

> *The essence of grief is a grotesque force that alters your existence. It is the harbinger of a changed person. You are at one moment the person before the death and then you are the person after the death, never existing in the same way again. The*

death of a loved one, the death of a marriage, a
relationship—it makes no difference. You are altered.
You are changed, without your consent. You resist,
you deny, you shout out against it—but it is there, in
all its complex and subtle forms.

She whispered the names of those she had lost—*Becky,*
Mommy, and Daddy. This is for you.

Kate left the patio doors open that night, letting the breeze lull her to sleep, cleansed yet again by tears and memories. A short time after setting up the coffee to brew, she heard the sound of tires crunching over the gravel of the driveway. She peered out the window. A uniformed driver got out of a black Mercedes and walked up to the door. Kate opened it before he could ring the bell.

"Can I help you?" she asked.

"Good morning, miss. I have a note from Mr. Max Evans. I am to wait for a reply."

Kate opened the engraved envelope and withdrew the note from inside.

Dear Kate,

It would be an honor and pleasure if you would dine
with me tomorrow at noon. My driver, Horace, will
escort you to the Woodlands.

Regards, Max.

It was an old-fashioned and formal gesture, but Kate was genuinely touched. She told the driver to let Mr. Evans know that she would be delighted to have lunch with him.

"Very good, Miss," he said, tipping his hat.

Kate knew why he was asking her to lunch. They had not spoken since his visit and this was his way, without pressure, to find out if she had made a decision on his offer to buy Howard's Walk.

She had given his offer a good deal of thought. It was the deal of a lifetime. She knew it could be months or even years before she got another offer that was as generous as his. This was what she wanted, wasn't it? To get out from under this place. To get back to her old life, her writing, her traveling. She was beginning to feel better with Sam and Martin's help, when they were there, and with Billy to cheer her up. She would miss them if she left, but even with Ben's encouragement, she couldn't shake the feeling that it was time for her to move on.

She turned and went to the kitchen where the aroma of freshly brewed coffee awaited her. She poured a mug and carried it out to the patio. The great expanse of lawn spread out skirt-like in front of her.

Well, if I do leave, I am going to leave my mark, Kate thought. *Something, however small, in Becky's memory that will always be here—growing, even if we aren't.* Spurred by her decision, she dressed quickly and headed out to find what she had in mind. At the second intersection off of Chilton-Franklin Road, she found the sign she recalled from her previous trips into town. *Eden Springs Garden Center.*

She pulled her car into the parking lot. Men were loading mulch and pine straw into trucks, bulk in some and bags in another. The commotion was a sign of a thriving business.

She heard Ben's voice calling out orders to his crew as she got out of her car, and she spotted him across the yard. She remembered how she had felt the day before, like she was adrift in the nearness of him, and realized that even from a distance the attraction was still as strong. He lifted large bags of soil like they were filled with air, tossing them into the truck with ease, his muscles rippling under his work shirt. His jeans hung low on his hips, accentuating a long torso.

She stood watching until he noticed her and waved.

"Hey, Kate," he said. "I see you found me."

"I did," she smiled. "I was hoping the sign I saw was your place."

Ben leaned up against the car. "What can I do for you?"

"I'd like to buy a tree—to plant in Becky's memory," she replied.

He nodded. "That's a great idea. Did you have anything in mind?"

"No, I was hoping you could give me some ideas. Something that blossoms, maybe?"

"I have some nice flowering ones. Come on, I'll show you."

As Ben guided Kate through the rows of burlapped trees, he described the different types, all of which Kate rejected until he showed her a small Redbud.

"This might not look like much right now," he explained, "but it's a great blooming tree in the spring. Butterflies love it. The birds will nest in it too, so it has a wildlife value."

"It sounds perfect," she decided.

"This one it is then." Ben lifted it easily and carried it over to the checkout area. "I can come plant this for you if you want," he suggested.

"That would be great," Kate said, quickly agreeing to his offer.

"How about tomorrow? I can come around lunch time?"

Kate hesitated. "I'm afraid I'm busy tomorrow," she answered, touching the leaves of the Redbud. "Actually, I'm having lunch with your father."

Ben stiffened and looked away. "Oh? I didn't know you were friends," he said as he tore the price tag off the tree.

"Well, not friends really," she explained. "He stopped by one evening and made me an offer on the house. I guess he wants to discuss it further."

"He made you an offer?" he asked. "And you are considering taking it? You didn't mention that yesterday."

"I haven't decided yet," Kate answered defensively. "It was a very generous offer though."

"I'm sure it was. Listen, Kate, I'm sorry. I have to get back to work." He stepped away and nodded to the cashier. "Rosemary can take care of you from here. I'll have someone deliver this and help you plant it."

"Ben, I know you mentioned you and your father weren't close, but I didn't think...."

Ben motioned for her to follow him to an empty corner of the lot and lowered his voice. "It's none of my business. My father and I have our own issues and they don't have anything to do with you. But a word of advice. Max Evans has made his way in this world by cheating and lying and I have no reason to think that he would stop with you. So be careful," he warned her and walked away.

Kate paid for the tree and left for home. She was stunned at what Ben had just said about his father. Max Evans had been very nice to her. Ben had said they weren't close, but what he had just described was on another level of resentment. She wondered how they had gotten to that point in their lives. It wasn't an appealing trait to her, and she knew she didn't need someone with baggage in her life. The friendship with Ben she was beginning to hope for was now in serious doubt.

Max Evans' driver arrived precisely at noon the next day. Kate had settled on wearing a sleeveless white knit shirt and tan slacks, a stark but pleasing contrast to her auburn hair and the darkening tan she had acquired from just a few days working in the sun. She wrapped a light cardigan around her shoulders and slid into the back seat of the Mercedes.

Kate stretched her hands out over the soft leather seat. The interior was impeccably appointed, the leather designed in a diamond cut pattern and the trim a rich polished mahogany. It was clear that Max Evans spared no expense in his possessions.

The driver followed Chilton-Franklin Road for about a mile and then after a few turns, approached a winding, tree lined drive. After a few moments, he slowed the car to a stop in front of a wrought iron gate. He entered a code on the keypad, the gate slowly opened, and they continued down the drive.

Soon the chauffeur pulled the Mercedes around a circular brick-paved space in front of the estate known as the Woodlands. Kate peered out the window at the imposing structure. Four two-story columns supported the portico. Flowering shrubs lined the circle of the driveway and lofty topiaries stood at attention, leading the eye up to a massive carved front entrance, a dark wood door that stood out against the bright white intensity of the rest of the house.

A man in a tuxedo approached them from the house. The chauffeur opened her door and Kate stepped out of the car. "Welcome to the Woodlands, Ms. Tyler. My name is Angus," the man in the tuxedo said.

"Thank you, Angus," Kate replied as she took in her surroundings.

"Please follow me." Kate followed him through the front foyer, a grand space flanked on either side by two graceful staircases. She tipped her head up and found herself underneath a massive chandelier and blinked at the shimmers of light that it reflected throughout the room. He led the way to the patio at the back of the house where Max greeted her, taking her hands in his.

"Kate, welcome to the Woodlands. I am so glad you decided to come."

"Thank you for inviting me. You have a lovely home."

"I plan on never leaving. Please, come. I hope you're hungry. My chef, Philippe, has prepared a delicious lunch for us. Can I get you something to drink?"

Kate agreed to a local estate Cabernet that Max recommended. He chose a crystal glass from the bar and poured the wine. Kate took the glass from him, commenting on its simple lines and shape. "Is it Italian?" she asked, swirling the dark-ruby liquid around in the bowl.

"I am pleased that you noticed, and you are correct. It is Italian. I was served a wonderful Italian wine in this style of glass in Rome and ordered a set for here at the Woodlands. It is a Bottega del Vino crystal, mouth-blown and hand-finished." Max took a sip from a glass he had poured for himself. "They say that if the wine matters, so does the glass. So, I only use the best, even for our local wines. And I must say, our local estate wines do stand up against some of the more expensive I have had."

"It is lovely. And a perfect wine for it."

Philippe approached them then and bowed slightly, his hands clasped tightly over a substantial midriff. He was swathed in white with the exception of a pair of bright orange boots.

"Ah, Philippe," Max said. "Tell us what you have prepared for us today."

"Of course, sir," he responded. He turned to Kate. "Today we have for our appetizer roasted garlic on French Baguette with Killer Shrimp. We will serve this with an August Kesseler Riesling. For the second course we have Garden Fresh Tomato Soup and with that we will have a Mulderbosch Sauvignon Blanc. The main course will be salmon with dill mustard sauce, Insalata Caprese and a Paul Masson Ruby Burgundy. And for dessert I am preparing a simple chocolate orange cake with Brachetto D'Acqui."

Max clapped his hands. "Bravo, Philippe!" He turned to Kate. "At first I was contemplating a simple southern lunch—shrimp and grits or barbecue—but with a world traveler like yourself, well, I wanted something very special, very international."

"It all sounds wonderful," Kate said. And she wasn't lying. Her appetite had been slowly coming back. She began to relax and enjoy being pampered and waited on in the beautiful surroundings of the Woodlands.

Max guided her to her chair and held it while she sat. He then sat across from her.

"I hope you don't mind my saying so, but you look lovely today, Kate. The last time we met, I was very concerned about your health. I hope you are feeling better?"

"I am feeling much better, thank you for asking." Max continued to chat about the weather and plans for the Woodlands. The conversation soon turned to travel, and he drew Kate into exchanging tales of their favorite places to spend time with good food, excellent wines, and great company.

"I recall you have been to France. Tell me, have you ever been to St. Tropez?"

"Yes," Kate replied. "But only briefly on one of my trips to Europe."

"I love the quaintness of it, don't you?" Max asked. "The narrow streets, the shops along Rue Georges Clemenceau."

"Did you visit the museum there?" Kate asked. "I did manage to see an exhibit of Paul Signac and Matisse. It was wonderful."

"Yes, the era of those great artists is hardly to be matched. In fact, I have several of Signac's works here at the Woodlands. Perhaps I can show them to you later."

Philippe began serving, and Kate was fascinated by his expert pairing of food and wine. Each was perfectly elevated by the other and each course was more incredible than the previous one. She ate everything in front of her, tasted each of the wines and was more relaxed than she had been in weeks. Max made her laugh with his talks of mishaps on a backpacking trip through Europe in his youth.

He sipped his wine and stared out over the balcony. "The Cote d'Azur is one of my favorite places because of that trip." Max was silent for a moment as he gazed into the distance.

"I have had a lot of misadventures on my trips, but none ended quite as wonderfully as that, I must admit," Kate said.

The sun was moving lower behind the house. Kate felt a chill and rubbed her arms. Max, pulled from his reverie, noticed her discomfort and immediately retrieved her sweater from a nearby chair. He put it around her shoulders, his hands lingering just for a moment. He sat down in the chair next to her. "Would you like to go inside?" he asked.

Ben's warning suddenly came back to her. *My father has made his way in this world by cheating and lying and I have no reason to think that he would stop with you. So be careful.* Up to this point, Kate could not think of one moment when Max had been anything less than a gentleman to her. But as a woman, she instinctively knew that Ben might not have been lying to her either. Max certainly was charming. Was she being seduced? What would happen if she said no or if she said she needed more time to think?

Kate felt uncomfortable under Max's keen gaze. But she had done a lot of thinking since her conversation with Ben the day before and she had decided that caution was the best approach. Most importantly, she would not let Max intimidate her. "No, I'm fine, thank you." Max moved to pour Kate another glass of the Brachetto d'Acqui but she covered the glass with her hand. He set the bottle back on the table.

"So, Kate... have you given any thought to my offer?"

"Yes."

"And?" he asked. He leaned in closer and looked intently at her. "Just between you and me. Will you accept my offer to buy Howard's Walk?"

She straightened her shoulders. "Max, I will be honest with you. I have just come through a very difficult time. I am just getting a grasp on where I am right now, today, let alone the future. I thought I wanted no part of the house and the gardens and I am still not sure that I do, but I think the right thing is to wait until the estate is more settled before I decide anything. I really appreciate the offer and I am not saying no to it. But I can't promise you anything."

He leaned back in his chair. "I see." He stood, walked to the stone railing of the patio and leaned up against it.

"I was thinking about our conversation the other day, and there might be another option. If you do agree to sell, which I hope you do, but you want to stay in the area, perhaps we can add something to the agreement. I would be willing to leave you the piece of property that the caretaker's cottage is on, help you fix it up. It could be quite cozy and comfortable for you, a place for you to return to between trips. And we would still be neighbors."

Kate started to reply. "Thank you, but..."

"Well," Max interrupted. "I have probably taken up too much of your time and unfortunately I have an overseas call coming in soon. I hope you have enjoyed your lunch today and the conversation. Perhaps we can do this again soon?"

"Of course," she said. "And thank you for the wonderful hospitality."

The butler escorted Kate out to the car, without another word from Max. She realized that their business had been concluded and her presence was no longer required.

12

COLLEEN CARROLL THREW A YELLOW CASHMERE SWEATER set on the bed next to a teal silk blouse, a white jean jacket and two pairs of crop pants. She admired herself in the full-length mirror. Toned and fit now after a recent boot camp workout, she found that her wardrobe was lacking. "Time for another trip to Atlanta, girl," she told her reflection.

She went to a large walk-in closet searching for something to wear. A potential client had called at the last minute for a meeting and she wanted to look her best. Colleen had discovered a passion for the real estate business; she liked her clients and the money wasn't bad either. The competition fueled her ambitious nature, and she did admit to a certain ruthlessness that served her well in the industry. The sky was the limit and with the right contacts, she envisioned a lucrative future.

She sifted through her wardrobe and finally settled on a red sleeveless shift that fit snugly, showing off her toned arms and contrasting well with her jet-black hair. Gold hoop earrings and a pair of nude ankle strap sandals finished what she considered her uniform—sexy, powerful, and successful.

The doorbell rang. Colleen grabbed her purse and walked to the door, ready to turn away anyone on the other side of it. She opened it and frowned. "Well, Max, twice in one week. What can I do for you?"

Max Evans looked her up and down. "Aren't you going to let me in?"

She stepped back and let Max come in. Trying to put some space between them, she walked behind the bar and took a bottle of Perrier out of the refrigerator. He had never come to her apartment before and she found it unsettling. Max sat down on a stool at the bar.

"Did you forget to tell me something?" he asked, after a moment.

"I don't know what you are talking about."

He pointed to her left hand. "What is that?"

"That is my engagement ring. What does it look like?"

"It looks like the headlight on a Chevy."

"Yes, Max, it is a very large diamond. Simon proposed to me last night." She spread the fingers on her left hand and turned it in the light to make the stone sparkle. "You said you liked Simon and you've always said you want the best for me, right?"

"Of course, I do, darling. So, congratulations on your engagement."

Max moved to the sofa, stretching his arms across the back. "But I didn't come here to discuss your love life."

"Make it short then," Colleen snapped. "I'm meeting a client."

"I want to know what progress you have made with Kate Tyler... and that house."

"I told you I would be in touch. What's the hurry?"

"Patience is not my strong suit, Colleen. You of all people should know that. Have you talked to her?"

"No, I haven't talked to her yet. I will... in my own time."

"Must I remind you that are on my time, not yours."

"I told you I would get it done. You don't need to worry about a thing."

"I hope you are right. Or things could get embarrassing for you—and your career—and your family."

Colleen froze and looked him in the eye. "You leave my family out of this—"

He stood. "You know I can do it, Colleen—and don't you ever forget it."

Colleen glared at him. She hated Max for threatening her, but she knew from experience how callous he was in business and the damage he could do to her career just by a few strategically placed comments to her clients. They had once had a brief affair during an out-of-town trip, and he would not hesitate to reveal it if he wanted to humiliate her. He could make things very unpleasant for her father, too, even with his spotless reputation. And even though she had kept her father at a distance in the last few years, admittedly because of her own issues, he would never deserve what Max could dish out if he chose to.

"I had lunch with Kate today and she's still waffling. I want that house."

"Fine. I said I would do it and I will. I'll see her tomorrow."

"That's better. Now, there's one more thing. What have you been hearing about Ben's sale of the garden center?"

"I know he has it up for sale. It's being handled by a realtor out of Winston-Salem, I think. Why do you ask?" she managed to ask, busying herself at the bar.

"From what I hear, he's pretty close to selling it," Max said.

"So? It will get him out of town. Isn't that what you want?"

"Yes, eventually," Max agreed. "But not this way." He went to the window and pulled back the curtain slightly to check out the pool area. No one was there so he turned back to Colleen. "The boy is a disappointment to me. I was ready to give him everything I have, teach him everything I know. But he threw it all away. And he was arrogant about it. He needs to be taught a lesson. He needs to know who's in control."

Colleen knew of the fractured relationship between Ben and his father. It had been the topic of many conversations during a brief but tumultuous relationship with Ben. But she had never known how to help him. Maybe in the end they were both just too damaged to be together. Colleen turned back to Max and shrugged. "So, what do you want me to do about it?"

"Find out what you can, who the buyer is, that sort of thing. Use your connections and let me know everything you find out."

"Fine. Anything else?"

Max smiled. "No, that's all... for today. I'll let myself out."

Colleen quickly locked the door behind him. She despised Max at that moment. She despised him for his threats, his manipulation, and his obsession with controlling everything and everyone in his orbit.

Later that afternoon, Ben's cell phone rang. Colleen's name came up on the screen. He let it ring twice more before answering. "Hello, Colleen."

"Hi Ben. I'm sorry to bother you but I wondered if you had a few minutes to talk."

Ben sighed and pulled the phone away from his ear. Colleen Carroll was not what he needed at the moment. But out of respect to her father, Wesley Carroll, he decided to hear her out. "What do you want—I'm really busy right now."

"I wanted to see if you were home. I need to talk to you about something."

He sighed. "I'm out in the garden center if you want to stop by—but I don't have a lot of time."

"OK. I'm near there now. I'll see you in about five minutes."

Ben ended the call. He was frustrated with himself for agreeing to see her, but it was done now. She sounded worried about something, which was unusual for her. A few minutes later, Colleen pulled into the parking lot. She got out of the car and walked over to him. He pulled off his work gloves and threw them on a display bench.

"So, what is it you wanted to talk about, Colleen?"

"Not out here. Can we go inside?"

She followed him into his office. He shut the door and motioned for her to have a seat.

"Ben, I won't waste your time."

"Good to hear."

"And you may not want to hear this from me. But your father has been asking me about the sale of your business."

"OK, I'll bite. What kind of questions has he been asking?"

"He wants me to check with my real estate contacts and let him know whatever I find out."

"I don't understand. So, he knows it's up for sale. What more could he need to know?"

"He wasn't specific," she said. "He just asked me to let him know whatever I hear about it."

"And will you? Are you going to do what he wants?" She hesitated. "I see," he nodded. "So why are you telling me this?"

"I wanted to warn you."

"Warn me of what you are going to go ahead and do anyway? Perfect," he said. He stood up. "I can take care of myself."

"I know that, but I am trying to help you." She let out an exasperated sigh. "OK, I won't tell Max anything about the garden center, I promise."

"Yeah, just like you promised some other things. Sorry, but you broke that trust a long time ago."

She flared. "Exactly! It was a long time ago, Ben. I was wrong, I know that. But you just can't forget it, can you?"

Ben was grim faced. "No," he said. "I wish I could forget, but I can't. You cheated on me. I forgave you and then you did it again."

"Well, I've said what I came to say. I am trying to help you out, that's all, but apparently you can't see that. Then it's not my problem anymore. It's yours." She stormed out the door to her car. The sound of tires spinning, and gravel flying filled his parking lot.

Colleen gripped the steering wheel of her Mercedes and stomped on the gas. She swerved around a sharp curve in the road hitting the straightway at top speed.

She knew more than she had let on to Max. The most likely buyers of Ben's garden center were a young couple with two children from Winston-Salem. But Max was a vindictive man, and Colleen was well aware of his distaste for what his son had become, although Ben was successful in his own right and a very well-respected member of the community. But for Max, life was not exciting without some drama and manipulation. The power it gave him over other people was his driving force— nothing else. Colleen knew that she and Max were alike in many ways. And Ben and her own father were alike in many ways, too: strong, dependable, honest. She had not treated Ben or her father fairly. And her outburst with Ben just now was proof of that. She had lashed out—again—for no reason at all.

Colleen had other lovers before Simon, always passionate affairs that ended abruptly. Ben Evans was one of them, but she had believed that they were truly in love. Despite that, she was the one to destroy the relationship. It wasn't a slow crumbling of their love for each other. It was an epic obliteration of it, and one that she was responsible for by cheating on him, more than once, each time after he had forgiven her. The wall that she needed to keep around her, that she never allowed to be breached, was like a fortress. And Ben had gotten too close to breaking through it. The wounds from it were deeper than she had ever let on. And she knew that she had hurt him deeply.

Simon wasn't going to be the one to breach the wall either. She would make sure of that. Colleen made the sharp left turn towards the interstate. The road ahead was empty, and she took full advantage, her whole body feeling the upward rhythm of the gears and the engine. She just wanted to drive, anywhere, it didn't matter. This was her release, an escape from the insanity of her life. She drew energy from its power, its speed propelled her when and where she directed it. And it was all in her control.

Colleen downshifted as she reached the entrance to the interstate and then sped up the ramp. This was one of those times when she desperately needed her mother. She would have unburdened herself and her mother would have listened and given her advice—whether it was what Colleen wanted to hear or not. But her mother had died of cancer when Colleen was in her junior year in high school. Memories of the day she was told of her mother's diagnosis still haunted her. The suddenness of it, the realization that she would only be with them for a few months more, and the pain of watching her in that brief battle was a burden that Colleen could never really face.

She watched her father tenderly care for the woman he loved so fiercely. He was a rock, for her and her mother, but Colleen had pushed back against them both. There was not enough time for her to even grasp the diagnosis and, too soon, the fight was over and her mother was gone. The guilt of that time persisted, even now. Colleen soon began to look for love where she knew she wouldn't find it. She hurt others before they could hurt her. Ben was proof of that.

Then, allured by Max's charm, infatuated with his power and what he promised her would be a successful and exciting career, she had gone all in with him after her breakup with Ben. It was a glamorous start to her career, moving in the right circles, meeting the wealthy and influential people that he did business with. But then there was a significant lapse in judgment; she knew what would happen on that trip to New York City with Max. She had even suggested the trip. What would be so wrong with a one-night stand, she thought? She wanted what he was promising. She was in control. She knew what she was doing—or so she believed. Now that one-night stand disgusted her. And it gave him a hold over her that she would forever regret. If Ben or her father ever found out—it would destroy them. Max was always there, never letting her forget that he was the one to give her a start, to make the right connections and that he could keep their secret—or use it against her.

She knew Max Evans didn't care about her and never had. Control. It was a weapon that he used with skill and cunning.

She had promised Ben she would not tell Max anything. And she was determined to keep her word this time.

13

KATE CONTINUED TO MULL OVER HER LUNCH with Max at the Woodlands. The meal was perfect, the wine pairings were extraordinary, and the conversation, at least at first, was light and enjoyable. It had been refreshing to share stories of her travels, and it intrigued her that Max had such broad cosmopolitan experience. But then the conversation had turned to the real reason he invited her, and it wasn't to share stories of his youthful adventures. He was a businessman and wanted answers. But now she had questions of her own.

The sun wasn't making an early appearance that morning. The trees around Howard's Walk dripped with the remnants of an overnight rain and the sky was the color of pewter from horizon to horizon. A light fog settled into the empty spaces in the gardens and woods.

No work would be done outside today, she was sure. Billy would be kept at home and she did not relish the thought of another rainy day stuck in the house. She grabbed a hooded parka and headed out the door. A few minutes later, she pulled into a parking spot in front of Wesley Carroll's office. The rain had returned and Kate drew the hood up on her parka and made a dash for the door where a woman greeted her.

"Come on in, darlin', it's coming down in buckets! We'll be gettin' out the rowboats pretty soon! Let's get that wet coat off you. We can hang it up right here," she said pointing to the coat rack by the door.

"Thank you," Kate said, shrugging out of her jacket. "I'm Kate Tyler. I wondered if Mr. Carroll would have a few minutes for me? I don't have an appointment though."

The woman's face lit up with a warm smile. "Well, hey there, Ms. Kate," she said. "We haven't met. I'm Brenda Gilbert. Mr. Carroll has been worried about you and hoped you would stop by again. Is everything going OK for you these days?"

"Thanks, Ms. Gilbert. It's nice to meet you, too. I am feeling much better. Is Mr. Carroll in?"

"Now, now—you call me Brenda—we're not big on ceremony here. And he sure is, hon, you just sit right down. I'll let him know you're here."

Brenda buzzed her boss on the intercom and announced that Kate was here to see him. "He'll be right out. Can I get you something, hon? Some hot tea to take that chill off?"

"No, thanks. I'm fine," Kate replied and took one of the cushioned chairs by the window as Brenda chattered on about the deteriorating weather situation.

"And we'll be getting into hurricane season before you know it and they're already talking about storms in the Atlantic. Never good for us even in this part of the state."

Wesley appeared in the doorway, ushering out his current appointment. After giving Brenda a few instructions, he invited Kate into his office.

"It's good to see you, Kate. How have you been?"

"Much better, thank you. I can only imagine how I must have looked the first few times we met."

"Under the circumstances, I think you were very brave for coming here. No one would have been any better off than you." He offered her a seat. "What can I do for you?"

"I hadn't heard from Mr. Tower in a while and I wondered if he had been in contact with you?"

Wesley shook his head. "As a matter of fact, he hasn't but I won't be involved in the estate. These things do take time, you know. I'm sure he will be in touch."

"I see. I don't have any experience with this. But I haven't heard from Mr. Hubert either about selling the property. But, oddly enough, I have had an offer on the house."

"Oh?" Wesley replied with a slight raise of an eyebrow.

"Yes, from an unlikely source, I suppose. But an offer all the same."

"May I ask who made the offer?"

"Max Evans. In fact, it was a very generous offer."

Wesley was silent. Kate was ready to gauge his response, wondering if he would feel the same way that Ben did or ally himself with Max, who appeared to be an important part of Eden Springs.

"I see." He cleared his throat. "I have been aware of his interest in the property over the years. Well, that does give you something to consider then doesn't it?"

"Yes, I guess it does. But I have one more question if you don't mind?" Wesley nodded and she continued. "Max was there at the meeting the other night. So, if he is interested in restoring the gardens, if I sold it to him, that is, it would still be good for Eden Springs, right?"

Wesley looked puzzled. "Max Evans has not involved himself in the discussions regarding the gardens—as a matter of fact, that is the first meeting he has attended on the subject. I expect he was only there as an observer. He has never been interested in the gardens, that I know of. I don't know what interest he would have in the property except it would give him more than he already has."

He stood up abruptly. "You'll have to excuse me, Kate; I need to make some phone calls." He escorted Kate to the door and for the second time in three days, Kate felt as if she was being brushed off.

She said her good-byes to Brenda. "Stay dry, dear!" she said as Kate faced the rain once more.

Kate hunched down against the rising wind and pointed herself towards the café. She shook herself off as she entered and slipped out of her dripping wet coat. It was late morning, before the lunch crowd arrived, and Kate took a booth along the side of the restaurant. She saw Rosie smile and wave from behind the counter. Rosie finished with a customer and came to where Kate was seated.

"Well, as I live and breathe, it's good to see you out and about, Kate! What can I get you?"

"Coffee would be fine, thanks Rosie."

"Michelle, bring us a couple cups of coffee, would you please?" she called out to a young woman behind the counter. She slid in across the table from Kate.

"I need to get off my feet for a while anyway. I'm getting too old for this, but I don't know what I would do without this place. The mornings come too early and the nights don't come soon enough for me anymore. Haven't had a vacation in years. But enough complaining. How are you?"

Kate smiled. "I'm a lot better. A lot has happened lately. Do you have a minute?"

Rosie waved her hand around the almost empty diner. "I have all the time in the world, dear. Not many people come out in this weather. So, tell me what's going on."

Kate began with Sam and Martin stopping by. She left out the part about her being so depressed that she didn't dress for days, but she did tell Rosie that they had been good company for her, and they had started to clean up the gardens. Then she told her about meeting Billy and Mimi and how Billy had been helping her, and that she had bought a tree from Ben Evans' garden center to plant at the house in Becky's memory.

"That's a wonderful idea! And I'm glad you met Billy, too. He's real special, and so is Miss Mimi. She's had a tough time without Calvin though. Did she tell you he passed a while back?"

"Yes, she did. It must be hard for her alone with Billy. But she doesn't seem like the type to complain."

"No, she's from tough stock."

"I've also met with someone else lately. Max Evans invited me to lunch the other day and has made me an offer on the house."

Rosie sat back in her seat. "Max Evans? Well, I'm not surprised. He'll try to get his hands on anything that's not his when he doesn't even appreciate what he does have—and he has a lot. I'd be careful about that one, dear. He's too slick for my taste."

"But he has been nothing but a gentleman to me, Rosie. Although when I mentioned it to Mr. Carroll just now, he seemed very upset, too."

"You told Wesley? Well," she chuckled, "I would have liked to see the look on his face. Look, Kate, there's a lot of history here that you don't know about. And not that it should make any difference to you one way or the other—you must do what you think is right—but I think it's only fair to let you know who all the players are. Now this isn't gossip—because I don't gossip—but here are the facts... and this comes from my mother, so I know it's true.

"Back when Miss Bessie and her husband Enoch Howard lived here, this town was booming. After the war, tobacco was big. Thanks to Enoch and Harley Evans—that's Max's father— Eden Springs prospered and grew. Enoch and Harley were in the war together and stayed close friends after. They were both town leaders here in Eden Springs. But from what I hear, the Woodlands started a big decline. I never heard what really happened, but it was bad enough that they almost lost the place. But then Harley died suddenly, and Max came back from Europe with his fiancée and took everything over. Well, things did turn around for him financially, but his fiancée left and went back to Europe—she and Pearl, Max's mother, never did get along, and then Max eventually married Elizabeth, that's Ben's mom.

"Then, when Enoch died, Bessie wouldn't have anything to do with Max. And when she moved back to England, and Max wanted to buy Howard's Walk, she absolutely refused. She could have sold it to him several times, but she kept her word."

"But why would he still want it now?"

"That's just his nature. He has to have what's not his."

"You mentioned a wife. Is he still married?"

"Why? Did he say he wasn't?"

"No, but he never mentioned a wife. And he wasn't wearing a ring. I guess I just assumed they were divorced."

"Elizabeth left him just before you came. Max had been cheating on her for years and she finally had enough, I guess. She lives in Charleston now. We all miss her. She is a fine lady. Ben takes after her."

Kate remembered Max's hands on her shoulders and a shiver went through her.

"I did get the impression that Ben and his father don't get along."

"That is true. Ben is more like his grandpa Harley than Max and they clash a lot, always have. But Ben is his own person and won't be swayed by his father. He'll go his own way. As a matter of fact, he is selling his place. He's going into business with an old college roommate in South Carolina."

"Yes, he mentioned that to me. So why was Mr. Carroll upset, too?"

Rosie hesitated, then continued quietly. "Like I said, I don't gossip, but it's kind of common knowledge around here that Wesley has had a thing for Elizabeth Evans for years. Wesley's wife's been gone for quite a while now—cancer, poor thing. It was real rough. Don't get me wrong—he and Elizabeth never had an affair or anything. He's too much a gentleman for that. But I think it broke his heart to see the way Max treated her for all those years, and then her just leaving like that? I know he must be hurting."

"I had no idea. I could have handled it better I think... if I had known."

"You couldn't have known. He'll deal with it." Rosie patted Kate's hand. "You didn't bargain for all this small-town stuff. It's our baggage to deal with, not yours. Unless you would consider staying? Then you can have all the baggage you want!"

She chuckled, and Kate smiled. "This just isn't my life, Rosie. To be honest, if I'd had a place in Winston-Salem, I probably wouldn't be here now. But, well, a few other things happened around the same time that Becky died, and I didn't have anywhere else to go. It's not that I don't like it here, but it all happened so suddenly. Everyone has been so nice, and it's given me time to pull myself together, but I can't seem to think long term. And I still don't have the money that Becky did to pull this off. So, I don't think I could stay even if I wanted to. And if I have a good enough offer from Max, don't I have to consider it?"

"Well, maybe. But there is something else you need to know. About ten years ago, Max closed up a textile plant just outside of town and moved the whole operation to Mexico. Put about three hundred people out of their jobs with not a penny for their trouble. So, Max got richer while those poor folks all had to look for other jobs or move away. That's when the town started going downhill again. So, when this chance with the gardens came up, I think it made people think back to when the Howards were here, and the factory was going strong and things were better. But not everybody is on board with fixing up the gardens as a public venture. Some of the farmers are still thinking it might be best for them to sell out, too. Lots of developers have been coming around and it wouldn't surprise me if Max was one of them, but I don't know that for sure."

The lunch crowd started trickling in despite the rain, and Rosie took the last sip of her coffee. "Guess I'd better get back to work. There's a trailer somewhere in Florida with my name on it but at this rate, I'll never get there!"

Rosie shuffled off, one hand on her back. Kate felt sorry for her. This place was obviously getting to be too much for Rosie but was probably so much a part of her life that she didn't know how to leave. Kate never wanted to be that tied down to something, and she wasn't sure how someone could let themselves get that way. But maybe she was the exception rather than the rule. Maybe most people did finally want to settle down.

14

KATE TIGHTENED HER HOOD AROUND HER FACE as she dove out into the rain. Predictions of a late spring storm hitting the area were coming true and the rain bore down on Eden Springs in torrents. The windshield wipers of Kate's Honda were no match for it but tried gamely on high speed to clear a view of the road. She turned the defogger on, voicing encouragement to the fan as it rattled and squealed in protest. Kate hunched over the steering wheel, peering through the wetness and the fog.

She followed a slow procession of vehicles along Columbia Avenue, all battling the storm, and almost missed the left turn onto Henries Road. Kate was startled out of her concentration by a notification on her cell phone warning drivers of flash floods. She slowed down and made a cautious right turn onto Chilton-Franklin Road.

After about a mile, Kate slammed on her brakes when she suddenly hit an area where the water had completely flooded the road. There was no good place to turn around, so she slowly steered her car into the water. At the last few feet, she gunned the engine and just as she came to more solid ground, the car wheezed and gasped and chugged to a complete stop. She turned the key several times, but the engine would not start. She turned on her emergency blinkers. She began to regret leaving town in the middle of the storm.

After a few minutes, Kate tried the engine a few more times but it still refused to start. As she debated her next move, an approaching car pulled up next to her. They each rolled down their window a crack.

"Do you need some help?" the woman asked.

"Yes, my car stalled. I wouldn't go through that flooded area if I were you," she warned her.

"Do you live near here?"

"Yes, I live at Howard's Walk." The rain and thunder almost drowned out her words, but the woman must have heard her as a look of surprise spread across her face.

"Have you called anyone?" she asked.

Kate shook her head.

"Listen, why don't you come over and wait in my car. I can call the tow truck."

Kate thanked her, grabbed her backpack, and ran to her car.

"My name is Colleen," the woman said, holding out her hand.

"Hi, I'm Kate Tyler. I can't thank you enough for rescuing me. I was getting a little worried."

Colleen called a local tow truck and gave him their location. "There, all set. He won't be long. Never hurts to have a friend in the towing business," she laughed.

"I can't thank you enough. You are a life saver."

"No problem. So, you live at Howard's Walk, right?"

"Yes, I've been there about a month."

"Well, as a matter of fact, I was just on my way back from there." She pulled out a business card and handed it to Kate. "I had heard that you moved in and might be thinking of selling so I thought I'd stop by and introduce myself."

Kate looked at the card. "Colleen Carroll, Realtor," was written in fluid handwriting across the card with contact information and a tagline: "Buying or selling ~ you deserve only the best." "Are you related to Wesley Carroll?" she asked.

Colleen smiled. "Sure, he's my dad. Have you met him?"

"Yes, as a matter a fact, I just saw him earlier today," Kate said. "I know him through, well, the house and everything. I guess you know I'm Becky Tyler's sister then. She had just bought Howard's Walk before..."

Colleen turned to face Kate. "Yes. I heard. And I am so sorry for your loss. I can't even imagine what you have been going through."

"Thank you." Just then, the tow truck appeared through the rain, which had finally begun to slow to a steady drizzle. "Well, I guess this is me then," Kate said. "Thanks again, Colleen. You really helped me out. If there is anything I can do for you, just let me know."

"Hey, not so fast. I'm not leaving until he figures this out. He may have to take your car into the garage. Let's go see what he says."

They both got out of the car and made their way across the road to the tow truck. The driver hopped down, pulling the hood of his yellow slicker over a Yankees baseball cap. "Hey, Colleen. Ma'am," he nodded towards Kate. "What's the problem?"

Kate explained the nuances of her ancient Honda and its aversion to the wet weather. "It just stalled out after I got through the puddle."

"Well, Ma'am, that's the one thing that you don't do—you don't drive through standing water. This spot always floods, sometimes worse than today, so in a storm like this, just don't even try it. Where were you trying to get to?"

"Howard's Walk, just down the road there."

"Well, OK, but next time if it's raining this bad, go around on Old Timber Road, take a left on Sandy Lake Lane, then three miles on the other end of Chilton-Franklin and you can avoid all this mess here."

Kate mentally tracked his directions and thanked him. "I'm new here so I'm not very familiar with the area. But I will keep that in mind."

Colleen interrupted. "Tony, that's all great but can you find out what's wrong with her car?"

Tony peered over his glasses at her. "She told me what was wrong, Colleen: it stalled, and it won't start. It got wet would be my guess at it." He turned back to Kate. "Like I said, don't drive through standing water, then you won't need me. But I'll take a look. Why don't you ladies just go back and wait in that pretty little Mercedes over there while I see what's goin' on here, OK?"

They quickly agreed and sloshed back to the car. Once inside, they both started to laugh. "Tony doesn't mince words," Colleen said. "I've known him since high school. He's one of a kind. But I wouldn't think of calling anyone else when I'm in a jam."

Kate agreed. "I should really get a new car, but that Honda and I have been through an awful lot together."

"Well, I just start them and drive them—anything more than that, I call Tony."

Tony approached the car and Colleen rolled down the window. He looked in towards Kate. "Looks like it's just going to have to dry out, Ma'am. I'd better tow it into the garage though and make sure there's nothing else going on." He looked at Colleen. "Can you get her home?"

"Sure, thing, Tony. That is, if that's all right with you Kate?"

Kate nodded. Tony handed her his business card. "Just give me a call tomorrow."

"Thanks Tony," Colleen flashed a smile at him. "You're the best."

He touched the brim of his cap. "No problem, you ladies take care." He waited until Colleen had navigated the car in the other direction and then waved as they drove off.

"Would you like to come in for a minute?" Kate asked as they reached Howard's Walk. "It's the least I can do."

"Sure, I'd love to. Thanks."

As they got out of the car and walked up the front steps, Colleen scanned the front of the house. She walked to the end of the porch and back, put her hands on the porch railing and jiggled it slightly.

"Excuse the condition of everything," Kate apologized, noticing the shaky railing. "Things are still in a bit of an upheaval right now, I'm afraid."

"Oh, don't worry. I've seen it all. I confess, though, I am excited to see the inside, too."

Kate unlocked the door and they stepped inside. Colleen looked around the meagerly furnished room. It was not appointed as it would have been in its prime, but the bones were there. The columns with their marble footers were majestic, the curved stairway to the second floor anchored the room perfectly. Even the chandelier, although dated, had been sparked to life, and gave abundant light to the room. "Actually, I think I like what you've done with the place so far."

They walked back to the kitchen and took off their coats. Kate hung them on the backs of the chairs. "Some tea or coffee? Or maybe some wine? I have all three."

"Some wine would be great; it's been that kind of a day, I guess," Colleen said.

Kate retrieved a bottle of Pinot Gris from the refrigerator and two wine glasses from the cupboard.

"How long did you say you have been here, Kate?"

"It's been almost a month actually."

"I'm sorry we haven't met sooner. I've been pretty busy with the real estate business and, also," she held her hand out to Kate, "I just got engaged!"

Kate stared at the ring. "Wow, that is beautiful! Have you set a date yet?"

"No," Colleen responded. "It all happened so fast that we haven't had a chance to think about that yet."

"Congratulations though."

"Thanks. I don't think we will have a long engagement, so I'll have to get busy planning the wedding. I am not expecting Simon to be any help at all. But he'll do what I tell him so it will all work out. But I want to hear about you. You've been here a month and I see you have been doing a little bit of work on the house. Do you have long term plans for it?"

Kate hesitated. Each time she was asked the question, she never knew quite how to answer. She sat down across from Colleen and took a sip of wine. "Colleen, I'll be honest with you, I don't have any idea what I will do. I have been here a month; I have gone through some dark times here. I'm feeling a little better now, but I am just stuck. And it seems like just when I think about packing my bags, I have someone telling me I should stay." She shook her head. "I really don't know."

"Kate, that is perfectly normal. I don't know your situation, but there's one thing I do know. Don't go by what anyone else tells you. And in your heart, you will know when you have made the right decision. But," she added, "I do know real estate. And I do have some history with this house, being an Eden Springs native, and all. So, I can at least see that you get an honest assessment on what it would take to fix it up for you to stay and what it would take for you to make it saleable for the best profit. Just facts and figures. Would you be interested in that information?"

"Yes, I would!" Kate exclaimed. "No one has really been up front with me about that part of it. People seem very emotional about the house, and the Howards. But yes, I would like an honest, unbiased opinion, pros and cons, about staying or selling."

"Fantastic!" Colleen said. "I can be here tomorrow with a contractor; he can give you an estimate and then you will have three choices—fix it up and sell, fix it up and stay, or sell it as is. Staying here without any improvements at all isn't really an option, if I am being perfectly honest."

Kate nodded. "Yes, you are right about that. Nothing really works well; I've just been making do."

"OK then, I will be back here tomorrow morning, say around 10?"

"Sounds great. And thank you, Colleen. You have saved me twice today!"

15

LATE THAT AFTERNOON SAM AND MARTIN RETURNED from Lakeville and found Kate on the patio off the kitchen, looking out across the lawn. The storm had moved through and the sunset was shaping up to be a beautiful one. Kate had dragged the only upholstered chair in the house outside so that she could curl up in it comfortably to watch the spectacle. Martin commented that she didn't seem to have a sense of where any furniture really belonged, what with a bed in the foyer and now a side chair on the patio.

"Nice to see you, too, Martin!" Kate teased. "I don't have much, so what I have, I have to use. And I might as well be comfortable." She greeted them both with a hug and then turned back to the view. The pink and red clouds exploded across the sky, streaking and shifting, reflecting the brilliance of the sunset.

"This is too good to miss. Just be quiet and watch."

The two men dutifully sat down on the stone railing and watched the display in silence. Finally, the air was still, and the evening darkened and cooled quickly. Kate shivered, got up and began to drag the chair back inside.

"Here, let me help," Sam offered. He took one arm and they squeezed the large piece back through the kitchen door and into the foyer, next to the bed where it had previously been situated. Martin carried several bags of food inside and began preparing their dinner.

Suddenly Kate announced, "I have something to show you and I can't wait any longer. Can you help me bring something down from upstairs?"

Sam quickly agreed and they went up to the second floor and retrieved the trunk.

Once downstairs, Kate opened the trunk and pulled out the photo albums and market bulletins for them to look at first. They went through all of them intently, delighted to see how the house and gardens had developed over the years and to read in Bessie Howard's own words her love of gardening.

Sam dug further through the trunk and in the very bottom found three large cardboard tubes. From them, he pulled several rolled-up drawings. As they carefully flattened them out on the table, the entire landscape of Howard's Walk was laid out before them. There were detailed site plans showing the position of every plant and structure, just as it was all those years ago. Yellowed pieces of paper were clipped to the plans with descriptions of each tree, shrub and flower that had been used on the property.

Sam let out a low whistle. "This is incredible."

Martin could hardly breathe. "Everything is here! Everything can be recreated, Kate, just as it was!"

Even Kate could appreciate the enormity of the find. She was quite sure Becky had not been aware of it. The trunk had struck Kate as being untouched, and the drawings were buried at the very bottom underneath everything else.

"It really is wonderful, isn't it?" she whispered.

Kate was the only one to notice the pasta boiling over on the stove, so she went to rescue it and left her friends to pore over the plans as she finished the dinner preparations. Instead of sitting down to eat, they simply grabbed plates of pasta and sauce as they continued to look over the drawings that now covered the table. They had begun to make additional notes of plant names and measurements.

"This is amazing, Kate," Sam murmured. "Like being able to step back in time. I mean, take a look at this—this is the back of the house. And this," he said, holding up another drawing. "This is the greenhouse." He moved around the room as he talked, then went out onto the patio. Martin and Kate followed and watched as he stood in the dim light, envisioning what had been and what could be again. Martin grabbed a rake as Sam began to explain where each plant could be positioned. Kate quickly stepped in.

"OK, you two," Kate said, taking the rake from Martin. "Time to call it a night. No digging or planting right now."

They both protested. "But, Kate..."

"OK, OK," she said, raising her hands in surrender. "You can take the plans out to the RV if that will make you happy! I've had a long day anyway, so I hadn't planned on looking at them anymore tonight."

"But we are headed back home tomorrow morning for a couple of days —we just wanted to stop to see you on our way home," Sam said. "Do you mind if we take them back to Lakeville with us?"

"How about the whole trunk?" Martin begged. "Can we take the whole thing? I'd love to read the market bulletins, too, please?"

"Well, I guess you can take it," Kate relented. "Just remember to bring it with you when you come back!"

16

BILLY HUDDLED UP AGAINST THE HOLLOW OF THE OAK TREE, positioning himself so that he could look out across the wide lawn up to the house. He had arrived there just in time to see her pull the chair out onto the patio and curl herself up into it.

She just sat and stared out at the trees and the sky. He didn't think she could see him. She would wave, he thought, if she could see him. Then he would go up to the house and she would give him some cookies and milk or lemonade. But he wouldn't go unless invited. His mama said not to anymore and that was OK. He saw her lots, almost every day.

He smiled and tucked his legs up, as much as he could, like she did, and wrapped his arms around them, like she had hers, and remembered how she had talked to him.

She talked to him a lot, more than anyone else had ever talked to him, except maybe Ben or his mama or Miss Bessie when she lived there. But he didn't see Ben very much and his mama, well, she was supposed to talk to him. And Miss Bessie had been away for a long time. His mama told him that she moved far away but he still liked to go to her house sometimes and knock on the door and pretend that she was there. The flowers had been pretty and it made him sad that they weren't there anymore. But now that Kate was here, he was helping her and maybe they could make it all pretty again.

Yes, Kate talked to him almost like he thought a grownup might talk to another grownup. And not loud, like some folks did, like he couldn't hear or something. And sometimes she would touch his arm and look right into his eyes when she talked to him and smile at him and that made him feel really good. Some people didn't like to touch him or look at him, at least people that didn't know him.

All in all, he liked living here in Eden Springs, and since Kate moved in, well, things had gotten a whole lot better. Billy closed his eyes for a moment and when he opened them, Kate had already gone back inside the house. It was dark. His mama would begin to worry. He waved at the empty patio and turned towards home.

17

THE NEXT DAY, COLLEEN ARRIVED right on schedule, contractor in tow. She had already informed the contractor that money was no object and the owner wanted only the best. She knew Max wanted the property as is, and that was what he would get. But she needed the renovations to be so cost-prohibitive and time-consuming that Kate would decide that her only option was to sell without making any improvements.

After about an hour, Colleen called Kate into the kitchen and they all sat down at the table. "Well, Joe, what are we looking at here?" Colleen asked.

Joe took his hat off and hooked it on the back of the chair. "Well, this house has been empty for a long time. I see someone's done some work here recently, but it needs a lot more." He went through the list of notes he had made on a yellow notepad—electrical work throughout and new lighting, finish the plumbing, complete redo of the downstairs bathroom and add a second upstairs in the master. The kitchen needed a complete remodeling, new appliances, and floors. The hardwood floors in the other parts of the house were still in good shape but all needed refinishing. And the entire house needed repainting inside, or, for the best effect, some vintage wallpaper in several rooms would be a nice touch.

Kate nodded as he went through the list, agreeing with each of the items as being necessary. She had been living there so she knew the house had its faults.

Colleen went through the list again. "So, let me make sure I understand. All new electrical? Is that really necessary?"

"Yes, ma'am, that needs to be your top priority. And your fixtures really need to be updated."

"And the plumbing; I suppose she does need a bathroom on the second floor."

"I would recommend it; houses this big never have just one bathroom. You could probably do with another half bath, too."

"And the kitchen, the layout isn't really great, what would you recommend in here?"

"Total gut job. New cabinets, granite countertops, stainless steel appliances, the works. Nobody wants a dated kitchen these days. And don't forget, this doesn't even cover the outside. I can see a lot of work needs to be done there. You've got yourself one heck of a piece of property here."

"What is your estimate for everything you've listed here, Joe?" Colleen asked, hoping that the cost would be overwhelming to Kate.

"Well, you're looking at about ninety to a hundred thousand to do it right. And that doesn't cover anything on the outside—you'd have to get a professional to fix up the greenhouse—if it's even worth saving. And the landscaping, well, like I said, you've got a lot of property here to cover."

Kate's mouth dropped open. "I had no idea it would be that much."

"Well, Kate," Colleen said, "I'm afraid I agree with his assessment. And this is what you should do even if you wanted to sell it fixed up. You can't afford to skimp on a place like this. And you could sell it for a lot more."

The contractor tore off the top sheet of his list and handed it to Kate. "I hope you decide to go ahead with the remodel though—this place is a hidden gem and we'd love to work on it." He shook hands with them, and Kate showed him to the front door.

Kate went out onto the patio where Colleen was waiting. After a moment, Colleen said, "I can see this is a little overwhelming for you. Do you have any questions about it?"

Kate sighed. "I just can't believe it would take this much money. It was nowhere near this much when the guys came to do some work when I first got here. But I guess they didn't really do much."

"No, it looks like they barely hit the essentials."

"I don't think I have that kind of money, even if I used all of what Becky left me. And it would be such a big undertaking. I just don't know."

"I understand," Colleen said. "I know we talked about three options and there still is one that doesn't involve fixing it up. I do have a buyer who would buy as-is, if that is what you want."

"Well, Max Evans did make me an offer. Is he the buyer you are talking about?"

"Oh, no," Colleen said. "This is an investment group out of Winston-Salem. They are pretty sharp about knowing a value when they see one."

"So, what do you think the house is worth?"

"Well, with the property included, which is valuable by itself, I'd say about three hundred and fifty thousand. Do you know what Becky paid for it?"

"No, but I could probably find out from Mr. Hubert."

"Don't worry, I can find it." Colleen took out her phone, accessed a website and quickly found the sale price. "Well, Becky must have been a shrewd buyer; she got it for three hundred. But I can easily see this going for three twenty-five to three fifty now, as-is, with no improvements. You've got a mortgage on it and this would really set you up for a nice profit after you pay that off."

"I need to think it over, if that's OK. I appreciate everything you've told me though. You've been so helpful with all of this, Colleen. I guess Mr. Hubert wasn't really anxious for me to sell it."

"No, he probably wasn't. But like I said before, this is completely up to you." Colleen went back inside, gathered her things and left Kate another business card. "But if you decide to sell, I can have it sold in a matter of days. Let me know what you want to do."

Colleen put on her coat. "Have you heard from Tony about your car?" she asked.

"Actually, yes, he called a little while ago; it's all ready."

"Let me take you into town to get it then; you can't be without a car out here in the sticks! And there's no Uber in Eden Springs!" she laughed.

Kate agreed, thanked her for the offer, and they headed into Eden Springs. A few minutes later, Kate turned to Colleen.

"Colleen, what would you do if you were in my place?"

"Kate, I really can't make that decision for you. But," she said, "this could be a very costly mistake for you if it didn't work out. You are very smart to realize what your financial limits are. And, honestly, is that what Becky would have wanted for you? To not be successful at it?"

Kate thought about this and finally shook her head. "I don't think so."

They arrived at Tony's Garage and Kate got out of the car. "Thanks again, Colleen, you've been so great about all this. And thanks for all the advice, too."

Colleen smiled. "No problem. You think about what I said, OK? And let's get together again soon."

Later that day, Ben arrived at Howard's Walk, his truck crunching over the gravel in the drive. Kate watched from the house as he unloaded the redbud. He leaned it up against the side of the truck and approached the front door. She opened it before he could knock.

He smiled crookedly at her, not quite able to look her in the eye. She stepped out onto the porch, closing the door behind her.

"Sorry to drop in without calling," he said, "but I thought it would be good for me to bring the tree over and get it planted for you. If that's OK, I mean."

"Sure, thanks for bringing it."

"I'm sorry it took me so long to get it out here to you. Listen, Kate..."

"Ben..." Kate started.

"You go first," Ben encouraged her.

"No, you go, please," Kate offered.

Ben took off his baseball cap and twisted it in his hands. "OK. Well, I want to apologize, again, for how I acted. My father is one of my hot buttons. I shouldn't have taken it out on you though. That was wrong. So, I'm sorry."

Kate nodded. "Apology accepted."

There was an awkward silence, and then she changed the subject. "Well, let's go take a look out back—you can help me decide where to plant it."

Ben grabbed a shovel out of the back of his truck, picked up the tree and followed Kate around to the back of the house. They chose a spot in the slope of the backyard that would be clearly visible from the patio where she liked to spend quiet time in the mornings and evenings.

"I've never planted a tree before," Kate said. "But you probably do this all the time."

"It's not hard once you've done it a few times. Here, hold this so I can dig," he said, tipping the tree towards Kate so that she could hold it. Ben eyeballed the size of the root ball and dug a hole large enough to contain it. He pulled out a utility knife and showed Kate how to cut the burlap away from the root flare. When she had finished that, it was ready to plant. He easily lifted the tree into the hole and asked Kate to hold it straight.

He stepped back to check it. "Perfect," he announced. "Hold it right there."

He removed the remaining burlap and shoveled the soil back into the hole, tamping the last bit into place. The young tree stood straight against the light breeze.

"Shouldn't we stake it or something?" Kate asked.

"Nah," Ben said. "It should be fine. But keep an eye on it and if it starts to lean, just let me know and I'll come take care of it. It needs to be watered though. Will your hose reach all the way down here?"

Kate grimaced. "I'm afraid not. The one that was here is rotted."

"No problem. You have a bucket, right?"

"Oh, yes," she laughed. "One doesn't have Billy around here for very long without having a bucket or two."

"I get it," Ben nodded. "You stay here, I'll get some water."

Kate watched him as he strode up the slope to the greenhouse. Every move Ben made was with purpose and self-assuredness. Even his apology, though she could tell it was difficult for him, came from a place of honesty and good heartedness. She wondered where a person learned that. Was it born in them? Was it in their DNA? Or was it from hard times, having to survive a difficult childhood with an unloving father? The more she saw of Ben, the more obvious it became to her where the genuine Evans man was. He wasn't at the Woodlands. He was right here in her back yard.

Ben returned with the bucket and generously watered the soil around the base of the tree. Kate watched the water soak into the ground, imagining how it would nourish the tree just as Becky had nourished her all her life.

Kate suddenly shivered and wrapped her arms close around her. There wasn't a chill in the air, but her heart was beating faster and faster. Suddenly, the memories of the last few weeks, the reason she was here in the first place, all came flooding back. Tears filled her eyes.

"Kate, are you all right?" Ben asked.

"I feel like I'm all in pieces," Kate said, softly. "I miss her so much."

She looked at the redbud they had just planted. She had wondered if it would be able to stand on its own but there it was, straight as they had planted it, ready to set new roots.

"I think I understand now—I mean, maybe what she wanted from this place," Kate whispered.

"What's that?"

"To bring it all back. To grab something from the brink and bring it back to life and share it with others."

Ben sat down on the grass and motioned Kate to join him. "Tell me about Becky," Ben said.

Kate began with her childhood, how she had always looked up to her twin and how Becky always looked out for her. She told him how her parents died and how she began to depend on her sister more and more, and to depend on others like Mitch, and other ex-boyfriends, instead of finding her own strength. She talked as the air stilled and as the sun settled behind the trees.

"But you are strong," Ben said. "And it must have been there all along or you wouldn't have it to draw on when you need it. You probably wouldn't even be here."

Kate allowed herself to relax slightly then. "I thought I had already grieved," she said after a moment. "I thought I was done with it."

"I haven't been through what you have but I lost my grandpa, my mom's dad, when I was thirteen. He was a big man, in my eyes anyway. I idolized him. I was his only grandchild. He taught me how to fish, how to build things, and taught me the name of every plant and tree in the woods. Now that I look back, I know that a thirteen-year-old has no concept of grief and how to handle it. I sure didn't. But I was lucky in that I had my mom to lean on. I guess what I am saying is that if I hadn't had my mom to help me through it, I would have had a harder time."

Kate thought about those that who had helped her share the weight of her grief since Becky's death—Mrs. Mims, Sam, Martin, and now Ben. Not family, not friends from her past, but complete strangers.

She looked at him. "Ben, you and Sam and Martin—you've been there for me. And Mrs. Mims and Mr. Tower back in Winston-Salem. But I've lost everyone else. I've lost everyone!"

Ben put his arm around her. "It's OK, Kate. It's going to be OK."

After a few moments, Kate said, "Ben, you don't have to answer this but what happened—between you and your father?" Ben hesitated and took his arm from around Kate. "I'm sorry, I shouldn't have asked such a personal question."

"No, it's OK. It's not something I talk about much, though. A lot of people around here don't like my father for a lot of different reasons, some business related, some personal. He's made a success of himself, but it's usually been at others' expense."

Kate didn't want to tell him that she knew some of the story already. She felt awkward knowing that Rosie had shared some rather personal details of their family situation. But she wanted to hear it from Ben.

"I told you about my granddad," Ben continued. "The reason I spent so much time with him was that I hated being at home. It was my escape, I guess, to get out of the house and spend time with someone who really cared about me, other than my mom, of course. She encouraged me to spend time with my granddad. I was either with him or here at Howard's Walk, helping Miss Bessie in the gardens. My father never had time, always traveling on some business deal. The only effort he ever made with me was to push me in the direction he thought

I should go—which I knew was not what I wanted. We fought about it a lot."

"I'm sorry. It must be hard to grow up with that pressure."

"It was. And my mom," he said, taking a deep breath. "My mom covered for me, I guess you could say. And she got the brunt of a lot of his anger. Especially when he was drinking."

Kate slid her hand into his and he entwined his fingers in hers. They were silent for a moment.

"I'm so sorry Ben. I had no idea."

He shrugged. "It was all I knew, up to a point. For a long time, I thought maybe all families were like that."

"And your mom?"

"She finally had enough. She should have left him years ago, but she wouldn't while I was still in the house. Even after that, she kept thinking it would get better, I guess. But it never did. And a custody battle would have been pretty nasty when I was little. She just moved out recently. Moved to Charleston. She's filing for divorce."

She leaned her head on his shoulder and he put his arm around her again. "You're easy to talk to, Kate. I haven't shared that with many people."

"You've helped me today too, Ben."

A light breeze ruffled the grass and the slender branches of the redbud. Kate shivered. "It's getting cold out here. I think we'd better go inside."

He moved first, reluctantly loosening his grip and helping her up to her feet. She welcomed his strength as they walked back to the house.

"Will you be OK, now?" Ben asked as they reached the door.

"I think so. But I would love to have you stay for dinner—that is if you want to."

"I'd like to, but I'd understand if you want to make it another time."

"No," she said firmly. "Absolutely not. And honestly, I'd rather not be alone right now. Please stay?"

"Only if you let me wash up and help you cook."

"It's a deal."

Kate retrieved two pieces of salmon, green salad, and wine from the refrigerator while Ben cleaned up. Kate soon learned that he knew his way around a kitchen, finding spices for the salmon and adding fresh vegetables to the salad.

They talked late into the evening, Kate telling Ben about her work as a travel writer and the places she had been. Ben nodded. "That explains all of those stickers I saw on your luggage when we first met," he said. "I have to confess, you made quite an impression on me that night."

"Oh, really?" Kate smiled. "Then I confess, too... you definitely made an impression on me."

As they talked, Ben began to share more memories of Howard's Walk and Miss Bessie's passion for plants. "There was this one plant, an Angel's Trumpet, that she had. She loved that plant. It's not here now though," he said. "Cuss-man Bill stole it from her."

Kate raised her eyebrows. "Cuss-man Bill?"

"Yeah, all the kids called him that because he cussed a lot. Especially when he found us on his property, sneaking plants back for Miss Bessie."

"Wait, what?" Kate laughed. "You were stealing them from his property?"

"No," he corrected her, grinning, "not stealing them. He stole them from Miss Bessie years ago. Lots of times. She was too nice to say anything, so we just took them back for her." He leaned towards her, his eyes narrowing with mischief. "What do you say, Kate? How about a midnight raid... you and me? We'll go get the plant back. One more time. For Miss Bessie."

Was it the wine from earlier or the dare or maybe both? "Sure," she agreed. "I'll do it. For Miss Bessie. Just tell me when."

"When? Why not now? Have you got something dark to wear?"

"I guess so."

"So, put it on and we'll go!"

Kate rummaged through a pile of clothes by her bed, ran to the bathroom and changed into a pair of black leggings, a black tee shirt, wrapped her hair up in a messy ponytail and jammed a baseball cap down over it all. "OK, I'm ready," she said breathlessly as she ran out to the truck where Ben was waiting. He had put on a dark colored jean jacket.

"Then let's roll!" They jumped into the truck and took off down the driveway.

Several minutes later they turned onto a one-lane dirt road that disappeared into a stand of trees. Kate had passed that turn off many times but thought that it was just an abandoned trail. Instead, she soon realized that it wound back and forth through the woods until it ended in a small clearing with what could only be described as a one-room shack situated in the center of it. Smoke circled from the chimney and the curtainless windows had an amber glow coming through them. Several abandoned cars were scattered through the yard and in the surrounding woods.

Ben turned off the headlights and slowed the truck to a stop as they approached the yard, staying far enough back so that they wouldn't be seen.

"Ben," Kate whispered, "are you sure we should be doing this?"

He turned to her with a serious face. "You're not backing out on me now, are you?" Then he grinned. "Come on, Kate. I'll show you how we do adventure in Eden Springs. Let's go... but be quiet!"

They eased out of the truck and silently closed the doors. Ben came around Kate's side of the truck. He pointed towards the right side of the shack.

"See there? That's what we want." Kate could barely see in the dark, but as her eyes adjusted, she could finally make out the object of their midnight raid. The plant stood about four feet tall and was draped with large golden yellow, trumpet shaped flowers that hung down from the top of the stalk. Ben reached up into the bed of the truck and carefully retrieved a short-handled spade. He crouched low and motioned for Kate to follow him.

They reached the corner of the shack, staying low to avoid the windows. They crawled on their hands and knees the rest of the way to the plant. There was no sound from the inside.

"You're on lookout, Kate," Ben whispered.

"Ben," she whispered back.

"What?"

"What am I looking for?"

He jabbed a finger towards the house. "Him!"

"Oh, OK," she nodded.

He started digging while Kate, her heart pounding, wondered to herself what in the world she was doing there, creeping up to people's houses and digging in their flower beds.

Ben worked his way around the base of the plant with the spade, careful not to damage the roots. Finally, the plant tipped out, loosened from its unlawful home. But the shovel tipped with it and fell out of Ben's hands, hitting a rock. The sound reverberated in the silence of the woods and Ben and Kate froze as they waited for warning sounds from inside that they had been caught. But there was no sign that Cuss-man Bill had heard the noise.

Ben handed the plant to Kate, signaled her to follow him to the truck and they slowly backed away from the house. Suddenly, the porch light went on. "Get in the truck!" Ben shouted. Kate scrambled in, dragging the large plant—leaves, flowers, roots and all—with her. Ben jumped in, started the truck and swerved in reverse out of the clearing.

Shouts and cursing came from the front porch as they raced down the lane. The sound of gunshots sliced through the air. Kate had a white-knuckle grip on Ben's arm, her eyes shut tight and her head down, her face buried in the fragrant flowers of the Angel's Trumpet, expecting the window behind her to shatter, along with her skull, at any moment.

Ben let out a whoop as he negotiated the tight curves and dips in the narrow lane and Kate herself finally let go a scream. Finally, as the panic of being shot at faded, so did her grip on Ben's arm. "Did you see the look on his face?" Ben screeched to a halt at an intersection then sped off again. Kate wondered why he bothered to obey the stop sign when he, they, had just committed a robbery. "He's pissed now!"

Kate took a few deep breaths. "Ben, what did we just do? That man was shooting at us! He knows who you are. What have you gotten me into?"

"Don't worry, Kate." He turned toward her, grinning. "Like I told you, he stole that plant from Miss Bessie. We're just taking it back. Besides, this isn't the first time."

"But this time he was shooting at us!"

"And he's shot at me before, too. At least twice. But it's worth it, just to see the look on his face!"

"You are insane. Over a stupid plant? I'm not going to jail over this, Ben. I'll tell them you forced me into it."

Ben pulled into the drive at Howard's Walk and they both got out, Kate gingerly holding the stalk of the plant. Clods of soil hung precariously to the roots. Dirt was all over the floor of the truck and all over her and Ben. He took the Angel's Trumpet from her.

"I know just where to plant this."

Kate followed Ben through the gate to the spot she had been clearing next to the greenhouse. It was just outside the French doors that led inside.

"How about right here?" he asked.

She agreed it was the perfect spot. Ben grabbed a shovel and started digging. When it was deep enough, he stood the plant in the hole and motioned Kate to help him hold it steady while he pushed the soil back in around it. Once it stood on its own, Kate knelt, too and they both finished filling in around the stalk.

The soil was moist and crumbled in her hands. It felt good to knead it between her fingers and press it down to secure the plant. Ben was gentle as he worked with it, and she began to understand a little more about him then and why he had wanted to bring the plant back to Howard's Walk where it belonged.

Kate sat back on her heels, her sandals long since discarded somewhere in the truck. Her legs were stained with water and dirt and her leggings showed the imprints of her hands as she had tried to wipe them off. Ben sat back, too, a look of satisfaction on his face. He took the corner of his tee shirt and wiped his face, smearing the dirt around.

They were a sight, she thought, but alive. And more alive than she had felt in a long time.

Ben got up and walked to the corner of the greenhouse where it joined the house, pulling off his tee shirt as he went. He turned on the spigot, rinsed his hands and splashed water on his face. Kate joined him and held her hands under the water. Ben reached for her hands and turned her to face him.

A streak of moonlight escaped from a clutch of clouds racing across the sky. Now unrestrained, it threw its rays to the earth, seeking darkened places.

"Kate," he whispered. "I think I'm going to kiss you."

Kate nodded and he kissed her, gently at first, then more hungrily, and she kissed him back, wrapping her arms around his neck and drawing him closer.

Suddenly, Ben pulled away. "Wow, I'm sorry, I shouldn't have done that."

"No, Ben, really," she said. "I wanted you to. I really wanted you to." She turned his face to hers. "It's OK."

He pulled her to him again and held her close. He kissed her forehead and her cheek, tenderly, with no expectations. "I think I should go though. It's late."

"OK," Kate agreed, and they walked to his truck.

"I'll call you later though?"

"I'm counting on it."

He got in, rolled down the window, held her sandals out to her and smiled. "We had a hell of a good time tonight, didn't we?"

"Yes, we did, Ben," Kate answered. *The best time I've had in years,* she thought. Kate watched him go and as she did, she felt a new element bubble up inside her, edging out the pain and anger that had been a part of her for so long now. She knew that she had only learned a small part of what made Ben into the man she now saw him to be. And maybe it was all happening too fast. The last thing she wanted was a rebound relationship. But she was sure of one thing. She wanted to learn more about Ben Evans.

Kate lay awake until the early hours of the morning, but then sleep finally came and she dreamed of the wild ride and the moonlight and the touch of Ben's lips on hers. It seemed to last only minutes, and then she was suddenly wide awake. She knew she would not sleep again, although the thought of dreaming about Ben again was tempting.

It was still a murky mix of night and day and she wrapped herself in the quilt from her bed, still warm from her sleeping, and padded into the kitchen. The night before, she had set up a pot of coffee to brew on a timer and the rich aroma began to fill the house. It was the same strong European brew that had gotten her through many episodes of jet lag on her travels overseas. She showered while the coffee finished brewing, pulled on sweatpants and a tee shirt and then layered it with a sweatshirt that she could shed as the day warmed. She pulled on a heavy pair of work boots, subdued her wet hair into a ponytail and tucked it through the back loop of a pink baseball cap.

Kate took a heavy brown mug from the dish rack and poured the coffee into it, blowing away the wisps of steam as it flowed into the cup. She tucked her free hand into the pocket of her sweatshirt and stepped out onto the front porch. It seemed that morning had been reining in the sun just for her because at one moment there was only a hazy glow behind the trees and then the sun, molten and golden, erupted into the sky.

She often thought of Becky on mornings like this and missed her, not as painfully as before, but with melancholy and a longing just to be with her again. She vowed never to forget that it was Becky who brought her here and she had paid a dear price for that to happen. And she was slowly realizing that out of this tragedy, she was healing. She had been sliding into an abyss but was clawing her way out. And it was this place and the people that she had met that were bringing her out of it.

Kate sat down on the steps. In her heart she knew that the decision regarding Howard's Walk was hers and hers alone. She could no longer depend on her sister to push her through life or count on Mitch or anyone else to fix her problems, not even Ben. She was here in this place, standing on her own two feet, surviving everything that had happened to her. Her future was up to her.

Whatever she decided, she would see it through. She could sell and walk away without regret, if that was what she decided. She could go back to the life she knew as a journalist, if that was what she decided. She had been drawn in by some of the small-town stories that she had been observing and hearing as she began to meet the locals. An article about Eden Springs and its unique charm had even been forming in her mind, and it could be worth pitching to some magazines. Becky would have understood.

But, truthfully, Kate's old existence was not drawing her back as it had been just a few weeks ago. She realized she was getting comfortable right where she was. Maybe there would be a way that she could stay and carry out Becky's dream of bringing Howard's Walk back to life, even if Colleen and others doubted that she could. The money would just have to work itself out. She would have Sam and Martin's support, and Ben's, too, if she decided to stay. Maybe John Hubert's dragging his feet in putting the house on the market was a blessing in disguise. Either way, whatever her future held, it was time to take it into her own hands.

18

KATE WALKED INTO EVE'S BEAUTY SALON the next day, not sure what to expect. She was used to her own stylist in Winston-Salem but when she saw the sign "Walk-Ins Welcome" on the sidewalk outside of the salon she decided to take a leap of faith. It had been over two months since her last visit to a salon and her curls were getting out of hand.

She was expecting to see little old ladies staring from underneath vintage hair dryers at the young newcomer, but she was pleasantly surprised to see a salon that was sleek and modern with three stylists of different ages. Taking a seat, she sifted through the pile of magazines—*People*, *Women's Day*, *Cosmopolitan*, and, surprisingly, *Premier Travel Magazine*. It was three months old, but she pulled it out of the pile out of curiosity and leafed through it. There, on the first page, was Jack Starner's picture as Editor. In his column, he talked about the economy and how people were taking fewer overseas trips and how it was a great time and opportunity for everyone to look closer to home. He promised that there would be more articles in the spring issues about where to go and what to see, called "In Your Own Backyard", focusing especially on places in North and South Carolina and Virginia, places readers could visit on one tank of gas or less.

"Well, Jack, if you need articles," Kate said under her breath, "I am more than ready to give you articles." And what better place to write about than Eden Springs, she thought, less than one tank of gas away from just about anywhere in each of those states: lovely people, beautiful scenery, and maybe, just maybe, a beautiful garden at Howard's Walk.

Kate looked up from the magazine and noticed an elderly woman approaching her, slowly, her tiny birdlike frame arrayed in bright pinks and reds, her white hair newly curled. She took the seat next to Kate and rested her hands on the top of her cane. Her eyes twinkled as she turned and tipped her head to look at Kate.

"My name is Emma Peese," she said. Her words came out slowly, like southern molasses. "We haven't met. What is your name, dear?"

"Kate Tyler. It's a pleasure to meet you Ms. Peese."

"Tyler. Hmmm. Would you happen to be related to Rebecca Tyler?"

"Yes, ma'am. I'm her twin sister. I moved into Howard's Walk a few weeks ago."

"Well, Kate, I am sorry I have not introduced myself sooner. I don't get out as much as I used to. I did happen to meet your sister Rebecca though, at John Hubert's office one day. I was very impressed with her accomplishments and what she was thinking about doing with Howard's Walk, and I told her so. I was so saddened to hear about her tragic accident."

"Thank you."

"I've been in Eden Springs ever since I married Mr. Peese in 1953. We came here from Greenville, South Carolina, and moved onto his family's farm to help out. Been there on the homestead ever since. We were married for sixty years. So, I was here when Miss Bessie and Enoch had the gardens. It was a wonderful time. The gatherings we used to have there in the summer—families came by and we'd have picnics and games on a Sunday afternoon." She appeared lost in thought and in her memories. Soon she turned her attention back to Kate and Kate felt she was being measured.

"You and your sister are very different in looks. But I

have a feeling you are just as passionate and strong as she was, with a vision for your future. I can see it in your eyes like I could see it in hers."

"Thank you, Miss Peese. I take that as a compliment."

"Well, you'll be doing a good thing, dear," she said, patting Kate's hand. "It will take some hard work, but you can do it. We need to keep this town alive and young, you know. We've been stagnating. And it's a shame really. But this is a very good thing. This will be good for everyone." She pushed herself up from the chair and smiled. "Like I said, I don't get out much these days, but if there is anything I can do for you, you just let me know." Kate thanked her and held the door as she slowly made her way out to the sidewalk.

Just then, the youngest stylist, Tammy, called Kate's name and raved about her wavy auburn hair. "Don't you worry, I've got a lot of experience," she said as she laughed and took off her bejeweled baseball cap, letting loose a torrent of red hair, brighter, curlier and shorter than Kate's but enough for Kate to give her a thumbs up.

In a few short minutes, Kate knew all about Tammy's life as a single mom who had worked her way through beauty school in Winston-Salem and moved to Eden Springs for this job. Her cousin, Karen, owned the shop and she lived with Karen and her two kids, age five and eight, and her own two-year-old son Kelvin in a small house not far from town.

"And men!" she exclaimed, as she settled Kate into a chair at the shampooing station. "Lean back, honey. I had one, of course, Kelvin's daddy. But he turned out to be a real jerk. How about you, Kate? You got a man in your life? I can tell you, there's not many good ones out there. And nowhere to meet them either. This town is really dead for night life. Karen and I go into Winston-Salem once in a while when we can get a babysitter for the kids. But you, wow, you sure are pretty. You could get a man easy in this town, but there's not much to pick from, like I said."

Her fingers were like magic as she massaged Kate's scalp during the shampoo and Kate found herself completely relaxed. Tammy finished, sat Kate up in the chair and wrapped a towel around her hair. "But I haven't seen you around before. Are you new to town, Kate?"

"Yes, I've been here about a month...." Tammy guided Kate back to her styling chair.

"Well, you'll like it here. People are real friendly and we all help each other out. OK, so what are we going to do here, just a trim or something a little shorter? Me, I would just do a trim, your hair is so beautiful. But it's up to you, whatever you want." In the end, Tammy trimmed a little more than Kate expected but she had to admit, the results were amazing. Tammy had mad scissor skills and lots of interesting life stories, and Kate rewarded her with a large tip.

Kate was never one to waste a new haircut, so she went into Eden Springs News and Cigars to look for more recent issues of *Premier Travel Magazine* and bought the last one on the rack. Chad, the young man behind the counter, stared a full thirty seconds before ringing up her purchase, calling her "ma'am" several times. She wandered through the Garden of Eden Florist, taking in the aroma of the floral arrangements and reminded herself to take flowers to the cemetery for Becky when she was back in Winston-Salem. Kimberly, the florist, was truly touched when Kate explained why she had stopped by and assured Kate she could help her with that any time, just give her a call. She stopped at Perkins Hardware last and picked up a thirty foot water hose for the backyard, some door knobs for the kitchen cupboards and a hammer and screw driver and hauled it all out to her car herself, although Burt, Jimmy, or Jimmy Jr. would have been happy to help her carry it.

It wasn't Rome. Or Paris. But it was getting to feel a little bit more like home.

At the hardware store, Kate noticed a flyer advertising a farmer's market at Cable Farms. The Grand Opening was that coming Saturday with music, food trucks, and bouncy houses for the kids but they were open during the week, too. On a whim, Kate dialed Colleen's number and asked if she wanted to join her at the market. Colleen put her on hold to check her calendar, but when she came back on, she said that she would love to meet her there.

Cable Farms was north of Eden Springs in the opposite direction of Howard's Walk. The road meandered through low but scenic hills, a change from the flat farmland that approached Eden Springs to the south, and Kate found herself enjoying the more picturesque scenery. The farms along the route seemed generally smaller than the ones she had seen near Howard's Walk. These were cattle and horse farms with larger, somewhat newer homes than those found on the tobacco farms.

After several miles, she saw a sign on her right for the turn off to Cable Farms and she turned onto a long dirt road that led to the main buildings of the farm. She drove past fields of strawberry plants on both sides of the road; long arms of mechanical sprinkler systems shot streams of water over the budding plants. Beyond that extended acres and acres of produce as far as she could see, with workers bent in the fields, harvesting vegetables that were now in season. She pulled into the expansive graveled parking area of the farm.

Kate got out and walked to a large open pavilion. Long wooden benches stretched out underneath it and she wandered through the shaded aisles taking in the lush colors of the vegetables, amazed at the many varieties in season this early in the year. She always assumed that the produce in the grocery stores was brought in from California, Mexico, or even South America, and a lot of it was. But this was all labeled as locally grown.

Kate was suddenly transported in her mind back to a time in Paris at the Saxe-Breteuil Market near the Eiffel Tower. She closed her eyes and willed the aromas of the open-air market to come to her—fresh bread, fish, apples, cheeses, and desserts. She could hear in her mind the sounds of friendly banter between vendors and customers, learning how to properly prepare the fish that was brought in from Normandy that morning, or how to use the apples in a special tart for dessert. It was commonplace to handpick flowers from the flower vendors to decorate your dinner table, adding a touch of romance to a delicious meal that included ingredients bought that same day at the market. Farmers from all over France came there to sell their specialties to the Parisians who had been shopping there for decades.

She opened her eyes and was struck by the vivid colors displayed before her with the same meticulous care and style of the Parisian markets. Towers of red-ripe tomatoes and baskets of red and yellow peppers, each one gleaming as if polished by hand; leafy greens of all sorts: russian red and dinosaur kale, creasy greens, collards, and purple mustard greens; crates of pale green cabbages, dusty orange sweet potatoes and red beets; multi-colored acorn squash and bundles of bright orange carrots. There were cartons of early strawberries, and flowers by the buckets full—sunflowers, camellias, and tulips.

"Kate." She felt a touch on her shoulder and turned, pleased to see that it was Colleen.

"Hi, Colleen! I'm glad you could make it."

"Thanks for inviting me. This was a great idea." Colleen took off a pair of large designer sunglasses in the shade of the pavilion and tucked them in her bag. "But you looked like you were off somewhere else just now."

"No, it's just this place," Kate admitted. "It reminds me of the open-air markets in Paris."

"You've been to Paris? Well, I'm jealous. I've always wanted to go but never seemed to be able to make it happen." She looked around the market. "I haven't been here in years."

"Really? I would have been here every weekend if I'd known about it."

They walked between aisles overflowing with produce, stopping to accept samples of early strawberries and tomatoes from the vendors. "Do they have coffee here?" Colleen wondered aloud. "I could really use a cup right now."

She spotted a vendor and they headed in that direction. They bought their coffee and sat at a small wrought iron table nearby. "So, when were you in Paris?" Colleen asked. "Were you there for long?"

"I lived there for two years, actually. But my favorite trip was when I went there to do an article for a magazine on the local scene around the Eiffel tower. This market reminds me of the Saxe-Breteuil Market there. You could see the Eiffel Tower as you were choosing the greens for your dinner salad. It was pretty spectacular. But what was it like growing up here? Have you always lived in Eden Springs?"

"Oh, yes, born and raised. And my parents, too. They were high school sweethearts and they came back here after college, law school for my dad. He's never wanted to be anywhere else or do anything else except be a small-town lawyer with his own practice."

"So, you came back here, too? After college, I mean?"

"Yes, eventually. Dad wanted me to go abroad to study after graduation, but I didn't—because of a guy, of course. It's always a guy, right?"

Kate laughed in agreement.

"So, when that guy didn't last, I came back home, kind of at loose ends. I tried a few different things but then got into real estate."

"Do you like it?"

"I do, and I've been doing OK with it. Still learning though. How about you?"

"I have a degree in journalism, and I have been freelancing since I graduated. I travel, and I write about the places I've been to. In fact, I am thinking about doing an article on Eden Springs and submit it to a magazine I've done some work for."

"Instead of Paris? Or Rome? I don't think Eden Springs even compares to those places. Eden Springs is barely a dot on the map. People forget we're even here."

"I don't see that at all. I mean, look at this market—the colors and how everything is displayed. To me, it's like art, and very much like the Parisian markets. And I saw cattle and horse farms on the way here, and the trees are in bloom. I think Eden Springs is quaint and friendly. And Howard's Walk must have been beautiful in its day."

"You and I are complete opposites," Colleen smiled. "You've been all around the world and think Eden Springs is a great place to be. I've been in Eden Springs pretty much my whole life and I'd love to go to all those places you've talked about."

"Well, I didn't think it was such a great place when I first got here," Kate admitted. "I didn't even want to come, to be honest. But I didn't have much of a choice." Kate shared her recent breakup and the issues with her trip to Rome. "So I am finding my way. Especially after losing Becky."

"Do you have other family?"

"No. We lost our parents to a car accident when we were in college. I don't have any other relatives. At least none that I know of anyway. Becky and I were adopted."

Colleen took another sip of her coffee and shifted in her chair. "I lost my mom when I was sixteen. She was my..." she hesitated.

"Your guiding star?" Kate prompted as Colleen's gaze drifted across the fields that surrounded the pavilion.

Colleen looked back at her and nodded, with a brief sad smile. "Yes. She was exactly that."

They were silent for a moment, each lost in memories of those they had left them, too early. "You remind me a little of Becky," Kate said then.

"Oh? How's that?"

"Your determination, knowing what you want and going after it. That's something I always admired about her. Did you ever meet her?"

"I'll take that as high praise then. No, I never met her. I wish I had, though. She must have been pretty ambitious to take on a project like Howard's Walk."

"Yes, she was. She was an attorney. She helped a lot of people in her job. And she did a lot for me, too."

Kate decided to lighten the mood a bit. She was enjoying getting to know Colleen, but she was hoping this outing would be a chance to just have some girl time, too. "So, I got my first Eden Springs haircut today. Tammy did it. She's lots of fun."

Colleen leaned back to assess it. "I meant to compliment you on it—it looks great."

"Thanks. Tammy seems to think there aren't a lot of guys around here to date. Not that I am really looking after the mess with my last boyfriend. Is your fiancé from around here?"

"No, he's from Winston-Salem. And Tammy is right, not too many eligible bachelors in this town."

"Do you know Ben Evans, though? You both grew up here, right?"

Colleen coughed as she finished her coffee. "Uh, yes, I know Ben. Have you met him?"

"Yes, a couple of times. He seems really nice," Kate admitted, keeping the details of their midnight raid and amazing kiss to herself.

Colleen twisted the diamond ring on her finger. "He is a very nice guy." She fell silent for a moment, then seemed to make a decision. "Ben and I dated a while back, but the breakup wasn't his fault at all. I just wasn't ready back then. He really is a good man, Kate. I don't want you to think anything differently about him now."

Kate wasn't surprised at Colleen's admission of dating Ben. Small town, young romance, it would seem natural for them to get together at some point. But there was a difference in her tone when she talked about him, and Kate wondered what the real story behind their breakup was. "So how is your wedding planning going? Have you set a date yet?" she asked, hopefully getting to a safer topic.

Colleen's phone sounded an alert and she pulled it out of her bag. "No, no date yet," she said, suddenly distracted. "I haven't had a lot of time to even think about it, really." She gave Kate a weak smile that told her she hadn't chosen a safe topic at all. "Well," she said suddenly, standing up. "Sorry to run, but I have to get back into town. I have some work to do. But this was a great idea, Kate. Maybe we can do it again sometime."

"Sure. I'd like that. I'm glad you came," Kate called as she watched her walk away. She finished her coffee and made a mental note regarding Colleen: keep it professional, don't talk about anything too personal, and don't ask about her relationships. Kate put her thoughts about Colleen aside and pulled out her phone. She snapped pictures of the displays under the pavilion and made notes and sketches in her journal for reference later. She selected several fresh tomatoes and greens, and a few ears of corn, for herself.

As she was preparing to leave, a woman approached her and introduced herself. She was tall and thin and dressed in black jeans and cowboy boots but had added flair with a stylish jean jacket and white blouse and scarf. "Hi, I'm Bonnie Cable. I'm the owner of Cable Farms." Kate shook her outstretched hand. "I noticed you taking pictures and notes. Are you a reporter? Not that it matters," she assured Kate, "but I'd be happy to answer questions if you would like."

"No, not a reporter. But I'd like to do an article for a travel magazine about the area. I'm Kate Tyler. From Eden Springs." She had never introduced herself that way, but it felt surprisingly natural. "Actually, I just moved to Howard's Walk. Maybe you've heard of it?"

"I grew up in Eden Springs, so I am very familiar with Howard's Walk. Technically, we are not located in the town of Eden Springs here at the farm. But I've heard some folks talking about someone new over at Howard's Walk, and maybe thinking of renovations there. Would that be you they are talking about?"

"Yes, that would be me. But plans are still up in the air about help from the town though."

"Would you like to see the farm?" Bonnie asked. Kate quickly agreed and they walked through the pavilion and out to the fields as she explained the different crops they would be producing throughout the seasons. "Everything fresh, grown right here on the farm for the most part. We do get a few of the more unique crops brought in from the smaller specialty farms that are starting up. And products like goat cheese, herbs, meats, things like that. We'll have beef for sale soon and it comes from Porter Family Farms, right down the road, all organic and grass fed. If you haven't been to Sunrise Gardens yet, you might want to check that out. It's a wholesaler for wildflowers that they grow and sell here at the market and to florists in Winston-Salem. That would be a great addition to your article. And there are a couple of wineries just opening up not far from here, too. And you can't miss picking strawberries—they will be ready real soon."

Kate was fascinated by all the unique family owned businesses in the area and felt a great article coming together that she could pitch to the magazine. And not only that, she was beginning to realize what an important addition the renovation of

Howard's Walk would make to an already prosperous agriculture industry. She would be living in her own "destination" spot.

"Bonnie, can I ask if you have been part of the town meetings about Howard's Walk and the gardens?"

"No, like I said, this place is outside the town limits, so we don't get too involved in their matters. But it seems to me that fixing up Howard's Walk would be a win-win for everybody. I'd be happy to come support you if you need me to. I wouldn't have a vote, but I could at least let them know I think it would be a great idea. I do have some pull in the area," she said, smiling. "And we could help out too, if you needed equipment or things like that, when you start renovating."

"Thank you! That sounds perfect. I'll keep you posted about the meetings."

"Great! Now tell me about this article you might be writing. We need all the good publicity we can get!"

19

SAM AND MARTIN HAD BEEN GONE FOR FOUR DAYS when they called Kate to let her know they were coming by and had something to show her.

When they arrived, they carried the trunk into the house and set it down in the kitchen. They were unusually quiet though and Kate asked them what was wrong.

"Well, Kate, we found something in the trunk that I don't think you saw before when you were going through it." Sam pulled a manila envelope out of the trunk with a note paperclipped to it. He handed it to Kate. The handwriting was immediately familiar to her and the note read "Show Kate."

"This is Becky's handwriting." She looked at the two men. "Where did you say you found this?"

"It was in the very bottom of the trunk. I don't know how we missed it, but I think we were so excited about the plans and other things we found, we just didn't see it. We didn't open it, Kate. We thought you should do it."

Intrigued, Kate removed the paperclip, opened the envelope and pulled out a folded piece of paper. It was a birth certificate with the words STATE OF NORTH CAROLINA imprinted across the top. An official looking stamp and the date of August 17, 1990 was in the lower right-hand corner. She quickly scanned the document. Place of birth, Carteret County, North Carolina; the child's name and father's name was blank; mother's name was Jenny Howard. She read the date of birth and stopped.

"Date of birth August 16, 1990," she read aloud. "That must be what she wanted to show me—Jenny Howard had a baby with the same birthdate as Becky and me. There was a picture of Jenny in the trunk, too. Wait a minute, though. Look at this. It says Jenny had triplets. Wow! That's something."

"That is something," Martin agreed. "Wonder what ever happened to them?"

Kate did some quick calculations with the dates. "Well, the other photo said she was 13 in 1986. So, Jenny was only about 17 when she had them. Maybe they were given up for adoption, like Becky and I were."

"Wow, Kate, you don't think..." Martin whispered.

"No, Martin," Kate said, quickly dismissing his question. "I don't think anything of the kind. Becky and I weren't born in Carteret county. I have my birth certificate to prove it. And ours say that we were twins, not part of triplets. No, I think she was just surprised that the dates were the same. I suppose a lot of people were born on that day in North Carolina, right?"

The men agreed. "But thank you both for showing this to me," she said. "I really appreciate it. Did you find anything else?"

"Nothing unusual but the plans are amazing. Thanks for letting us look at them."

Sam added, "It's a shame that this place was let go for so long. Becky obviously must have seen them, too. Now we know she went through the trunk since she left you the note. I wonder if she shared them with anyone else?"

Kate said, "I doubt it."

"Kate, Sam and I were talking. And we were wondering..."

Martin hesitated. "Oh, I am just going to come out and ask you. Have you decided to stay?"

Kate shook her head. "So much has happened since you left. I had a realtor and a contractor come by. Bad news. The cost to fix the place up right could be as much as a hundred thousand."

Sam let out a low whistle. "That's a chunk of change all right."

"But," Kate continued, "I'm still looking at all the options. Fixing it up to sell, fixing it up to stay or selling it as is. I wish I had an answer for you. But if I do decide to stay, would I have your support?"

"Of course!" they both said.

Kate heard Ben calling from the front of the house. Kate lit up and met him with a hug in the foyer. Sam and Martin exchanged glances. "Ben, I want you to meet my friends, Sam Bingham and Martin McDonough. Guys, this is Ben."

"Nice to meet you both," Ben said as they shook hands. "Kate's told me a lot about you."

"Well," Martin frowned, "she has told us nothing about you." He turned and glared at her. "So why is that, Kate?"

Kate laughed. "You two breeze in and out of here like the wind and wonder why I don't tell you every detail of my life?"

"Yes, we do wonder about that!" Sam exclaimed. "But we will let it go, now that we have met Ben."

"Good, but in the interest of sharing, Ben owns a garden center here in Eden Springs, so you have a lot in common. He knew the Howard family back when they had the gardens and would be really interested in seeing what we found in the trunk," Kate said.

"Well, we have a lot more to show you, then. Wait until you see what we have been working on! Come on, Martin, let's bring it all in."

The two men went out to the RV and came back with a long folding table, a card table, two folding chairs and an artist's easel, which they arranged in the foyer. Then Sam carried in two large boxes, one with drawings, books and catalogs that he and Martin had been collecting, and the second one containing the carefully preserved original renderings and handwritten notes they had found in Miss Bessie's trunk. They put out laminated copies they had made from the originals for use as working copies and had then carefully marked each one with codes to match the notes with the drawings. Kate rolled the originals back into their tubes for storage.

"It's about time we got all of this together in one place—and out of the RV!" Sam said, as they laid everything out on the long table.

Ben was stunned at what was laid out before him on the table. He approached reverently and let out a low whistle. "This is amazing," he said, as he traced his finger across the first rendering, a drawing of the original site plan of the gardens. "It's all there, exactly the way it used to be."

Martin picked up the drawing and taped it on to the easel. Ben scanned across the other drawings and notes, growing more fascinated with each illustration.

"OK," Sam said, "as you can see, we have been busy. And I know you just said you still weren't sure if you were staying yet or not, Kate, but this was so exciting, we went a little wild. Anyway—just in case, mind you—this is what we found. As this site plan shows, there were several distinct gardens on the property." Sam pointed to the different markings on the plan. "Some were specific to certain tree species such as the Crepe Myrtle Garden and the Magnolia Garden. We can tell that they wanted interesting plantings for all four seasons. And I can see the English influence that Bessie must have wanted to maintain but in a twentieth century style."

"You are exactly right, Sam. This is just how I remember it," Ben said.

Kate shook her head. "I'm afraid I don't know what I'm looking at. Can you describe what it would be like?"

"Well, you don't see the grid plans of gardens typical of the 18th century," Sam explained. "The plans here followed the contours of the property itself. It was more natural. I see she liked lots of colors in her gardens, too. But comparing these original renderings to the current state of the gardens dated earlier, it appears that over the years, but before Bessie left, some modifications were made, but nothing drastic... mostly to the hardscapes."

"Hardscapes?" Kate asked.

"Paths, trellises, fences, arbors, retaining walls—things like that," Ben explained.

Sam continued. "As the hardscapes deteriorated, they were replaced or just torn down. We have quite a bit that is missing, according to these plans, but we are very fortunate that we can see what it once looked like."

The remaining site plans were tacked up one by one and discussed. In total, they covered the entirety of Howard's Walk. The group was quiet as they began to take in the sheer enormity of what the project could become. Martin finally broke the silence. "The big question is what can be done..."

"If you stay," Sam interrupted.

"Yes, if you stay, what could we do while staying within a budget—and I'm just throwing ideas out here, mind you—but maybe with the volunteer help we can get, some fundraisers? What would be easy, but still be as true as we can to the southern garden style, and with a big impact?"

"And?" Kate asked when no one replied.

"And, it's a tall order," said Ben. "We would have to make some really tough decisions."

"Ben's right," Sam said. "There are at least seven stages to completing each of the gardens we decide on, not to mention all of the work that needs to be done on the areas that won't be part of the gardens. Tree removal would help a lot. Have you thought about repairing the greenhouse? It could be a big attraction itself."

Kate nodded, her creative mind racing ahead of her. "Maybe the greenhouse could be a place for horticulture classes and generate some money that way." They discussed other ways to add revenue to the project and Kate mentioned her visit to

Cable Farms and the article she was writing. Sam and Martin had never been to the farm but were eager to see it. Ben said that he knew about it but had never thought to connect it to their project.

"Bonnie had some great ideas about how Howard's Walk could be linked with other agricultural businesses north of here," Kate said. "And she said she could come to the next Town Council meeting and give us her support if I needed her to."

"Great idea," Ben agreed. "Wait a minute," Ben said as he pulled out his phone. "There is a town council meeting tomorrow night. Kate, you said you wanted to reach out to people in town. Do you think you could get Bonnie to come on short notice?"

"I can call her and ask. But I won't be going alone, right?" she asked, looking at the three men.

"Absolutely not," Martin and Sam both said. "Anything you need, Kate, we are here for you."

"OK, then," Ben said. "I'll call John and let him know we will be there so he can put us on the agenda."

Sam turned to Kate. "We can lay out the concepts we have, Kate, but the decision is really up to you. You knew Becky best. She never gave us any formal plans or ideas when she asked us to help. What do you think she would want to see done at Howard's Walk?"

Kate paused for a moment. Considering that she had learned about the gardens only after Becky had bought them, it was hard to try to envision what Becky would have wanted.

"I guess Becky must have had her own ideas about this property," she said. "She was very creative, and whatever her plans were I am sure they were ambitious. But I don't even know if she wanted to create something new or stay true to Bessie and Enoch's original gardens."

Kate looked around at her friends. Then she made up her mind. "Becky was a visionary—that much I know. She didn't leave any plans except for the few arrangements she made with the contractors. But she was also very practical. And she would expect us to be practical about it, too. I think we would need to go ahead with a new vision, our vision. In the end, that's all we can do, and I think she would expect that from me."

At 6:45 PM the next evening, Kate, Ben, Sam and Martin walked into the Community Meeting Room in the municipal building of Eden Springs. Kate saw Bonnie Cable across the room and waved. Rosie told them to help themselves to coffee and cake. Kate introduced her to Sam and Martin and explained why they were there. John Hubert arrived a few minutes later and Kate approached him. "Mr. Hubert? Excuse me, could I talk to you for a minute?"

John turned and his face lit up when he saw her. "Of course, Kate! It's so good to see you. How have you been?"

"I'm doing better," she said, although it occurred to her that she had been living there for over a month and he still had not reached out to her about the sale of the house.

"Good, good. Now what did you want to talk about? I see you are on the agenda tonight."

"Yes. It's about Howard's Walk. I thought I might have heard from you about putting the house on the market. At the very least I thought you might let me know about whether there was any interest from people to help fix up the gardens."

"That's true enough," he apologized. "But I wanted to give you enough time to, well, you know, just give you some time alone there. But you're right. I should have been in touch before this. Are you still thinking of selling?"

"I am trying to decide that. That's why I am here tonight. But you need to know I have also had another realtor look at the property. Actually, it was Colleen Carroll."

"Oh, I see," he said, his face reddening. "Well, she is a good realtor." Others started arriving and taking seats. John began to step away from Kate. "We'll get through our agenda quickly and then we'll give you a chance to talk, OK?"

Kate noticed his embarrassment but was not sorry that she had approached him; after all, business was business. She spoke to Bonnie Cable briefly and stopped to say hello to Emma Peese who was sitting in the front row like a queen holding court; all she was missing was a crown, but the flowery hat she wore over her new hairdo seemed perfectly adequate. She then returned to her seat next to Ben. "How did it go?" he asked. Kate gave him a thumbs up.

The meeting agenda had been placed on their seats before the meeting and Kate looked it over. Four other items were planned before her, including how to deal with bands of wild dogs that were roaming just outside of town limits, and the need for better upkeep of the Veterans' Memorial Gardens. Then it read, "Discussion of Gardens at Howard's Walk... Kate Tyler."

She'd never been on a meeting agenda before and her stomach started knotting up. Ben reached over, squeezed her hand and gave her a quick smile.

Just then, John banged the gavel and called the meeting to order. The first three items were moved through quickly; the final item involved installing a traffic light at the intersection of Wood Street and Cross Street. Despite Snap giving a passionate defense of why he wasn't going to sit at an intersection and wait for the light to turn when there was no one in sight for miles, the motion was ultimately passed.

Then it was Kate's turn.

"The next item on the agenda is Kate Tyler regarding the Gardens at Howard's Walk," announced John Hubert. "Kate, welcome and you can go ahead any time."

Kate stood shakily, twisting the agenda in her hands. Her friends looked at her encouragingly and she began. "Mayor Hubert, thank you for letting me speak tonight. l want to introduce some friends of mine, Sam Bingham and Martin

McDonough." The two men turned and waved at people seated around them. "They own Martini's Marvels, a landscaping business in Lakeville. Actually, they were friends with Becky for a long time, and we've gotten to be good friends, too.

"I've also gotten to know many of you, and I wanted to say that I appreciate your support and friendship to me during this time. I'm doing much better and I... well, I appreciate it more than you know." Kate stopped for a moment and realized that all eyes were on her. But she knew the words she spoke came from her heart and that was all that mattered.

"But what I wanted to talk to you about tonight is really how to go forward. I have some decisions to make, and to be honest, I am still not sure if I will stay in Eden Springs or not. You see, a lot of it depends on all of you. Becky's vision of the restoration of the gardens was not something she was going to do by herself. Her vision was that this would be everyone working together to make it a focal point for the community, a tourist attraction like it was in the past.

"But there is something else I've learned. I've learned, through reading some of Miss Bessie's writings and hearing about the Howards, that she and Enoch loved this town and they loved the gardens. And many of you that remember those days, remember the joy that it brought to tourists when they came here. And they did come. From all over." As Kate talked, she realized she needed to share what she knew as a professional, from personal experience. She was sharing the truth with them and gained confidence from that knowledge. She straightened her shoulders and went on.

"I've traveled all over the world and I can tell you that the Gardens at Howard's Walk, at their peak, must have been among some of the finest that I've seen. Maybe not as big, but just as beautiful. People will come to enjoy a place that will lift their spirits, give them a quiet place to meditate, a place to learn, a place for families to share in the beauty of nature. I know that for a fact. And with the beauty of this area, and the wonderful people here, there are so many possibilities to explore. People deserve a good place to visit like Eden Springs. It's not the beach, it's not the mountains—but it's close, and it can be affordable for everyone.

"I met Bonnie Cable the other day, from Cable Farms," she said, pointing out Bonnie, who raised her hand in acknowledgement. "She told me about several other interesting places that are starting up near her farm that would be great destination spots for visitors. So, I think that adding the Gardens at Howard's Walk again would be an opportunity that we shouldn't pass up.

"I guess that's all I have to say. I think this project would be great for Eden Springs. But to do it right, I would need your help." There was a moment of silence and then Sam stood and started to applaud; Martin, Ben and others followed.

Rosie spoke first when the applause ended. "Kate, you can count me in! And the rest of you better think about what she just said. This town needs a boost. You've all been talking about selling, walking away. But this is your home, your legacy—and once it's gone, it's gone for good. I've thought about giving up—no different than anyone else in this room. But this gives me hope. Hope for our futures. So yes, count me in, Kate."

There was more applause until Miss Peese stood and raised her hand, quieting the crowd. She steadied herself with her cane and began to speak, slowly and deliberately. It was clear that when Miss Peese spoke, people listened.

"Everything she says is true, folks. I met Kate the other day and told her I thought this would be a great idea. I met her sister Rebecca, too, and I think it would be special to do this in memory of someone who really wanted to bring something wonderful back to Eden Springs." Her gaze fell over each person in the room. "So, I say, let's get organized and get this project going!" She tapped her cane on the floor and sat down.

Bonnie raised her hand to speak next and was recognized. "I agree with everything Kate said. We have an opportunity here that will be great for everyone in the area. With the new wineries and specialty farms starting up north of here, if we have Howard's Walk south of town, it would make Eden Springs the epicenter for tourism. I have told Kate I would give her my support in any way that I can. Thank you." And she sat down.

Two women stood up next. "Kate, we're from the Eden Springs Garden Club and we've been talking, and we want you to know that if you decide to stay, we can help raise money. And we know as much as anyone in the area about the local plant life that thrives here, no disrespect to our guests," one of the women said, nodding to Sam and Martin. "So, you can count us in, too. Mayor Hubert, on behalf of the Eden Springs Garden Club, I propose that our club be the official committee for the restoration of the Gardens at Howard's Walk."

John Hubert put that in the form of a motion to the town council, and cheers went up as the vote was unanimous in favor of it. Kate was overwhelmed. People approached her after the meeting was over, and thanked her and shook her hand, showing their support. The words of a journalism professor suddenly came back to her. *Words have power, Kate. If you choose them wisely and let them spring from the heart, people will listen. But the burden of what comes from those words—that burden is for you to bear.*

The burden was now hers.

20

BEN AND KATE DROVE BACK TO THE HOUSE with Sam and Martin settled into the bed of the truck with strict instructions to Ben to take it slow so they wouldn't bounce out in the dark.

Kate was quiet for several minutes. Ben finally broke the silence.

"I'm very proud of you, Kate. You gave a wonderful speech back there."

Kate smiled. "Thanks—I'm not sure quite what to make of it. I mean, I guess I found out what I needed to know but I wasn't quite expecting that."

"You inspired them. But I'm a little curious about what inspired you. They were hanging on every word."

"I've been wondering that myself. But I was looking around and here were these people, who didn't have to be there, at a routine Town Council meeting in this little town." She turned to Ben. "They were sad at first, Ben. They were there, but they weren't happy. But something drew them there. And I thought, they must care about the town, even the mundane, everyday issues like the traffic light. But they were still in a bad place, like I was when I came here. I guess I can just relate to what they are feeling."

They heard a knock on the back window of the truck and Kate slid it open.

"Drop us off at the RV, OK?" Martin said.

"Sure thing." Ben slowed down as he approached it and dropped them off. They signaled Kate to roll down her window.

"Kate, you were amazing tonight. See you in the morning, OK?"

"Thanks guys. See you tomorrow."

Ben pulled up in front of the house. "Time for a glass of wine?" Kate asked.

"Absolutely," Ben replied. A few minutes later they were settled in on the back patio, Kate snuggling next to Ben.

"Kate!" Billy's voice suddenly pierced the silence. They stood and looked across the back lawn. Billy was running towards them. "Miss Kate, Miss Kate!" Billy shouted.

"Oh, no," Kate said as they ran to meet him. "Billy, what's wrong?"

"It's Mama, Miss Kate—I ran here, through the woods. It was dark, and I'm scared!"

"Billy, just slow down and tell me what's wrong."

"It's Mama. She fell and I can't get her up!" Billy cried.

Ben took Billy's face in his hands to make him focus. "OK, Billy, we're going back to your house and check on your mama now, OK? Everything's going to be OK."

"OK, Mister Ben. I ran all the way here, Miss Kate." Billy rubbed his wet face with his sleeve. "I'm sorry, I shouldn't have run in the woods, but Mama needs help!" Kate comforted him and told him it was OK, no one was mad at him.

Kate and Ben took Billy to the truck and sped off to Mimi's house.

Billy gripped the dashboard, peering through the windshield. They soon approached the Zink's small brick ranch home and pulled into the driveway. The front door was open, and they ran inside and found Mimi lying on the kitchen floor.

"Miss Mimi!" Kate knelt beside her. "Are you OK? What happened?"

Mimi was conscious but obviously in pain. "I fell. Where's Billy? Is he here?" she asked, trying to see her son.

"He's right in the next room, Ben is with him. He's calling EMS now so we can get you to the hospital."

Mimi nodded and winced in pain as she tried to move her leg. Kate noticed she couldn't lift her right arm. EMS soon arrived, the team acting quickly to take her vitals and check for obvious injuries, noting the severe pain as they assessed her leg and hip.

"It might be broken, Miss Mimi. We'll get you to the hospital." Minutes later they had her on a stretcher, covered with blankets and securely strapped in. Billy became agitated at the sight of his mother being taken away, something he had never seen in his life and didn't understand. Mimi motioned to him to come near. "I'm OK, Billy," she whispered. "Stay with Miss Kate and Ben for now, OK?"

"No Mama, I want to go with you!"

Ben stepped in. "Billy, we'll take you to the hospital in my truck so you can be with her, but you need to go with us, OK?"

"OK, Mr. Ben," as he moved to follow the stretcher. But Ben took him by the arm and gently guided him back inside to the kitchen. Billy sat down at the table with his hands fisted, rocking back and forth, unable to understand why his world had suddenly been turned upside down. "Where are they taking Mama?" he finally asked.

Ben knelt in front of him and took his large hands in his. "Billy, you know how sometimes you don't feel good and your mama would take you to see Doc Bartlett?"

"Yeah," Billy said softly. "I like Doc Bartlett—but I don't like shots!"

"Well, those shots are to make you feel better even though it hurts a little bit. Your mama isn't feeling good so she's going to see Doc Bartlett at the hospital. Do you understand that, Billy?" Billy nodded, but his face was still wet with tears. Kate hugged him and the two sat with him as he cried.

Kate soon took Ben aside. "He might need to stay with me for a while. I'll pack a few of his things." Ben agreed and Kate left them alone to find Billy's bedroom.

A handmade sign on the door pinpointed his room. It was sparsely furnished. A large bed was situated against one wall. A low bookshelf next to the bed held children's books, a box of random train set parts and tracks. A picture of polar bears was tacked over the bed. Kate found an old suitcase in the closet and opened it up on the bed.

She packed a few shirts and pants, underwear and socks, all that would fit in the suitcase. She laid a couple of the books on top of the clothes and closed the lid, snapping it shut. As she was looking around for anything else that might help Billy feel at home, she noticed a photo album on the bookshelf. She sat down and opened it.

It was a mixture of photos in no particular order. Pictures of his mother and what must have been Calvin, his daddy; Billy as a little boy and then others as he was growing up. There was a wallet size studio photo of Mimi and Calvin taken many years earlier, before they adopted Billy, she guessed.

Then Kate saw several pictures that looked like they were taken at Howard's Walk. The colors were faded somewhat but the surroundings were familiar to her. She recognized one of the faces as Bessie Howard, whom she knew from the photo albums she saw back at the house in the trunk. The first photograph looked like it was taken at a birthday party; perhaps for the same sullen faced teenager she saw in the other pictures.

Suddenly, she stopped and looked closer at the picture. People were gathered around the table and a cake lit with candles was set in the center, everyone ready for the birthday girl to make a wish and blow them out. But it was not that image that caught her attention. Because on the table in the photograph lay a tablecloth with poppies and green leaves and vines and flowers scattered across the center. Her hands shook as she stared at it. It couldn't be—not the same one that she now had tucked away in the side table at Howard's Walk; not the one that Becky must have left there since she had had it in her possession for many years.

"But that's impossible," Kate murmured to herself. The next photograph was similar, taken at Howard's Walk, but this time everyone was standing around a small child in a highchair. The mop of blond hair was strikingly familiar. She pulled the photograph out of the tabs at its corners and turned it over. The words brought tears to her eyes. "Billy's first birthday—August 16, 1991."

Ben came to the door. "Is everything OK?" Kate quickly closed the album and looked up at him. "Everything's fine. I think I have everything." She opened the suitcase, laid the album inside and closed it again. She put her feelings aside. There were more important things to think about now, and Mimi and Billy needed her. "Let's go."

They drove to the hospital. Kate answered a stream of questions from Billy as they parked and walked into the Emergency Room.

"Is this where my mama is? Why isn't my mama home?"

"Yes, Billy, this is where your mama is because she isn't feeling well and the doctors and nurses are helping her here," Kate reassured him.

"OK. Can she come home with us, Kate?"

"I don't think so, Billy, but we'll see. You want what's best for her, don't you?"

"Sure, I do. And it's best for my mama to come home. Right, Kate?"

Kate knew it was hopeless to try to explain to him any further. They asked at the desk if they would be able to see Mimi Zink, Kate explaining the situation to the clerk. She said she would check with the nurse and after a few moments returned to say that only she and Billy could visit, and only for a few minutes.

"You wait here with Ben, Billy," Kate said. "I'll make sure she isn't sleeping, OK?"

"OK. I hope she's not sleeping!" Billy hopped from one foot to the other in anticipation.

Kate followed the clerk back to the room, then pulled back the curtain and entered quietly. Machines stood on either side of the bed, blinking and beeping out Mrs. Zink's current vitals' status. This was not the place for Mimi, Kate thought. She should be home, cooking, caring for Billy, working in her garden. She took a deep breath and put a smile on her face.

Mimi appeared small and frail in the bed. Kate approached her and took her hand. "Mimi, it's Kate."

Mimi's eyes opened slowly. She smiled.

"Kate, dear. How nice of you to come." She looked around the room. "Is Billy here? I don't want him to see me like this. Where is he?"

"He's here, Mimi. He is with Ben in the waiting room. I think he needs to see you though. I know it's hard, but he doesn't understand what's happening. I think he needs you to reassure him."

"Well, I guess. I don't want him to worry though."

"Can I ask what the doctors say?"

"They think I broke my hip when I fell. They will take X-rays soon and let me know what they need to do. I don't remember exactly what happened though. It was all so sudden. Kate, I need to ask you a favor, dear."

"Of course, Mimi, anything."

"Can you keep Billy for a while? I know he will stay with you. It's a lot to ask but I might be here a few days."

Kate smiled. "Mimi, of course he can stay. In fact, I already packed some clothes for him. I'll keep him as long as you need me to."

"Bless you, dear. You are an angel."

Kate thought back to the photograph. Now was not the time to ask Mimi about it. She needed her rest. But soon she would have to get some answers.

"I'll bring Billy in now, OK?" Kate left the room and found Ben and Billy waiting in the hallway. Billy was very quiet. "Is everything OK?" Kate asked.

"I told him he needed to be very quiet and gentle with his mama when he saw her because she was not feeling well. So, he is trying to be very quiet."

Kate took Billy's hand. "That's very good, Billy. She wants to see you now, OK?"

"OK, Miss Kate," Billy whispered.

He followed Kate quietly into the room, but his face lit up when he saw his mother. "Mama!" Billy tiptoed to the bedside and took the hand that Mimi reached out to him. Tears ran down their faces. "Mama, are you OK?"

Mimi nodded. "Don't cry, Billy. I'm going to be just fine and home before you know it." She put her hand on Billy's cheek and wiped away his tears.

Kate slipped out of the room to let them have their privacy. Once in the waiting room, Kate broke down. Ben took her in his arms. "What will happen to him, Ben? What if she can't take care of him?"

"She will do what's best for him—she always has. She knew this day might come." He lifted her chin and wiped her tears away. "I'll do whatever I can to help, too, I promise."

The nurse approached. "They'd like to see you both now. I think it will be OK, under the circumstances."

Kate and Ben returned to the room. Mimi took Billy's hand and Kate's and put them together. "Billy, you will be staying with Miss Kate for a few days, OK? I want you to be good for her and do what she says."

"Yes, Mama."

"Kate, you are my angel. I know this is a lot to ask of you, dear."

"I am so honored that you would trust him with me, Mimi. I won't let you down, I promise."

Just then, Dr. Bartlett came into the room. Billy's face lit up when he saw him, and the doctor gave Billy a big hug. "Well, here is my favorite young man. How are you, Billy?"

Billy looked puzzled. "I'm OK, but my mama is not so good. Can you help her Doc?"

"Billy, that's exactly what I am going to do. Your mother will be up and around before you know it. So, you have to be strong for her, OK?"

"OK," Billy said solemnly. "Mama says I am strong, Doc."

"OK, then. I am going to talk to Mr. Ben here and then we'll be back in. You stay with your mother for a few minutes."

They walked out of the room. Ben introduced Kate and told him that she would be taking care of Billy while Mimi was in the hospital. "Well, as long as that is what Mimi and Billy want, then that sounds good to me. But she won't be coming home as soon as Billy would like, I'm afraid. She has broken her hip, so she'll need surgery and then a stint in rehab. And I am concerned that she might have had a mild stroke. We'll do more tests on that tomorrow."

"That's no problem, doctor," Kate reassured him.

"OK then. We'll do the surgery in the morning and let you know how it goes."

Back at Howard's Walk, Kate fixed Billy a snack. He ate slowly and watched Kate as she moved around the kitchen. Finally, his eyes grew heavy with sleep. Billy let Kate lead him to her bed where he crawled under the covers and fell fast asleep. Kate sat with him a few minutes and then went back to the kitchen where Ben was waiting for her.

"I fixed some tea," Ben said. Kate just put her arms around him and whispered thank you.

"Listen, I have a blowup mattress and a couch and some chairs I can bring over, if you want. If you think it would be more comfortable, I mean."

Kate smiled. "Sure, that might help Billy feel more at home, and give me something to sleep on." She hesitated, but then said, "Ben, I have something to show you. I'll be back in a minute."

Kate got the album out of Billy's suitcase and the box out of the side table in the foyer and brought them into the kitchen where she laid them out in front of Ben. She opened the album to the two photographs she found earlier and pointed at the first one. "Have you ever seen this picture before? Or these people, other than Bessie and Mimi and Calvin, of course?"

"No, I don't think I've ever seen the picture before. Not sure who that is. Probably Bessie's daughter, Jenny, though?"

"That's what I thought. And you've never seen this tablecloth, here in this house, I mean, when you used to visit?"

Ben looked at it for a moment. "I don't think so. The only holiday we ever came was one Thanksgiving she invited me and my mom over since my father was out of town. I was real young. I remember thinking how everything was so comfortable and cozy here, not formal and cold like Thanksgivings at our house. My mom and I had a great time. But I don't remember anything else. Why? What's so special about the tablecloth?"

Kate slowly opened the box and pulled back the tissue paper. "Becky and I have had this tablecloth for years. Our adoptive parents gave it to us. Becky had it, so she must have left it here. I found it the first day I came to see the house. And when I saw it, it was what made me decide to stay for a while—I guess I thought maybe Becky wanted to make Howard's Walk be like the homes we had growing up."

"But, how... I mean maybe it's just similar to the one in the picture?" Ben asked.

Kate shook her head. "Look closer though." She pulled the photo out of the album and held it next to the tablecloth. "See here, right along the edge. There is a burn mark that's been there as long as I can remember." She pointed to the photo.

"There is the same mark, right there on the corner. Ben, it's handmade and one of a kind. Our mother always said it was an heirloom and that if we didn't keep anything else of theirs, we should keep this tablecloth. Knowing that and just seeing it here in the picture, it makes me feel like we must be connected somehow—to Bessie, to this house. And there's something else." She turned to another page of the album. Tears began to roll down her cheeks. "This picture was taken on Billy's first birthday. August 16, 1991."

"What's wrong?"

"Ben, that's my birthday—and Becky's birthday. August 16. We were all three born on August 16, 1990." She started to sob. Ben put his arms around her.

"Maybe it's a coincidence. Maybe..."

"I don't think so. And there's one more thing." She pulled the yellowed paper out of the manila envelope and spread it out on the table in front of Ben. "This birth certificate was in a trunk here at the house. Sam and Martin were looking through it and found it in this envelope. There was a note attached in Becky's handwriting that said, 'Show Kate'." She showed him the note and unfolded the birth certificate. "Look at this birth certificate, Ben. Triplets. Jenny Howard had triplets on August 16, 1990. And there were three baby blankets in the trunk, too."

"But you and Becky were twins, right? What does your birth certificate say?"

"It says we were twins, I'm sure. And the place of birth is a different county in North Carolina. This is all too much to be just a coincidence, though. I have felt such a connection to Billy, from the very beginning. Maybe this is why. I feel like he is part of me. And I think he feels the same connection to me, too. I need to talk to Mimi about it, but I can't do that right now." She wiped her eyes with her sleeve. "Ben, I don't know what to do."

"OK, well, we'll figure it out then. And I think you are right; you need to talk to Mimi about it. It's too important not to know the truth."

"Ben, no one ever talks about Jenny. Whatever happened to her?"

"I really don't know. I was little when she would have been around. I know she was never here while I was growing up. Maybe my mom would know more. I can ask her if you want me to."

"Thank you but maybe not right now. I need to absorb all of this. Please don't say anything to anyone."

"Of course not. Listen, we're both tired. Why don't I go get that air mattress and bring it over? You need something to sleep on tonight."

"Thanks. I guess I wasn't expecting I would ever have overnight guests."

Ben was back soon with two extra chairs and the air mattress which they set up next to Kate's bed. "I saw a light on in the RV, so I stopped and told Sam and Martin that you were here with Billy. They're here if you need anything, too," said Ben as he covered the mattress with a sheet and blanket and situated a pillow on one end. "Try to get some sleep, OK?"

"I don't think that will be a problem. I don't know when I have been more exhausted."

"You've had a lot to tackle today. Are you sure you don't want me to stay?"

"No, we'll be fine," Kate assured him. She hugged him. "Thank you for everything, for being here for us."

He lifted her chin. "I'd do anything for you—and Billy, too, Kate. Just remember that. I'll check on you in the morning. Call me if you need anything though."

Kate assured him she would and watched as he drove away.

21

THE NEXT MORNING BEN ARRIVED EARLY, but he had already checked with some people in town and made sure the Zink's farm work was taken care of. He knew everyone would want to help. He had a few more arrangements to make for the farm but didn't leave until he was satisfied everything was OK with Kate. Billy was still sleeping.

After Ben left, Kate curled up again on the mattress. Suddenly she felt hot, and beads of sweat erupted on her face and neck. She threw off the covers. Her breathing quickened into short, shallow breaths. *No, not again,* she thought. *I am not going to do this again.* She stood up and grabbed onto the door frame. *Slow, slow, breathe slow, take a deep breath,* she said to herself. *You are stronger than this. You have to keep it together. Billy is depending on you...* She slowly walked to the kitchen sink, turned on the water and splashed some on her face. *Just take one breath, one deep breath.* She felt her body shudder as she slowly gained control. She wiped her face and arms with a towel and fought back a queasiness in her stomach. *You're not alone... Billy is here... he needs you... Ben will come if you need him... don't let Billy see you like this. ...*

"Hey, Miss Kate." Kate turned around when she heard Billy's voice behind her.

She took one more swipe at her face with the towel. "Billy, you're up."

"Is my mama coming home today?"

"No, not yet. But we'll call the doctor today and see how your mama is doing." Kate led him to the kitchen table and sat him down. She took another deep breath. "How about some breakfast first?"

Billy laid his head on the table. "OK. Can I go home today, Miss Kate?"

Kate sat down beside him. "Billy, look at me." Billy raised his head. "How about if you stay here with me until your mama comes home. Even if it's for a few days, would that be OK? We have a lot of work to do and I need you to help me while she is getting better."

"You got stuff to move?"

"Yes, Billy, I might have some stuff to move." Kate smiled. "And you are the only one who can help me with that."

"Miss Kate?"

"Yes, Billy?"

"If I stay with you instead of Mama, where's my family?"

His question surprised her. "What do you mean, Billy?"

"Well, I live with my mama and she's my family but if I don't live with her and I live with you, are you my family? Mama says I should always be with my family. But I'm not with her today."

Oh, Billy, Kate thought, her eyes moistening. *You are wiser than you know.* Out loud, she said, "Billy, we are going to be family for today, and then as long as you need to stay with me, OK?"

"OK, Miss Kate," he said, brightening a bit. "I'm hungry. Can I have some pancakes?"

"Sure. As a matter of fact, why don't you help me today? I will teach you how to make your own pancakes, how about that?"

The concept of measuring ingredients was lost on Billy but dumping and pouring and stirring were tasks he picked up on quickly. He was distracted for the moment, and for both of them, Kate was glad.

Sam and Martin knocked on the kitchen door. "Just checking to see how you are doing," Sam said. Billy said "Hey" and they stopped in their tracks.

"Hello, young man," Martin said, holding out his hand. "My name is Martin, and this is my friend, Sam." Billy held out a floured and battered spoon and shook it up and down. "Hey, Mister Martin and Mister Sam. I'm Billy. My mama's sick."

"We are very sorry to hear that, Billy. I'm sure everything is going to be OK, though. Right Kate?" Martin looked questioningly to Kate as Billy turned back to stirring the pancake batter.

She took them aside. "That's Billy, Mimi's son. He's going to be staying with me while Mimi is in the hospital. She broke her hip and may have had a mild stroke."

"Well, if there is anything we can do, Kate, please let us know."

"I think right now we just need to keep him busy, so he isn't thinking about things too much. Why don't you have some pancakes with us?"

They agreed and offered to help clean up the kitchen which looked like they had been cooking for a crew of fifty.

Ben returned at lunch time and found Billy and Kate working in the greenhouse, hauling out old wooden work benches and broken clay pots that would go into the trash. Sam and Martin were walking around the property with the old plans in their hands, gesturing and pointing. He took Kate aside. "How's he doing?"

"OK, I guess. He's been very quiet. He wanted to go home but I convinced him he needed to stay here for a while. I talked to Dr. Bartlett. He said the surgery went well but she's had a slight stroke and has some residual weakness on her right side. She will need to be in rehab for quite a while. Did you find some people to help at the farm?"

"Yes, Buzz and Snap are going out there today—not that

they'll be able to do any of the hard labor, but they know what to check on. Mimi has some hired hands that should be able to handle things, too. And all my guys at the garden center will help if they need to. Oh, and Rosie said she'd round up the ladies from church to make some casseroles, whenever Mimi comes back home. They won't have to worry about fixing anything to eat for a long time!"

"I feel like I haven't contributed to anything then."

"Kate, you're watching out for Billy. That's the most important thing."

"Well, you can take that over while I go take a shower. I'd like to visit Mimi this afternoon. Can you keep Billy busy while I'm gone?"

"Sure, no problem. I'll take him to the garden center for a while. It will be a change of scenery for him. And I think there are some things he could learn to do there. Might be good for him."

Kate quickly agreed. She needed to talk to Mimi alone to learn more about Billy's history. Any information she could get, as hard as it might be to learn, she would be better off knowing the truth.

At the hospital Kate learned that Mimi had been moved to a room after her surgery. She found the room and knocked softly as she opened the door.

"Mimi how are you feeling today?" she asked, as she approached the bedside.

Mimi's eyes fluttered open and she smiled on seeing Kate. "Kate, dear. Thank you for coming. I'm OK, I guess. They take good care of me here. But I thought I'd be up and around by now. They tried to get me up, but I am just too weak."

"Well, you need your rest and you need to take time for your recovery so you can come home."

"How's my boy? Is he here today? I miss him so much!"

"No, he's with Ben today at the garden center." Kate pulled a chair up closer to Mimi's bedside. "Mimi, I wanted to come and talk to you alone today. Would you mind if I asked you a few questions?"

"Well, you know I love to see you. And I guess I can answer some questions."

Kate pulled the photo album out of her backpack. "When I was packing Billy's things, I saw this album on his bookshelf and thought he'd like to have it with him."

"Well," Mimi said, "you're right. He looks at that album a lot. He likes the old pictures for some reason."

Kate turned to the photo taken at the birthday party. "This picture... it looks like Billy's first birthday. Do you remember that day?"

"Oh, of course I do, dear. You're right, it was Billy's first birthday. Calvin and I had a party for him, but Miss Bessie wanted to have one too. Real nice of her, I thought. Calvin had got me a new camera as a present and I wanted to try it out. That's why I wasn't in the picture."

"Do you remember anything about Bessie's daughter, Jenny?"

"Oh, yes, what a wild one she was. Bessie had her hands full with her."

"No one ever talks about her. Do you know what happened, where she is?"

"Well, dear, rumor had it that she got mixed up with some young man and got herself in the family way. But I don't know that for a fact. That would have been before this photo was taken. She had already left the area. I know Bessie and Enoch didn't see her very much after she left. Really broke Bessie's heart, I do know that."

"Mimi, can I ask you something else?"

"Sure, dear."

"Who handled the adoption for Billy?"

"Well, we had a pastor around here back then that used to handle these things—kind of on the quiet, you know, but all legal, of course. Calvin and me mentioned in passing to him one day after church that we were getting on up in years and it didn't look like we were going to be blessed with children of our own so if he ever heard of any babies that needed a home, well, we would be interested. Not a month later he gave us a call and said he had a little boy, a baby, that needed a good home. Well, we drove over to the parsonage, did the paperwork, and took Billy home with us that very night. Best day of our lives, if you ask me."

Mimi teared up. "Goodness, I haven't thought about that day in a long time. But it's so clear to me now. And, you know, there were two other babies there—I would have taken them, too, but Calvin said, no, we'd have our hands full with just the one."

Kate felt the blood drain from her face. The room seemed to shift around her, and she gripped the arm of the chair. "Did you say two other babies?" she whispered.

"Yes, dear, two little girls, I think."

Kate sat back in her chair, stunned at Mimi's words.

"Kate, what is it dear? You look like you've seen a ghost!"

"Mimi, I need to tell you something." She took a deep breath. "Billy's birthday is August 16, 1990, right?"

"Yes, that's right."

Kate took Mimi's small hand in hers. "Mimi," she whispered, "my birthday and Becky's birthday is August 16, 1990." She pulled out the birth certificate and showed it to Mimi. "Jenny Howard did get pregnant. And on August 16, 1990, she had triplets. Mimi, it is very possible that Becky and I might have been those two baby girls you saw that night when you adopted Billy. And if we were, then that might mean that Billy is our brother and Jenny Howard was our mother."

Mimi cried out, "Oh no, no, no! You mean we took Billy

and split up triplets? We didn't know, Kate—we didn't know, and they never said anything about that! Oh, Lord forgive us, we didn't know!"

"It's OK, Mimi," Kate quickly reassured her. "Becky and I went to a wonderful home and I know your home was the perfect place for Billy. You've raised him with so much love."

"But maybe it's just a coincidence, dear. Isn't that possible?" Mimi asked, still not fully grasping the evidence that was in front of her.

"Yes, but there is one more thing." She pointed to the photograph. "Do you remember this tablecloth?"

Mimi peered at the picture. "Why, I sure do. I always admired the handiwork in it. I think Bessie said it had belonged to her mother in England. Why do you ask?"

Kate pulled the box out of her backpack and opened it. "Mimi, this is the same tablecloth that's in the picture. It has been in our family ever since Becky and I were little. My parents told us it was an heirloom, but I never realized what they really meant by that. But now I think I do."

Mimi fell back on her pillow. She reached for the tablecloth and Kate took it out and laid it next to her. Mimi's hands caressed the fine embroidery. "Oh, this brings back so many memories. Bessie and I were good friends and this tablecloth was always on her dining room table." She looked up at Kate. "I don't know what to say, Kate. If this came from your parents, maybe they got it from Bessie somehow?"

"I think that must be what happened. Maybe she wanted our new parents to have something from them. She understood that she might never see us again, of course. But this was something she could pass on. An heirloom from Bessie's family, maybe? And she didn't want to let you know that Billy's siblings were also adopted."

"Oh, dear, Bessie must have been so heartbroken to know that. And all those years that we knew each other, she never spoke a word about this."

Mimi thought for a moment. "Maybe that's why Billy took to you so quick?"

"I think so," Kate agreed.

"This has been such a shock, Kate. I don't quite know what to say." She smiled. "But you know, the first day you and I met, I told you that the good Lord would show the way someday. And I think he has. But are you happy about this, Kate? You don't need to feel any responsibility for Billy if you don't want to. And I don't blame you if you needed proof, either. Why, maybe you can both take one of those DNA tests, you know? I give my permission for Billy to have that done."

Kate smiled. "Thank you, Mimi. I'm thrilled that you would be OK with that. And I don't want you to worry about Billy while you are recuperating. He is always welcome in my home; I promise you."

"That makes me so happy, Kate. You are a wonderful young woman."

"Mimi, one more question, is the pastor that handled the adoption still in the area?"

"No, I think he's in an Alzheimer's unit in Winston-Salem and his wife passed years ago. Kate, dear, I am going to be home someday, real soon, I hope. And Billy will be back with me and things will be back to normal. But it gives me such peace of mind to know that, no matter what, he has you for a friend."

"Mimi, it is my honor."

Kate drove home slowly, drained from the emotional meeting with Mimi, her mind swirling with the revelations that she and Mimi had shared. But the one person she wanted to share it with, more than anyone, was Ben. He had been there for her through all of this. She was touched by the way he treated Billy and Mimi, and most of all, her. It was a sign of a man with character; Mitch and the other men she had had in her life came up woefully short when she measured them against Ben. She never expected the happiness she felt when she was with him.

But she finally realized that it was real, and it was something she did not want to lose.

Kate saw the RV and Ben's truck in the driveway as she arrived at the house. She got out of her car walked around to the back. The four men were sitting on the patio drinking lemonade. "Well, I guess no work is getting done today, is it?" she teased.

Billy grinned. "Miss Kate, we worked at the tree place and then came here, and Ben said there's nothing more to move so he said we could take a break!"

She walked up the steps and looked at Ben. Her look told him she needed to talk to him. "Sam and Martin, I don't think Billy has seen your RV yet; would you mind taking him out to see it?"

They quickly got the hint. "Sure, Kate. Come on, Billy," Martin said as they walked around to the front of the house where it was parked.

"What's up, Kate?" Ben said, reaching out for her hand. "You look exhausted. And a little... panicked? What's going on?"

"I talked to Mimi." She sat down next to him. "And she told me about the day that she and Calvin adopted Billy." She took a deep breath. "Ben, you won't believe this—I can hardly believe it myself—but she said there were two baby girls at the pastor's house when they picked up Billy. Two baby girls, Ben!" She broke down in tears and Ben gathered her in his arms. "And Becky and I have the same birthdate as Billy! It must have been us! Mimi told me she would have taken the two little girls, too, but Calvin said no. Oh, how I wish he'd said yes, Ben! We would have had a wonderful life with Mimi and Calvin and Billy, all of us together!"

"But are you sure about all of this?"

"Yes, it must be. I showed her the tablecloth and the birth certificate from Jenny for the triplets. The dates. It all makes sense now. I don't know if Becky realized all the connections or not, but she must have at least been curious about the dates. She put the note on the birth certificate to show me, right?"

"Kate, do you know what this means? I mean, if you are all Jenny Howard's children?"

Kate smiled through her tears. "If Billy and Becky and I are the children of Jenny Howard, that means this is our home! This is my family home, Ben! My home!" She looked across the yard, the gardens, the woods beyond. For the first time since she had arrived, she realized that this, all of this, was truly hers. She was not a substitute for Becky. She was not a temporary resident. This was her home. "You knew, Ben, didn't you? Somehow you knew that I belonged here."

"I guess I did, but I sure didn't know why I thought that. It was just a feeling." He tipped her face to his. "But are you happy about this, Kate? This would be a huge adjustment for you."

"I can't really describe what I am feeling right now. I think I am still in shock. But, honestly, Ben," she admitted, laughing, "I feel like a weight has been lifted, the black cloud that I have been under for the longest time now, is just gone. My stomach is in knots, my brain is whirling, but it's more like excitement, for what the future might hold. Does that even make sense?"

"I think so and I couldn't be happier for you."

Kate's cell phone rang, and she dug it out of her backpack. Colleen's name appeared on the screen.

"Hey, Colleen," she said as she answered. "I was just about to call you."

"Kate, how are you?"

"I'm great Colleen. Couldn't be better."

"That's great. Listen, I'm on my way to see you. But I was wondering if you had made a decision. Like I said, I have a buyer right now. We can get this taken care of very quickly. Are you thinking of doing some of the repairs first or sell it as is?"

Ben put his hand on Kate's arm, his eyes questioning her.

"I'll tell you after," she mouthed and returned to the call.

"Colleen, I'm sorry, but neither of those two options will work. I've decided to stay."

There was silence on the phone. "Are you sure? This is going to be a huge undertaking, you know. You've got a mortgage to meet, plus the repairs—selling would be the smart move in this instance. Listen, I'll give you a few more days to look at the numbers."

"I appreciate it, but I've made my decision. This is my home now and I intend to do whatever it takes to stay here."

"Well, OK, then but if you change your mind..."

"I won't. But thank you again, Colleen."

When Kate got off the phone, Ben questioned her. "You talked to Colleen about selling the house?"

"Yes, why?"

"I thought John Hubert was handling it."

"He never got in touch with me, and then I met Colleen when she helped me out during the storm last week. She stopped by with a contractor and he told me what it might cost to fix this place up. She's really been great. In fact, we went to the Farmer's Market at Cable Farms together last Wednesday. We had a good talk." Kate put her phone away and went into the kitchen. Ben followed her.

"Listen, Kate, you might as well hear this from me. Colleen and I dated a while ago. But it's all over, believe me."

"I know, Ben. Colleen already told me."

"Oh?"

"She didn't go into a lot of details. But she said you were a good man."

"She did?"

"Yes, she did." Kate gave him a quick kiss. "But I already knew that."

22

COLLEEN'S NEXT CALL WAS TO MAX. She had been surprised by the confidence in Kate's voice. Only a few days ago she had been unsure of what she wanted. This was a different woman. And there would be backlash from Max when he found out.

She took a deep breath and dialed his number.

"Max, it's Colleen. I'm afraid I have some bad news for you."

"Oh? And what's that? I hope it's not about Howard's Walk."

"Yes, it is. Ms. Tyler has decided to stay. She is not selling the house."

Max was silent. "You had one job, Colleen. And that was to deliver that house to me. I didn't care how you did it. It doesn't sound like you tried at all. I thought you were a better negotiator than that."

"I did, Max, and I almost had her. But something must have changed between the time I talked to her and today. Suddenly, she is determined to stay. She said it was her home and she would do whatever it took to stay there."

"I see. Well, there is more than one way to get what I want. I will own that house one way or the other, do you understand? Our collaboration is over, Colleen. You might find you have a hard time selling anything after today."

"Don't you dare threaten me, Max Evans," Colleen hissed into the phone. "Why don't you just let this go? What did she ever do to you?"

"She is just a fly in the room, Colleen. Just a bug buzzing around my head. She doesn't mean a thing to me. I am tired of this little inconvenience and I will see it removed so that I can have what I want. Revenge is sweetest when you can get what you want and make money, too. Always remember that." Colleen sat back, stunned, as Max ended the call.

Colleen turned around at the next intersection and went back to her apartment. Simon had called and told her he had some news to share. She wasn't in the mood after the conversation with Max, but he was there waiting for her.

She went in and poured herself a glass of wine.

"So, what did you want to tell me?"

Simon flopped down onto the sofa, twisted the top off a cold bottle of beer and took a swig. "Max offered me a job in sales for his development company and I accepted his offer."

This was the last thing she needed to hear. "Well, you can just un-accept his offer," Colleen retorted. "You are NOT working for Max Evans."

"I thought you wanted me to get a job. Isn't that what you have been bugging me about all this time?"

Colleen moved to the sofa and set her glass on the coffee table. She needed to convince him that this was a very bad idea. "Simon, you have no idea who you are dealing with. You get in with Max and you will never get out. And what happened to the manager's job at your dad's construction company? I thought that was all set."

Simon shrugged. "That wasn't really my thing. My brother's got that sewed up anyway. There isn't room for both of us at the company. Max Evans is the only other one really making it around here these days."

"But, Simon..."

"Listen, Colleen," he interrupted. "Eden Springs is a dead-end town the way it is now. You of all people should know that, but with Max, at least we have a chance to make some money. And what's the big deal? Didn't he get you started?"

Colleen stiffened. "Yes, but..."

"Max has got big plans for me and you, too. That house—that land. It's going to be his pretty soon. We're building something big there, and I'm going to be in charge of it all."

"I'm not so sure about that, Simon." After her conversation with Max, she was sure none of the plans involved her. But she needed to know more. The exchange with Max had chilled her. She knew he was ruthless, but she had never heard that much hate in his voice.

She got up, went to the bar and poured another drink. She decided to take another approach. "So, this is a big deal, right? Lucrative, I hope?"

"Yeah, a really big deal. It should set us up for life."

"But you are already set, right? The Barclays have quite a name for themselves around here."

A look of exasperation came over his face. "I told you before, it'll be years before I see that money. My father won't give up any of it before he kicks the bucket. Why, are you just marrying me for my money?"

"Of course not." Colleen thought for a moment and changed the subject. "So Max is going to get Howard's Walk? I heard Kate Tyler wasn't selling."

"Oh, she'll sell all right. And it's going to happen soon. He's not going to let her get in his way. He's got it all planned out."

Colleen took another beer out of the refrigerator and set it in front of Simon. "So, tell me the plan."

"Max tells me he'll tear it all down and develop the land, commercial and residential. He says Eden Springs is prime development area. I'll be in charge of sales."

"But, Simon, honey, you don't know anything about sales or developing properties. I'm not an expert but I have some knowledge of the business." She shook her head. "I'm not sure this is what Max has in mind for you."

"Well, he says I'm perfect for it. I thought you'd be more supportive of me." He stood up. "I can't figure you out, Colleen. I thought this is what you wanted." He put on his jacket. "I'll see you later."

Colleen suddenly realized that Max had just found the perfect person in Simon to do his bidding for him. Simon was good looking, and his family was rich and connected, but he didn't have the ambition to make anything of himself with an education or hard work. Max had not told Simon the whole story. She knew there was something else going on in his vengeful mind.

A bride's magazine on the coffee table caught her eye. She and Simon had not set a date, they had not talked about wedding plans, she had not been thinking about her wedding dress or who her bridesmaids would be. Truthfully, the wedding was not even on her radar. Her fiancé had just left her apartment and she suddenly realized that she hadn't even thought about confiding in him or telling him what she was going through. She couldn't tell him the truth about Max or their history, information that he had tucked away to be used whenever he chose to.

She had ruined the one potentially good relationship she ever had—with Ben. She knew she could never have him back. But no one, not Ben or Kate or anyone, deserved to be screwed over like this. Kate had been through enough, losing her sister like she did. She had to think. Ben probably wouldn't speak to her so she couldn't go to him. Max was history. Her career was potentially over—she knew Max had the power to make anything happen... or not happen. She hadn't been able to confide in her father in years.

She took a deep breath. Everything was falling apart, and she had no one to turn to.

23

"BE CAREFUL, BILLY," Kate instructed Billy later that afternoon. "The bucket is right by your front door, so get it and come right back, OK?"

"Yes, Miss Kate," Billy said, as he waved and then lumbered off into the woods.

He hummed to himself as he followed the well-worn path that he had used so many times between his house and Kate's. Suddenly, he heard a loud noise. He stopped and looked around.

"Who's there?" he asked quietly, but only the sounds of the woods responded.

There was another crack, then another. Billy backed up against a tree, frightened as the noises got closer and closer. Then he heard a voice.

"I can see you Billy. You can't hide from me."

Then Billy heard a noise from the other direction.

"I'm not over there, Billy. I'm over here."

Another gunshot popped in the air and this time the bullet came right above Billy, showering bits of bark down on his head. Billy slid down the tree to the ground, tears in his eyes.

"Kate, Kate, help me!" he called.

"Kate can't hear you, Billy," the voice said. "And she won't help you. 'Cause she's going away, Billy. Did you know that?"

"No," Billy whimpered. "She wouldn't leave me."

"She doesn't even like you, Billy. She just wants you to help her, 'cause you're big and strong, that's all."

"No, she likes me!"

"Well, get on back there then, if you think she likes you so much. But you better stay out of these woods, you hear? 'Cause I'll be waiting for you, Billy. You git, now."

Billy lifted himself up, trembling, and backed away from the noise. Then he turned and ran headlong back through the brush, stumbling over tree roots, branches slapping at him. He splashed through the stream and scrambled up the bank on the other side, his hands and feet muddy from the climb. Finally, he broke through the trees and found the open lawn. With the house in sight, he ran towards it.

"Kate, Kate!" he called out. He reached the house, ran up the steps to the patio and banged on the kitchen door. "Kate, it's me!"

Kate had heard him calling her name from a distance and met him at the door. "Billy, what's wrong?" He was wet and muddy, and his face tearstained. "Come in here," she urged. She led him to a chair at the table where he sat, rocking back and forth. When he didn't answer her, Kate knelt in front of him and held his hands.

"Billy, look at me," she ordered. "You have to tell me what happened."

Billy shuddered, remembering. "The man in the woods— he scared me, Kate. He said you were leaving but I know you're not leaving, right Kate?"

"No, I'm not leaving Billy," she quickly reassured him. "Now tell me, what man, where—who told you this?"

"The man in the woods," he insisted. "He scared me. There was loud noises."

"Loud noises? What kind of loud noises? Tell me exactly what happened."

Billy was still wide eyed and scared and breathing hard. Kate took off his wet shoes and socks as she talked and got a towel to dry him off. She ran water in the sink and brought a washcloth to clean his hands and face.

"Billy, I'm here and I am not going anywhere. You believe me, right?"

Billy smiled a little. "I knew you wouldn't go away. But the man said..." Suddenly he stopped, remembering. "I never got the bucket, Kate! I forgot to get the bucket!" Billy covered his face and sobbed.

"OK, Billy, just calm down and then we'll talk some more about the man. Don't worry about the bucket. We'll get that some other time. You don't have to worry about a thing, OK?"

Kate grabbed her phone, dialed Ben's number, and told him what happened. He said he would call the sheriff and come right over.

Kate turned her attention back to Billy. "Everything's going to be fine. Ben is on his way and we'll take care of everything." Kate pulled a chair close to him and tried to calm him. A few minutes later, Ben and the sheriff arrived. Kate let them in but kept them out of the kitchen until she had told them what she knew. "He just said that a man in the woods scared him and there were loud noises. The man told him I was leaving. Who would do this to Billy?"

"Well, first we have to figure out what Billy really saw and heard," the sheriff said. "Then we'll take a look out there and see if we can find any evidence. Did you hear anything, Ms. Tyler?"

"No, I was right here in the house, but I didn't hear anything like he is describing."

"OK, let me talk to him." They went into the kitchen where Billy was still seated at the table.

The sheriff pulled up a chair next to him. "Mornin', Billy. I'm Sheriff Bailey."

"Hey, Sheriff Bailey," Billy responded.

"Miss Kate tells me you heard something in the woods today, is that right?"

Billy stiffened. "Yes, sir."

"Can you tell me what you heard?"

"Well," he began. "I heard some loud noises."

"What did they sound like?"

"Just loud. They hurt my ears."

"OK, was it like 'crack-crack' or boom noises?"

Billy got excited and covered his ears. "Like 'crack-crack' noises."

"OK, that's real good, Billy," the sheriff said soothingly. "Now was it a man you heard talking?"

"Yes, sir."

"OK, do you remember what the man said?"

Billy teared up again and looked at Kate. "He said I couldn't see him and then I said, 'Kate, Kate,' and he said she couldn't hear me and she wouldn't help me anyway and that Kate was going away, and I said no she wouldn't go away, and he said she only wanted me to help move stuff 'cause I'm big." He brightened a little. "I help her move stuff. You want to see?"

The sheriff smiled. "No, Billy, that's OK. I'm sure you've been a big help to Miss Kate. Do you think you could show me where you were when you heard the man?"

"NO!" Billy exclaimed. "He told me not to come back into the woods and I'm scared to go there!"

"OK, Billy," the sheriff said, patting Billy's arm. "You don't have to go anywhere. From now on, you have Miss Kate or Mister Ben bring you wherever you need to go, OK?"

"Yes, sir," he nodded vigorously.

"Good. Now I'm just going to talk to Miss Kate and Mister Ben for a little while, OK? Can you just stay here for a while?" Billy nodded. The sheriff then took Ben and Kate aside. "We need to check this out. If Billy was running through the woods like I think he was, it shouldn't be hard to find a trail. I'll take one of my men along and see what we can find out."

"I'm coming with you then," Ben said. The sheriff agreed and he made a call to get a deputy. When he arrived, the men went back down across the lawn and saw immediately where Billy had come crashing out of the woods. They tracked his trail back to a disturbed area by a big tree. It didn't take them long to find where a bullet had grazed the tree, right above where Billy must have been sitting.

"Well, I'll be damned," the sheriff said. "Who in the world would threaten Billy?" He turned to his deputy. "Let's get some investigators out here and search the ground. There's got to be a casing somewhere. If he was calling to Billy, he couldn't have been too far off. Secure this area and let's see what we can find."

Ben went back to the house after making the sheriff promise to call him with any information. Billy and Kate were still in the kitchen. He took Kate aside.

"The sheriff will call us when they find something."

"But Ben, something's not right. He wasn't just trying to scare Billy. The man said I was going away. Why would he mention me?"

"I don't know. But I don't think it is a coincidence. The only person I know that wants you to leave here is my father. If he can't get it one way, nothing will stop him from doing whatever he has to. But I don't have any proof. And I hate to think he would do something this frightening to Billy. We need to let the sheriff investigate and see what happens."

24

THE NEXT EVENING, KATE SETTLED BILLY IN FOR THE NIGHT after another long day of worry and reassurance. She went out through the French doors to the small garden that ran along the edge of the greenhouse. She closed the door quietly behind her, pulled her hair back and picked up a flat of annuals Ben had brought earlier for planting. She was expecting him at any minute and soon heard his truck pull into the driveway.

He came around the corner, saw her and settled himself next to her, their arms touching, his thigh pressed against hers. She smiled at the closeness of him. A soft light from the kitchen spilled out over the lawn, tucking itself into the edges of the garden, illuminating a small plot Kate had made fertile and prime for planting. She gently shook a fiery red Mexican Sunflower and its collection of soil and feathery roots free from its temporary home.

Ben dug his hands into the moist soil to widen the place that she readied for the plant, and Kate carefully placed it in. Together they pressed the rest of the soil in and around it.

"Did you know that nighttime in a garden is the best time of the day—sensual, fragrant, and alive?" Ben asked. "Nothing really sleeps in a garden at night."

Ben brought Kate's hands out of the soil, gently brushing it away. She relished the feel of his hands on hers and his soothing voice, a welcomed moment of peace after the events of the last two days.

"It involves all of the senses—sight, sounds, taste, touch, smells. Everything is alive, growing, expanding."

Ben turned her face to his and kissed her lightly.

"Ben..."

"Shh," he whispered. "Close your eyes. Tell me what you hear."

Kate closed her eyes, sat back on her heels and listened.

"I hear your voice," she whispered. "I hear crickets. I hear the wind blowing through the trees."

"Do you hear the colors?"

Kate tipped her head. Coming from anyone else, she would have laughed. But this was real, heartfelt, by a man who loved nature. And in that moment, she suddenly wanted to understand everything about him. She shook her head.

Ben reached out and pushed back a tendril of her hair that seemed to glow in the softening light. "If you give each color a note, you can create sound from the colors. Open your eyes." Kate did as he asked. "Look at the red of the Mexican Sunflower here. And then the yellow Erysimum 'Moonlight' over there. The colors are like music in the night."

Her eyes swept over the moonlit glow of the garden, settling on patches of reds and yellows and soft purples nestled intimately within the deep green leaves. Ben waved his hand through the air as if directing a symphony. The wind seemed to follow his lead and the grasses moved back and forth in rhythm, gently, then slowing as the darkness dissolved the remnants of light. "Your hair is like gold tonight," he whispered, shifting slightly until he sat facing Kate. "Sometimes it almost shimmers. Did you know that?"

Ben loosened Kate's hair and as it fell around her shoulders, he pulled her to him and kissed her. He leaned in harder as Kate responded hungrily to his kiss and to the feel of his hands on her. He found the soft curve of her neck with his lips and murmured her name as she moaned with his touch.

They were urgent with their kisses now, not tentative like the first time.

The silence lengthened as they looked at each other. Kate got up and walked to the corner of the greenhouse where it joined the house. She turned on the spigot and adjusted the hose that she had rigged up a few days earlier so that she could rinse off before she went into the house. The water was cold but felt good against her skin and she tentatively put one hand in the spray, then the other, getting used to the temperature.

She felt Ben come up behind her, but she didn't turn around. He stood close behind her, almost touching. He reached around her and took her hands in his as she wove them in and out of the water. He intertwined her fingers in his and held her palms upward in the spray until they were both rinsed clean. She felt his body move against her as he drew her in closer to him and she leaned back into him, relishing the feel of the muscles of his arms around her. He folded his arms around her waist and kissed her neck.

She let go of her doubts one kiss, one touch, at a time. The air filled with quick breaths and soft pleadings.

She turned to face him, and he drank the water as it poured off her body like life-giving holy water from a fountain. He kissed her deeply and she let herself go, giving in to the incredible taste of him.

She felt his hands slide over her wet skin, caressing and exploring as she wove her fingers through his hair, pulling his mouth to hers again and again. The water sizzled off them as they became inextricably tangled in each other's lives and hearts.

"Ben, we can't. Billy..."

He pulled her close. "I know. We're not exactly alone, are we?"

She smiled. "No. He's sleeping but we just can't."

A breeze blew through the narrow courtyard. It cooled them as it blew over their wet skin. Kate untangled herself from his arms and turned off the water. She took his hand and led him inside the house, tiptoeing past Billy's sleeping form. She slid the kitchen door closed. "You go shower, I'll pour some wine."

Kate poured them wine and escaped to the shower when he was done. When she rejoined him on the patio, he had set the air mattress and blanket out and motioned for her to sit with him.

"Good idea. It's a beautiful night." She curled up next to him. "Ben, there is something I need to talk to you about."

"Sure, what is it?"

"I'm going to talk to Mr. Tower, Becky's executor, and tell him I need all the cash I can get so that we can start working on the house and gardens. I don't need a lot to be happy. Not money, not possessions. I was always able to leave things behind; we moved so much that I got used to it, I guess. I always thought I'd never want to settle down. Don't get me wrong, I love to travel. I always will. But in reality, I have been running—from something. But now, despite everything that's happened, I feel at peace here." She took Ben's hand and entwined his fingers in hers. "And if it turns out that this is my ancestral home, *my* heirloom—if I have been led here by fate or coincidence or whatever, then I have to stay. I have spent my entire life being rescued. By Becky, by Mitch, by so many other people. I don't know what the future holds for Billy, but I know that I need to be here for him, and Mimi, too. I thought I had lost all my family but instead I found them. I'll never know if Becky knew about Billy or not, but it doesn't matter anymore—I know this is what she would have wanted. Things happen in the right time, in the right way, and I can see that now."

Ben raised himself on one elbow and looked at her. "Kate, I understand what you are saying. I really do. But whatever you decide to do, just know that I want to be a part of it. You are an amazing woman—you have the biggest heart of anyone I have ever met. To do this for Billy—not everyone would take that on.

Maybe you are right. Things happen at the right time, when they are meant to happen. And I am not leaving."

"But what about your garden center? All the plans you had?"

"I'm taking it off the market. It will all work itself out. Kate, I don't want to leave you. And I don't want to be your rescuer. I just want to be with you."

"And that's all I want, Ben. That's all I really need."

25

THE NEXT MORNING BEN AND KATE WERE FINISHING their breakfast when they heard a knock at the kitchen door. Martin poked his head in. "Are we decent?"

Kate groaned. "Yes, Martin, why wouldn't we be?"

"Leave them alone, Martin," Sam chided. "It's none of our business. I'm more interested in what's for breakfast here, because no one is cooking in the RV." He gave a sidelong glance at Martin.

"No, because no one wanted to go to the market last night, so no one had anything to fix for breakfast," Martin replied.

"All right, all right, you two. I will fix more pancakes, if you will all just stop!" Kate laughed and started mixing more batter.

"Oh, good, and I just happen to have some blueberries with me," Sam said, "because if we don't use them today, they will get moldy in our kitchen because no one is cooking there... as I mentioned before."

They poured themselves coffee and sat down at the table. "Where is your young man this morning, Kate?"

"He was up at the crack of dawn and is outside already. There is enough work to keep him busy for quite a while. He doesn't like to be cooped up indoors." Then Kate filled them in on the events of the last few days.

"Well, that's it then, we're not leaving again," Sam said. "At least not for a while. The store can run by itself for a bit longer. That van will be parked right down the road. Just let anybody try to get by us."

Suddenly Martin slapped his hand down on the table. "Sam, we need to get a dog!"

"No dog, Martin."

"Oh, yes. A big bad-ass Rottweiler or something."

"No Rottweiler, Martin."

"Well, a bad-ass shotgun then."

"No gun, Martin. No bad-ass dog, no bad-ass shotgun."

"Whatever." Martin waved his hand at Sam. "I'm just trying to give Kate some peace of mind, that's all."

"I'm fine, you two. And peace of mind would be not worrying about you guys accidently shooting each other. So, I agree. NO GUNS!" She waved a spatula at them.

Martin raised his hands. "OK, OK. No dog, no guns."

He was silent for a moment. "We need to take karate lessons, Sam," he said, knocking over a bottle of syrup on the table as he sliced his hands through the air. "So, no karate lessons, I guess," he said, setting the bottle upright again.

"Now that we have that settled," Kate laughed, "I have something to tell you both."

"Tell us!" Martin exclaimed.

"I've decided not to sell Howard's Walk. I'm staying!"

"I knew it!" Sam said. "This is great, Kate. Ben, you don't look surprised. You knew already?"

"Yes, we've talked. But this was Kate's decision," Ben replied. "But I am glad. And just so you both know; I'm not selling the garden center—at least for now. So, I'll be staying, too."

"So, what happens next?" Sam asked.

"I really haven't thought about it, seriously, anyway. It's all happening so fast."

"Well, before we start," Ben said, "I would like to make a suggestion."

"Sure. Go ahead," Kate said.

"We've looked at these plans, we've all walked the property at one point or another, and we've already worked on cleaning some of it up. And we've planted a few new things already," he said, smiling at Kate. "But since we still aren't quite sure how we are going forward, let's look at what we do know, get that on the table and then narrow it down to the gardens themselves. Trust me, it's not a waste of time. I'm afraid if we don't get the big picture, we will miss something."

"I agree," Sam said. "Should we think about the house first or the gardens?"

Ben thought it should be the house but looked to Kate to answer.

When she hesitated, Sam encouraged her to close her eyes and envision the front of the house and what she might want to do with that.

"Well, it can't be left as it is," she began. "The porch is basically falling down. It's one of the first things that visitors will see so it needs to be completely removed and rebuilt. I want it to be welcoming, to really reflect southern hospitality." She opened her eyes. "But it would cost so much..."

"Don't worry about the cost. Just envision what you would like to see," Ben encouraged.

Kate continued, "OK. We need to decide what to plant out front so I hope you all can come up with some ideas. I think the fountain in the center of the drive can just be cleaned up and after the porch is done, we can do plantings around it. I want it really colorful."

"How about yellow yarrows, marigolds, and nasturtiums?" Martin chimed in.

"Sounds great!"

They continued bouncing ideas off each other. They agreed that all areas of both the house and gardens would be completely accessible for those with disabilities so that no one would feel unwelcome at Howard's Walk.

Kate continued. "OK, so I am thinking in the future—a gift shop, but for right now, we can house it here inside, right in this room along with maybe a Visitor and Educational Center until we can raise funds for a more suitable building."

Ben chimed in. "The original plans can be displayed here along with any old photographs that we can find. I'm sure people have pictures of the gardens to add to the collection. We can put photos of the post-war period of the town on display, too. Now that I think of it, the Eden Springs Historical Society might want to get involved with that."

Kate continued. "We can't forget the greenhouse work that needs to be done, too. Maybe the garden club could handle the inside work on that. And lastly, I want an herb and kitchen garden. But I don't have a clue about how to do that. Any ideas?" she asked.

Martin said, "It can be a container garden on the back patio."

Sam added, "Just think, rosemary, parsley, chives, basil, thyme, sage, and oregano..."

"And French tarragon," Martin chimed in.

"...all at your fingertips!"

"And I expect all of them to end up in our dinners, Sam!" Kate said, smiling. "And, lastly, I'd like us to keep a spot open for a much larger vegetable garden, maybe next spring. I want the place to be sustainable and that is a good start."

They discussed their ideas, making notes on all the steps needed to make the gardens a reality and prioritizing what could be done in a very short amount of time. Kate was overwhelmed by the amount of detail that was needed, and she wondered what she had gotten herself into. But whenever she expressed doubts, the others encouraged her, reminding her of how far she had already come.

The next evening, Kate gave the spinach salad one more toss with a light dressing and then added some fresh wild strawberries she had found in the woods. She placed the bowl in the refrigerator next to a platter of salmon fillets, marinating and waiting to be grilled.

She poured herself a glass of crisp Riesling and went out onto the back patio. Ben and Billy were cleaning up after another long day of work. Sam and Martin had retreated to the RV but said they would be back for dinner.

She gazed out across the lawn trying to envision their plans.

Down the sloping lawn to her left, there was a scattering of trees. The lawn itself, parts of which had not been mowed in years, grew wild. The trees were in relatively good shape, but at their full growth and untrimmed they were now blocking a good view of the pond which lay just beyond them.

On the far side of the pond, the woods began, and Kate followed the tree line across to her right. She had found that a partial path remained in the woods, but again, overgrown bushes and grasses and smaller tree shoots blocked much of the way. Billy's path was still visible although he had not used it since his experience in the woods.

The more formal gardens began off to the right side of the house, extending from the greenhouse down to meet the trees at the far end of the property. Flagstone walks led from the greenhouse in several winding paths throughout the gardens. Some had been replaced with Billy's help but many of the stones were still cracked and grasses had sprouted in the spaces between the stones and gravel. Wooden and wrought iron benches were scattered here and there along the paths, clearly weather worn.

There was a rose garden in the center of the lawn with sparse, sad blooms clinging to the stems, neglected over the years. In the middle of the rose bushes stood a Grecian statue and fountain, now moss covered and still.

Her gaze fell on much of the old gardens from this vantage point and, now that she was ready to take the plunge and start the work, she could see the true condition of the property.

Kate walked down the steps and sat on the last flagstone step at the bottom. She looked off to her right and saw the small redbud tree that she and Ben had planted in Becky's memory. The area around it was completely clear of weeds and tall grass. It stood straight and tall, and, while it was not yet part of any bigger scheme, it spoke volumes to Kate.

There must be memorial gardens here, she thought. *Gardens in memory of the Howards and of Becky.* And then, there would be gardens that taught, gardens that gave peace and gardens that surprised.

A sudden breeze brought a scent with it that made Kate turn her head. She recognized the scent from somewhere deep in her past, but she could not place it, nor could she tell where it was coming from. She followed the scent down the flagstone path, and it led her to the old rose garden. She gently lifted one of the haggard roses, leaned in, and breathed its scent. The petals were scant and pale and yet somehow exuded a sweet, extravagant aroma that brought back a memory from her childhood.

She closed her eyes and it came flooding back. She and Becky were about seven years old and traveling with their parents on holiday in Germany where her father was stationed. They visited a castle where she and Becky walked hand in hand through the formal gardens and then played hide and seek in a maze of carefully pruned shrubbery. Suddenly, they came upon a beautiful rose garden. They pretended to be princesses curtsying to each of the rose bushes. The roses nodded back at them, swaying in the light breeze.

With the castle looming in the background, its grand steps leading down to the gardens, they played princess for the rest of the afternoon. In their imaginations, princes stood watching over them instead of trees, soldiers and ladies-in-waiting lined the walks instead of neatly trimmed hedges. The grand sculptures were carriages waiting to whisk them away to the ball. Animal shaped topiaries rounded out the retinue. The two girls twirled and turned, their skirts swirling around and around, and they laughed and played until they fell to the soft grass in exhaustion.

Kate remembered looking up at the sky and finding shapes in the clouds. "Someday I am going to live here," Rebecca had said. "I am going to find my prince and live here forever, with gardens and flowers and trees."

"Me, too." Kate said. And she truly believed that they would be together forever.

Rebecca's Rose Garden, Kate determined now, would be the first garden to be planted.

Ben and Billy soon joined her, and Sam and Martin came a few minutes later.

"A penny for your thoughts?" Ben asked.

"Roses. Lots and lots of roses," she said, waving her hand over the entire lawn.

"You want everything roses?" Sam asked, hesitantly.

"No, not everything. But at least one garden full of them; one section completely roses, and not the small, single ones we have now, I want bushes and bushes of them. The existing ones will have to be taken out; if we can use them, fine, if not, then they go. Right, Billy?" she asked.

"All roses!" Billy mimicked her, waving his arms wide.

Ben hesitated. "Some of these roses are heirlooms, Kate. They are worth saving; even if they might not look like it right now."

"Fine, save them, but this is not what I am picturing."

"Right, lots and lots of roses."

She pointed to different areas. "Starting from the left side of the house here towards the pond." She turned to them. "And I want a walkway through it, with benches," Kate said, waving her finger through the air as if trailing through the yet imaginary garden. "So, what can we do?"

The men pondered, sifting through the different rose varieties they had tucked away in their minds from years of experience.

Ben started. "Well, let's start from the tallest to the shortest of the plants when they reach their mature height. In the back, for the tallest, I think maybe a Rugosa Rose?"

Ben looked to Sam and Martin for their thoughts. Martin nodded. "It's tall enough for a background and we can use it like a hedge. It can take the sun, too."

"What color is it?" Kate asked.

"If I remember correctly, it is a deep wine color, with kind of a creamy center," Sam said, looking to Ben who nodded in agreement. "And a strong fragrance, if that's what you are looking for."

"Yes, that's right."

Sam and Martin exchanged looks. "Are you thinking what I'm thinking, Sam?" Martin asked.

"Rose hips," they both said at the same time. The ideas began to tumble forth simultaneously.

"Rose hip jellies..."

"...and teas and soups..."

"...we could sell them," Martin said. His eyes widened. "Kate's Rose Hips!"

"And a cookbook! We could write a cookbook. I've always wanted to write a cookbook..."

"No, no, no!" Kate interrupted. "Wait a minute. Let's go back to 'Kate's Rose Hips'! I will not be selling anything on this property that has 'Kate' and 'hips' in the same sentence! Besides, what in the world are you talking about?"

Ben interrupted. "Then we can't spray the roses with any chemicals. Not if we are using the hips in the kitchen."

"That's fine," said Martin. "We should be going organic throughout the gardens anyway, right?"

"OK, can someone please explain what rose hips are and why I would be using them in the kitchen?" Kate asked.

"The decorative hips, or fruits of the rose plant are actually edible and a great source of vitamin C," Martin explained, "so we can use them in cooking—or for jellies or tea and lots of other things, but in order to do that we can't spray the plants with any chemicals."

"That's fine with me," Kate said. "I'm totally on board with going organic—and I'm not opposed to a cookbook but that really is way out there, guys—so let's focus on just getting things in the ground for now, OK? So, what else then?"

Sam and Martin gave advice on different varieties of roses that could be used, and Ben agreed with their recommendations. Kate was fascinated with their vision of Rebecca's Rose Garden. The Rugosa Rose would contrast with the flowering maples next to the house. The Felicia shrub rose would bring an apricot hue and scent to the mix. There would be yellow English roses and white carpet roses. Roses would be in bloom throughout the entire season for everyone to enjoy.

"Draw up the plans then," Kate said. "Rebecca's Rose Garden will be our first project."

"Rebecca's Rose Garden and Restaurant," Martin said. "And the spec-i-al-i-ty of the day is Kate's lovely 'Rose Hips'! I am going to put that in my notes." Martin danced around the patio until Kate finally chased him back into the house.

26

WESLEY CARROLL QUICKLY STRODE past the third-floor nurse's station of County General Hospital. He had an intense dislike for hospitals since his wife passed years before and avoided them when he could. But Mimi Zink had summoned him, and he knew it must be something important when she had asked him to come as soon as possible. He had been concerned about her health for quite some time, and this recent episode suffered by his longtime friend and client caused him some alarm.

He reached Room 348 and tapped on the door. "Miss Mimi," he called and slowly opened the door. Mimi looked frail and small in the hospital bed, but her grip was strong as she shook Wesley's hand.

"Wesley, how good of you to come on such short notice. You are too good to me," she said.

Wesley smiled. "I am sorry I have not been to see you sooner than this. I was sorry to hear of your fall."

She waved her hand in dismissal of his concern. "It will take more than this to keep me down. Come, sit." She motioned to a chair at the side of her bed and Wesley complied. They chatted for a few minutes about the fall and her prognosis, which, at least according to Mimi, was promising. "Doc says I will have to go to rehab for a little while but then he thinks I can go home after that. Oh, I do miss the farm and I miss Billy so!"

"And I am sure he misses you, too, Mimi. How is he doing? Is he being taken care of?"

"Oh, he is doing fine. He's staying with Kate Tyler. There was an incident, though. She and Ben are having the sheriff look into it. Sounds like he got scared in the woods one day. Oh, I am sure it's nothing. Sometimes his imagination runs away from him. And all the more reason for me to get home. She says he's fine now. She has been a peach for taking him in while I am here."

"Well, I am glad to hear it."

"Actually Wesley, that is why I asked you to come here today. There is something I need you to take care of for me."

Mimi proceeded to tell him about Kate's visit and the surprising discovery she had shared about her history. "I just couldn't believe it, Wesley, when she told me about the things she found and how it made her think that she and Billy might be siblings! But I guess it makes sense, right? What do you think, Wesley? Is it possible?"

Wesley thought for a moment and chose his words carefully. "Mimi, it certainly does sound feasible although an unbelievable coincidence. And Rebecca never indicated that she had any family interest in Howard's Walk in our conversations. So, it is likely that she didn't know herself. But," he continued, "the pieces all seem to be there, although I would like to see Kate's birth certificate. And there are other ways to make sure; that is, if you are willing."

"Yes, that's what I thought," Mimi said eagerly, her eyes bright with anticipation. "I already told Kate that I would be willing for Billy to take a DNA test. But after I thought about it, this needs to be done legally and all. This is where you come in. I asked one of the nurses about it—of course, I didn't tell her why I was asking. But she said you can buy kits online to test DNA. I thought it would be a lot more complicated than that. But these days, I guess you can buy anything with a computer. Anyway, I would like you to order the DNA kit and take care of the testing. The results would come to you, Wesley, so it is confidential. Would you do that for me? For Billy?"

"Of course, I would," Wesley reassured her, "if that is what you want. But you need to think about what happens when the results come back."

"I already have, and this is what I would like to do. If Billy and Kate are brother and sister, then I want my will changed to leave everything in a trust for Billy with Kate overseeing it. And if it turns out he isn't her brother, then, the will stays as is. If she still wants to be involved in his life, then I am OK with that, but you would continue as executor of the trust for him and he would have to have a caretaker at the house. I don't want him to leave his home unless he has family to go to."

Wesley nodded. "You don't need to worry about that, Mimi. You and Calvin have made a good plan for Billy. I will take care of the DNA testing for you though, if that is what you want."

"Yes, that is what I want. I knew I could count on you, Wesley."

Wesley patted her hand and stood. "I'll take care of it right away. And I will keep you posted on progress. But I must go now. It's been good to see you. I hope you continue to improve and can get back home quickly."

"Thank you, Wesley. I hope this all gets resolved soon."

Two days later, the DNA kit arrived at Wesley Carroll's home. Wesley's first call was to Mimi to confirm if she wanted to go ahead with the testing. When she wholeheartedly agreed, he called Kate and arranged for her and Billy to be available that afternoon.

The test was simple; a cheek swab from Kate and then one from Billy who complied after encouragement from Ben and Kate. Wesley took the samples and, at his home, prepared them for shipping.

The Eden Springs Garden Club, AKA the Committee for the Restoration of the Gardens at Howard's Walk, descended on the gardens that afternoon. Stella Burns was in the lead, her bulky frame dressed for serious garden work from the large purple gardening hat on her head to the grass-stained sneakers on her feet. As President of the club for twenty-two years—except for the year she turned forty, divorced her husband, and moved to the beach only to come back with a new husband and baby—she clucked her way through the greenhouse, the gardens, and the back yard with Sam, Martin, Kate, and Ben not far behind, and then followed by Carmen DiMartino, Kevin Knight, Sarah Poole, and Nellie Tuttle. Billy was bewildered with the activity and hid in the house, only risking an occasional peek out the kitchen door.

"It's a shame, for sure," Stella proclaimed. "A downright shame. To let it go for all these years. Well," she said, brushing soil from her hands after expertly identifying and pulling weeds here and there along her tour, "nothing that can't be fixed. Kevin, we need some measurements. Here, there, and there," she instructed, pointing around the yard. "Sarah, Carmen, take notes for Kevin." Kevin looked at Kate, Sam, and Martin in turn for their approval. They nodded, and he pulled out his tape measure.

"Stella, while they are doing that, there's something I think you should see inside," Kate said.

"Well, I guess I could step inside for a minute. If you think it's important."

"Oh, we do," Martin said, and guided Stella up the steps to the patio, through the kitchen and into the foyer.

Stella's eyes landed on the displays of the original garden plans that had been laid out. She was silent for a long time as she peered at each of the detailed drawings. "Oh, my," she breathed. "I had no idea. No idea at all. I thought it would just be a few plants, here and there, some bushes maybe, or a few trees, but this..." She turned to Kate. "Is this what you want to do?"

"Not at first," Kate assured her. "I really appreciate you and the others jumping right in. But I think we all need to sit down and think about where to start and then come up with a real plan for how we can do this in stages as we get funding. Do you think that would be OK, Stella?"

"Oh, absolutely, of course, that makes so much sense." Stella looked relieved. "And will you help, too?" she nodded in Sam, Martin, and Ben's direction. They promised her they would be helping wherever needed.

"Stella, you mentioned in the meeting the other night that you and the club might be able to do some fundraising?"

"Sure, Kate, that's no problem, you just leave that to us. Bake sales, raffles, dances, we've raised a lot of money over the years, so we'll get started on it right away."

"That sounds great; we appreciate it. I need some advice on the front of the house, you know, the fountain area. What do you think would be the right thing for that spot?" Kate steered Stella out the front door and onto the porch where they surveyed the area needing to be worked on. Stella recommended a simple green and white approach with Patriot hosta, which would stay nice through the summer. "We can add flowerpots with annuals if you want, for color of course, change it up once in a while, keep it fresh," she declared, and Kate agreed.

"And what about the greenhouse? Do any of you have experience with greenhouses?"

"I don't but Kevin and Carmen do—they both have degrees in greenhouse production so that would be perfect for them to work on. What did you have in mind?"

Kate and Stella continued around the house, discussing ideas, going through the greenhouse and then around to the back of the house where the others were still measuring and taking notes.

"Well, everyone, gather round!" Stella announced. "We have our work cut out for us! The greenhouse is a mess, so Carmen and Kevin, that will be your job. Nellie, you are in charge of fundraising—and none of that small stuff, we have to think big! Sarah, you—well, we'll find something for you to do." She turned to Kate and grabbed her hand. "Don't you worry about a thing, Kate. We'll take care of this in no time. OK, let's go everyone. Lots to do, lots to do!" And she shooed them all back to the waiting van.

Martin spoke first. "What just happened?"

"Hurricane Stella just blew through Howard's Walk," Sam sighed.

Two days later, an envelope arrived at Wesley Carroll's home. Wesley set aside the rest of his mail and slit the envelope open. The results were in.

Mimi had been moved to a rehabilitation center in Winston-Salem, so Wesley drove there immediately. She had just finished physical therapy and was being taken back to her room. "Wesley, how nice to see you," she said.

"And you as well, Mimi. You are looking much better. Are they taking good care of you?"

"Oh, yes, I am doing physical therapy and they say I should be going home soon if I continue to improve."

"That's wonderful."

They arrived at her room and the orderly assisted her back into bed. "Wesley, you know I love to see you any time, but I think maybe your visit here was for business. Is that correct?"

Wesley nodded and pulled an envelope out of his pocket after the orderly had left the room. "Yes, I have the results of the DNA tests here."

Mimi took a deep breath. "Well, then let's have it. What does it say?"

"Billy and Kate are a DNA match. Mimi, they are brother and sister without a doubt."

Mimi clasped her hands and raised them high. "Oh, thank you, Lord! I should never have doubted that You would show me the way with Billy, and You did, You did!" Tears sprang to her eyes. "Thank you, Wesley. Thank you so much for doing this for Billy and me!"

"Of course, Mimi. I am glad you are happy about it. Now we must tell Kate. And I assume you want to tell Billy?"

"I've thought a lot about that, but I'm not settled yet in my mind how to do it. And I guess there's no real rush. I want to get back home and have him with me while I have the help coming in and I think the time will present itself."

"I think you are right. There is no rush for this. He's your son, Mimi, and you will know the best way to handle it. But we do have to tell Kate, wouldn't you agree?"

"Oh, yes, as soon as possible. You see, this isn't just about Billy being her brother. She just seemed like such a lost soul to me, without her sister, without her parents. Why, this will mean the world to her to know that she has family. But this doesn't prove she was Jenny's daughter, does it?"

"No, but I have something else to tell you, Mimi. I hope I didn't overstep but I made a phone call to Bessie's family in England. Since Bessie had passed, and they thought it was all right to share with me, they confirmed that Pastor Corcoran was the one who handled the adoption for Jenny Howard and the triplets. Bessie had told them that soon after she moved back to England. I didn't share a lot with them, for confidentiality reasons, but I do think Kate has a right to know. Would you agree?"

"Yes," Mimi confirmed. "Absolutely. If you would tell her that, I would certainly appreciate it."

Wesley called Kate and asked if she could meet him at his office that afternoon. He told her he had the results from the DNA testing but wanted to share it with her in person. She agreed and drove into Eden Springs. Brenda greeted her and showed her into Wesley's office. Kate sat in front of his desk and clasped her hands tightly to stop them from shaking.

"Well, tell me the results, Wesley. I am prepared for anything here so just tell me. The suspense is unbearable."

"I hope this is good news, Kate. The results show that you and Billy are a DNA match as siblings."

Kate's hands flew to her face. "I knew it, I just knew it," she cried. Wesley came out from behind his desk with tissues and sat beside her. "Does Mimi know?" she asked as she wiped her tears.

"Yes, I saw her this afternoon and she is very happy, too."

"Oh, that is such a relief!"

"There is one more thing, Kate, and Mimi knows this too. I made a call to Bessie's family in England. They confirmed that Bessie told them that the pastor that handled Billy's adoption was the same pastor that Jenny turned the three of you over to for adoption. So, without direct DNA evidence to prove you are Jenny's daughter, this is, at least, in my mind, proof that you are a Howard—with the birthdates matching, and the heirloom that you have been left, and the information from Bessie's family. I think you have found your home, Kate."

Kate's tears, tears of happiness now, continued to flow. Years of doubt and wondering were finally over. She and Becky had often questioned whether they should search for their real parents although the time never seemed right. But they had both admitted a feeling of emptiness in not knowing. Now, a void had been filled.

When she finally wiped the last of her tears, she asked, "Does Mimi plan on telling Billy?"

"She wants to wait until the time is right. Perhaps after she is home and can spend more time with him. She has asked that you don't say anything. I need your word on that."

"That's a good idea. I promise I won't say anything to him." She took a deep breath. "I only wish Becky was here to talk to, you know. She would have been thrilled, too."

"I am sure she would have been."

Kate stood. "Thank you, Wesley, for all you've done. I need to go home though. I've promised Billy I would take him to see Mimi tomorrow so it will be an early night for us."

"I understand." Wesley stood and took Kate's hand. "I really am happy for you, Kate. I am glad this turned out like it did. When we first met, I know you were going through a lot. I was actually very worried about you. But I hope that you now feel like you are at home here in Eden Springs. I know we are very glad you are here."

"Thank you for saying that, Wesley. I plan on making this town my home now, no matter what."

The next day, after sharing the news of the DNA results with Ben, they took Billy to see his mother in the rehabilitation center. Kate saw clearly that the reunion made them both happier and Billy especially brightened up. Mimi talked to him about when she would be coming home and how she would be having people come in to help. "I'll help you, too, Mama," he reassured her. "I can make pancakes now! Kate showed me!"

"I am so proud of you, son. I miss you and I can't wait until I can come home."

"Me, too, Mama," Billy said.

"Billy, can you go with Ben for a few minutes? I want to talk to Kate alone. Is that OK?"

"Sure, Mama," Billy answered and left the room with Ben.

Kate sat in a chair beside Mimi's bed. Mimi spoke first.

"Kate, I knew, deep in my heart, from the minute we met, that I liked you and that you were a good person. So, I never worried when Billy was with you, and it's done him a lot of good to meet other people and do different things. And you know that I was worried about his future. But now," she beamed, "God has answered all my prayers! He sent you to me and Billy."

Kate shook her head. "I was so lost when I got here. I didn't know what my own future held. But I remember thinking that I had traveled the world looking for new people and places but now people were finding me. I am so glad we met each other!"

27

AFTER DINNER, SAM AND MARTIN RETREATED to their RV and Ben and Billy left to check on the garden center. Kate finished up a few chores in the garden and then settled in for the evening with a glass of wine, waiting for Ben and Billy to return for the night. There was a knock at the door. Kate peeked through the window and saw Max Evans standing on the porch. She hesitated. But this was her chance to set the record straight once and for all about her decision to stay at Howard's Walk. She took a deep breath and opened the door. "Hello, Max," she said stiffly.

"Hello, Kate. I am so sorry to bother you, but I wonder if we could talk?"

"It's late but there is something I want to discuss with you, too," she replied.

Kate started to move out onto the porch, but Max stopped the door with his hand. "Too many mosquitoes out here—could we go inside?"

Kate stepped out and closed the door behind her. "What is it you wanted to talk about?"

"The last time we met, you hadn't made up your mind about my offer. I hope you have had time to reconsider. It is a very generous offer and one you won't get from anyone else."

Kate took a deep breath. "I have decided not to sell, to you or anyone else. I am staying and going through with the plans for renovation of the house and gardens just as Becky wanted. I think I owe it to her. And I have found that I am very happy here. So, I think it is the right thing to do."

"I see," he said. "There is still a lot of work to be done. How do you expect to pay for all of it?"

Kate crossed her arms. All the warning signs were there in his tone, in his questions. This man would go to any lengths to get what he wanted. She chose her words carefully. "There is money available and more to be raised. And I don't plan on doing it all myself. The town..."

"The town?" Max laughed. "Don't depend on those people. I have lived here all my life and trust me, the 'town' will tire of this just like they do everything else and you will be left holding the bag. They are not dependable and really don't know what they are getting themselves into, as always."

"I've heard that you're the one who's not dependable," Kate said soberly. "You employed a good number of them at one time, didn't you? And then just moved your company to Mexico, leaving them with no jobs, no future? Not to mention how you have treated your own family..."

Max grabbed her arm and yanked her to him. "Listen here, you have no idea what you are talking about. Has my son been filling your head with these ideas? Or is it Wesley Carroll?"

"Let go of me, Max." Kate hissed. She stared at him until he released her arm. "You need to leave—now."

Max's demeanor changed in a split-second. He laughed again. "You really are pathetic, Kate. You didn't even know your sister bought this place until after she was dead. So, you don't know what went on behind the scenes—with us, I mean."

Kate stiffened. "What are you talking about?" she whispered.

"She was a very attractive woman, and smart, too. She saw the value of an alliance with me. I didn't tell you about it before because I thought you were smart enough to sell to me. And no one's opinion of Rebecca would have had to change. But you're a big girl. You deserve to know what she was really like." Max leaned in closer to Kate. She could feel his breath on her. "She couldn't wait to get to my place..."

Kate drew back and slapped him across the face. "You are a monster," she said fiercely. "And a liar. My sister would never have anything to do with someone like you. Get off my property! And never come back here again!"

Max put his hand on his cheek. "Your sister liked it rough, too."

"Get out!!" Kate screamed at him through her tears.

Max smiled thinly. "You will be begging to go back to your old, pitiful life before I am done with you. Trust me on that. Oh, and one more thing. I hear that Ben has been spending a lot of time here. But he's not right for you. He'll break your heart. Just ask Colleen."

Max turned and strode down the steps to his truck. Kate suddenly felt a clarity of resolve that she had never felt before. "Max Evans!" Kate called his name, her voice commanding that he face her. He slowly turned, a smug look on his face. "I know you don't want me here. But there is something you need to know. I am a Howard, Max Evans. My grandmother was Bessie Howard and my grandfather was Enoch Howard," she called out. "This is not just my house, Max. It is my HOME, my FAMILY home. And you will NEVER take it away from me!"

Max glared back at Kate with shock on his face that slowly transformed into a mask of loathing. A long moment passed as Kate locked eyes with the man she now knew to be her enemy. He finally turned away, got into his truck and drove off with a squeal of tires.

Kate began to shake as she watched the truck's taillights disappear down the road, her bold convictions suddenly transforming into anger as she stormed into the kitchen. She heard a key rattle in the lock at the front door. Ben ran into the house and called out to her. It only took one look at her to know something was wrong.

"What was my father doing here? I passed him on the road."

Kate was seething. "I can't talk about it, Ben. Not now."

"Kate, what did he do?" Ben put his hands on her shoulders, trying to control his emotions. "Did he threaten you?"

"Where's Billy?"

"I told him to go around and wait for us on the patio and we could do some star gazing. Don't worry about him. I want to know what happened with my father."

"I'm just too mad right now, Ben," Kate pulled away from him.

"Kate, tell me what he said. Please, don't push me away."

Kate rocked against the sink taking deep breaths. Finally, she said, "He asked me if I had decided about his offer or not."

"And?"

"I told him I had decided not to sell, not to him or anyone."

Ben took a step toward her. "How did he take it?"

Kate turned to him and folded her arms tightly across her chest. "He didn't take it well. We had... words."

"I'm so sorry, Kate," Ben said gently. "I told you, he'll do anything..."

"Maybe he's right!" Kate flung the words at him. Feelings that she thought she had conquered and buried came flooding back to her: the need to flee when life got hard, the urge to run away and not look back. "Maybe I should just leave! This is not what I bargained for, Ben. People have been threatened. Even Billy, for God's sake! Maybe this is too much for me." She shook her head. "I don't know what I'm doing. I've upset everyone's life here..."

"You haven't upset anything," Ben interrupted. "But you have made an impact—especially on me, Kate. And Billy. You can't leave—you can't let him win," he implored.

"The look on his face was just... hateful! It was like he was challenging me. But I don't know how to fight this, Ben! I have no idea how to fight someone like him!"

"Then we'll do it together."

"No, I can't keep going through this. After he left, I couldn't even breathe, I was so mad."

"Kate, you aren't alone anymore. You have me and Sam and Martin and everyone in town will help—they're good people." Ben took her by the shoulders. "Kate, I'm not leaving, and I don't want you to either. Please?"

Kate finally let him put his arms around her. He held on tightly. "I told him I was a Howard, Ben. He knows now. I never should have said it, but I did, I was so angry! Now everyone will know."

"It's OK, Kate," he whispered to her. "What's done is done. No more running. For either of us. We stay and fight."

Ben got in his truck and tore off down the road towards the Woodlands, angry and scared for those he cared about. The gate to the Woodlands was open and he sped down the long drive to the house. He pulled up in front of the house, slammed the truck door behind him and strode up the steps. He banged on the door and then punched the doorbell. "Open up!" he shouted.

The butler answered the door. "Master Benjamin?"

"Where's my father?" he demanded. "I want to see him! Tell him to get out here, now!"

The butler hesitated. "Mr. Evans is not available."

Ben shoved his way into the house. "He can make himself available. Or are you too afraid to talk to me face to face?" he shouted to the empty room.

"Please, Master Benjamin, he's not available."

Max appeared at the top of the stairs. "It's OK, Angus. If my son needs to talk to me, I am more than happy to oblige." He walked down the stairs and approached Ben. "I'm sure we can have a calm discussion about whatever is bothering you, right?" He motioned towards the library off the foyer. "Why don't we talk in here? Can I get you something to drink?"

"No, we're talking right here, and I don't want a damned drink. What were you doing at Kate's house just now? She said you threatened her. And I want to know who threatened Billy last week—out in the woods. Who was shooting at him?"

"Yes, I just spoke to Kate, not that it's any business of yours," Max said coolly. "She overreacted, I'm sure. And I have no idea what you're talking about, someone threatening Billy? Why would you think I would know anything about this anyway?"

"Because you want that land, and I think you'll do anything to get it."

Max laughed. "Oh, really? I have many legitimate ways to get what I want. I made a fair offer for the property and she has turned me down. So, there is nothing more to discuss."

"I don't believe you. I don't think you are done yet. Because you just can't give it up. You have really reached a new low."

Max's face turned stone cold. He stepped up to his son, his voice menacing. "You are the one at the low point, boy. You could have had everything. But you, and your mother, you both chose your own way. Now you will have to live with it."

Ben shook his head. "Don't you dare talk to me about mom. She is finally rid of you, and I couldn't be happier for her. And why does it matter to you that I chose my own way? I run a successful business, I have friends, I have a future. I am not you. And don't try to make me to be like you because that will never happen. I can live with myself and I can sleep at night with no regrets."

Max raised himself up straight at that, his face a mask of rage. "We get one chance in this world, Ben," he shouted at his son. "Just one! I have worked my whole life to build up something for you, to leave to you. Success like that doesn't just happen. You have to work for it, and I have put everything I have in my soul to make Woodlands a success, to leave you a legacy."

"A legacy?" Ben laughed. "Good for you! You have lots of stuff, possessions, money. But you don't have what really matters—people who care about you! You can sit in this house counting all your money. But you'll be alone while you do it." He turned to go.

"I gave up my own dreams, my own future, to come back here and make something of this place," Max shot back at Ben, his voice steely. "Do you think that's what I wanted? Do you think that was the plan I had for my life? I had to come back here and pick up the pieces, rebuild after the destruction that Enoch Howard caused my family, my own father, and I will never apologize for the way I have handled my life or what I have done for you. It was my legacy to you, but you will never get it now, do you understand me? Never!"

Ben shook his head. "You can't forget that, can you? Whatever you think the Howards did to our family is in the past—gone—finished! And whatever it is that you think happened—you can't change it! And what if Kate really is Enoch Howard's granddaughter? Is that what pushed you over the edge?"

Max's face returned to one of calm, steely composure. "In the end, I will get what I want. You go tell that to Kate." Max turned and strode up the staircase. Ben stared up at the figure that walked away from him—his own father, his flesh and blood—now, irrevocably, a stranger. All those wasted years, his father had been haunted by Enoch Howard's betrayal, a betrayal he had perverted in his own mind to justify how he lived—controlling, vengeful, and distant. It had consumed him and turned him into the twisted man he was today. And Ben knew that in the end, somehow, it would be his downfall.

"Here's the address." Max handed a piece of paper to Simon, who was seated next to him. "Don't burn the place down. We just want to make a little commotion, got it?"

"Got it, boss. And thanks for giving me the job, Mr. Evans. I won't let you down."

"Well, you'd be wise to get out of town for a while when you're done. You can use the campgrounds in upstate New York for a few days."

"Anything else?"

"Yes. I can't be connected to this in any way. You do this for me—and keep it quiet—then I know you can be trusted. This is big—and very profitable—when we get this land. So, don't screw up. The police will be the least of your problems if anything goes wrong."

Simon didn't hesitate. "You can count on me, boss."

28

THE NEXT DAY, SAM AND MARTIN WERE HUDDLED over drawings again, sketching more of their ideas for the gardens. Sam looked up from his work and saw Kate at the back door, looking out across the lawn. She had shared the results of the DNA test with them and Sam thought about the emotional journey they had all been on. From their first meeting with Becky as their attorney, to this day, he knew that he and Martin were exactly where they needed to be and doing exactly what they needed to be doing.

His phone rang. He pulled it out of his pocket, answered and listened for a moment.

"Jimmy, calm down, what's wrong?" Martin diverted his attention from the drawings when he heard Sam's urgent tone.

"What? A fire? Now calm down Jimmy and tell me what happened." He motioned to Martin. "We need to leave now," he whispered.

"We're on our way. Is everyone OK? Fine then, we'll be there as soon as we can." He clicked the phone off.

"What's going on?" Martin asked.

"There's been a fire at the store."

"What? Oh no, is everyone OK? What happened?"

Kate came in from the kitchen. "What is it?"

"We need to go, now, Martin." He spread his hands out to calm the situation. He turned to Kate and explained. "He said it wasn't bad, just a lot of smoke and water damage. We'll see when we get there." Martin began to gather up the drawings.

Kate put her hand on his. "Martin, don't worry about this, just go."

"Thank you, Kate." He hugged her and hurried after Sam.

"Get your things packed, we're going away for a few days." Simon Barclay walked into Colleen's bedroom, went to her closet and started throwing clothes on the bed. "Pack something slinky; you and me are going to be all alone in the woods for a while."

Colleen pushed past him and slammed the closet door. "What are you doing? And what are you talking about? I'm not going anywhere unless you tell me what's going on."

"OK, OK. So, I did a little job for Max. And he's rewarding me with some cash and a few days in his cabin up north. And you are going with me."

"Is that what you needed my car for—some job for Max?"

"Yeah. So what? I couldn't use mine."

Colleen strode to the bedroom door and yanked it open.

"Get the hell out, Simon. I told you he's trouble.

"Oh, yeah? You making me choose? Is that what this is?" Simon's face darkened. "Yeah, I have a choice. I can either make a lot of money with Max and keep it or make crap at any other job and have you spend everything I've got. So, what do you think I'm going to do?"

"Then we're through." She pulled the diamond ring off her finger and slammed it down on the dresser. "Take it. I don't want anything to do with you—or Max. The wedding's off."

Simon grabbed the ring and put it in his pocket.

"Have it your way. Like I said. This way, I get to keep what's mine. And you're the one that's trouble, sweetheart, not me!"

He walked out, slamming the door behind him.

Colleen was seething but felt no regrets for kicking Simon out. It was what Max really wanted—to control her by manipulating her in a marriage to Simon. No, she was done with both of them, once and for all.

She waited a few minutes to make sure Simon was gone and then went down to her car. As she tossed her purse onto the seat beside her, she noticed a crumpled slip of paper on the floor and picked it up. The note had the name of a business and its address on it: Martini's Marvels, 605 West Harbor Road, Lakeville. It was Max's handwriting.

The name was familiar, but she couldn't quite put her finger on why, or make a connection with the address. Suddenly she remembered seeing an RV with that name and logo on it around town. There had been two men with Kate.

She bit her lip and ran her hand through her hair. With Max involved, and Simon, too, there would be nothing good about this information, she was sure of that. Now she just needed to figure out how to fix things, if it wasn't already too late. It was her chance to redeem herself. It started now.

Kate's phone rang and she saw Sam's name displayed. "Sam, are you OK? How's Martin?"

"Everybody's fine, Kate. We've gotten through worse things than this."

"What happened? Do they know?"

"There was a small fire. Lots of smoke and water damage. Nothing that can't be repaired. But Kate, you need to know something."

"What, Sam?"

"The police think it was intentional. They are calling it possible arson."

"What? Who would do... Oh, no. You don't think..."

"We don't know anything yet. They are still investigating. It could be anybody, but, Kate, please keep a sharp eye out for anything suspicious at the house, OK?"

"Thank you, Sam, we will be careful," and she ended the call.

"Well, what did he say?" Ben asked. "Are they OK?"

"Yes, everyone is fine. Nothing that can't be repaired."

"Good. Do you know what caused it?" Kate hesitated. "Kate?"

"He said it might be arson."

"What? Why do they think that?"

"I don't know." Kate slumped down in the chair. "I don't know anything anymore." She began to cry.

Ben knelt in front of her. "Kate, what's wrong? Talk to me."

"Ben, do you think Max... do you think he could possibly... just to scare us? I mean after all that's happened..."

Ben's face dropped. He stood up. "I don't know. Oh, God, I hope not. But from now on, I'm not leaving you and Billy alone in this house. And we stick together wherever we go. At least until they figure it all out. I'll let the sheriff know about this, too, just in case."

The next day, Ben, Kate and Billy drove into town. Ben had spoken to the sheriff and filled him in on what had happened to Sam and Martin's business in Lakeville and finally admitted to him that his father might be involved. Sheriff Bailey didn't seem surprised and assured Ben he would follow up with the police and fire department there but would have to wait for their assessment before making any real connections.

"I'm ready for some burglers!" Billy exclaimed as they went into Rosie's Café. "And some treats from Miss Rosie!"

Kate smiled. "Treats? Miss Rosie must like you, Billy."

"Yes, I like Miss Rosie and I like the junk box, too."

Ben quickly explained, "He means the jukebox. Mimi and Calvin would bring him in on Friday nights sometimes and he always picked out his favorite songs."

"Can we play songs, Kate?" Billy asked excitedly.

"Sure, Billy." Kate pulled several quarters out of her purse and handed them over.

Rosie approached the three as soon as she saw them walk in the door. She took Billy's face in her hands and kissed him on the cheek. "My favorite young man! It is so good to see you, Billy!"

Billy blushed. "You are my favorite, too, Miss Rosie." He suddenly looked confused. "But Kate, she's my favorite, too." Since he couldn't sort it out in his head, he asked, "Can I play some music? I have quarters!"

"Sure, you go right on over there and pick out your songs." She turned to Kate and Ben as soon as Billy moved to the juke box. "How's Miss Mimi doing? Have you heard any news?"

"She's doing well in the rehab center. She hopes to be home soon," Kate answered. "I know Billy will be happy to have her back home."

"It's a blessing that you are keeping Billy. That's a load off her mind for sure. Now what can I get you?"

They found a booth near the jukebox and placed their order. Billy hummed along to "Forever and Ever, Amen" by Randy Travis.

The bell on the door jingled and Ben looked up. Colleen caught his gaze and walked towards them.

"Hi, Ben, Kate," she said as she reached their booth. "May I sit with you for a minute?"

"It's not really a good time, Colleen," Ben answered.

Kate gave Ben a puzzled look. "Ben, it's fine. Please sit with us," she said, motioning to Colleen. "Billy, why don't you go up to the counter and talk to Miss Rosie for a little bit."

"OK!" Billy eagerly went over to the stools at the counter.

Colleen slid in opposite Ben and Kate, taking Billy's place. She bit her lip and ran her hand nervously through her hair.

"Thank you, Kate. But I have something to say and I think you'll both want to hear it. Please, Ben?"

"Go ahead, then."

"Ben, you might not have heard but I am, or was, engaged to Simon Barclay. But I've broken it off. I found out some things…" She took another deep breath. "I found out that…" She gathered her thoughts and dove in, turning to Kate. "You know Max wants your land, Kate. You've known that from the beginning. Bessie Howard would never sell it to him, and it became an obsession. At first, I thought he just wanted it for development. And he still does. He wants it and all the farms around here. Businesses will be built up all the way to Winston-Salem if he has his way. It will be worth millions to him. Kate, I'm sorry, but I lied to you about who I was negotiating for. It was Max all along."

"You didn't need to lie, Colleen. You could have just told me the truth. I don't know what to say."

"You're right, and I am so sorry."

"And we both know he will do anything to get it." Kate glanced at Ben, but he shook his head and Kate decided not to share any more details about their recent incidents with Max.

"But there is something else."

"Just tell us, Colleen," Ben said.

"I think I know who started the fire at your friends' business." Kate's eyes grew big. "I saw it on the news—about the fire, I mean. I can't say anything here, but I'm going right now to talk to my father, and we'll go to the police and tell them everything I know."

Kate whispered, "Was it Max?"

Colleen shook her head. "I really can't say anything more. And you can't say anything to anyone before I take care of this, please?"

Kate and Ben nodded in unison. "Will you be safe?" Ben asked, his tone softening.

"I'll be fine, don't worry. Just take care of yourselves—and each other. And Ben, I am so sorry about all of this." She stood up.

"Colleen, I don't know what to say," Kate began. "Thank you."

"No problem. It's time I started doing the right thing." She smiled. "You two make a nice couple, you know. Good luck with everything."

29

COLLEEN STEPPED OUT OF ROSIE'S into the blistering after-noon sun. She shaded her eyes and scanned to her left across the familiar storefronts on First Street that were woven into her childhood memories. The newsstand where she had begged her older boyfriend to buy her cigarettes. Eve's Beauty Salon where she had stubbornly told them that, yes, she did want her hair streaked with purple for prom night.

Next door to Rosie's at the Garden of Eden Florist, a young couple emerged, holding hands and laughing. They looked happy and she watched as they clung to each other and kissed. She had worked at the florist during the summers in high school and recalled Ben lingering around the flower buckets in the back room, trying to get her attention. But she had ignored his attentiveness then. She knew he was one of the good ones, but he hadn't been her type, not then. Time enough for guys like Ben later, she had thought. When she and Ben finally did connect, she was already jaded about men and angry after her mother's death and immediately set out to ruin the first real love of her life.

She suddenly couldn't decide whether she loathed this small town or loved it. Perhaps it was all just too familiar and held too many memories and secrets. But here she was, still in Eden Springs, playing the same games she did in high school and making the same bad choices. All she had to show for it was a broken engagement, broken relationships with people who deserved better, and a career on the verge of being destroyed. Worst of all, she had been a disappointment to her father and a slap in the face to her mother's memory.

She clutched at her stomach, suddenly hit with a visceral reaction to the reality she faced. Her eyes filled with tears and she wiped them away with her fist. She shook her head and turned her back on First Street. "No more," she murmured to herself. "No more."

She gripped her bag close to her and began to walk down towards her father's office. Her father had made Eden Springs his home. He could have moved on, too, but these were his people, his friends. He had made a difference here, a positive contribution to his friends and clients and the community.

They had shared the pain of losing her mother. Colleen had not made things any easier for him after that loss, but he was always patient with her and tried to be understanding. She knew that he had feelings for Elizabeth Evans, though he had never expressed them outright, not once. He was too principled to cause her any humiliation or compromise her reputation by asking her to leave her husband for another man. Her father was never comfortable with expressing emotion, but with something as powerful as what he felt for Elizabeth—it simply could not be contained and it could be seen in a glance, a word, a touch.

Now that Elizabeth had left Max of her own accord, maybe they finally had a chance at happiness.

Her own life was about to change, too. She was officially going to accuse Max Evans of attempting to intimidate Kate into selling her land and doing unspeakable things to make that happen, including arson. And this accusation fell on Simon, too. What would this do to her father and Elizabeth now? Sooner or later Max would be held accountable, she was sure of that. But now she would be the catalyst because she was the only one who knew the truth.

The door to her father's office opened. Colleen saw Elizabeth step out first. From a distance, Colleen watched as the two shared a brief touch on the cheek, a hand on her shoulder, and a smile. Her father held the car door for Elizabeth and waved to her as she pulled out into the street.

Colleen grabbed a light post to steady herself. The heat was oppressive, and she felt as if it emanated from her. She saw her father look towards her and raise his hand to wave at her, but she could not respond. She heard him call her name as he ran towards her. By the time he reached her she was sobbing, her body shaking in heartbreak and misery.

"Colleen, what's wrong? What's happened?" Her father pulled her to her feet just as her knees began to give way beneath her.

She grabbed on to him. "Daddy, I am so sorry!"

"Come on, let's get you to the office," he said calmly. "We'll talk about it there. Everything will be OK, honey."

They reached the office, stepped into the cool interior, and Wesley guided Colleen to a chair. He brought her a glass of water, sat down in the chair next to her and held her hand. Colleen clung to it tightly. He pulled out his handkerchief and gave it to her.

She turned to face him. "I'm so sorry!" she repeated.

"Sorry for what, honey?"

Colleen slumped back in the chair. "Just for everything," she sighed. "I've been a real pain, haven't I?"

Her father hesitated for a moment. "Well..."

Colleen began to laugh through her tears and her father joined in. "Well, I guess that says it all, doesn't it?" She sniffled and blew her nose.

"Why don't you tell me what's going on," her father urged.

"Where to start," Colleen began. "Well, I've broken off the engagement with Simon."

Wesley glanced at the hand he was holding. There was no ring. "Oh, honey, I'm so sorry."

"No, you're not," she said simply and laughed again. "He was a real jerk and you knew that all along. I should be mad at you for not stopping me, but then I'm not easy to stop when I've made my mind up about something."

"Well, you are a grown woman now and can make your own decisions. But... I think this is for the best," he said helpfully.

"Mom would have told me in no uncertain terms what she thought of him."

"You're right," Wesley agreed. "She spoke her mind, too—that's where you get your... confidence from." This brought another smile to Colleen's face.

"I've missed you, Daddy," she admitted. "I feel like I put a wedge between us since Mom died. But that's changing," she said determinedly. "As of right now."

"I'm glad to hear that," he nodded. "But there is something else that's bothering you, isn't there?"

Colleen shifted in her seat and faced her father.

"Before I tell you, I need to say something else."

Wesley looked at her questioningly. "Go on."

"I saw Elizabeth just now."

"Yes," he said. "She was in town and stopped by to say hello."

"Really, Daddy? Did she just stop by to say hello?" Colleen asked dubiously. "Just admit it—you are in love with Elizabeth." Her father's face reddened at his daughter's astute observation. "It's OK, I've known for a long time. In fact, I think it's just perfect."

Wesley shifted in his chair. "Is it that obvious?"

Colleen smiled. "Real love shouldn't be hidden away—it needs to be expressed. Everyone deserves happiness, and you and Elizabeth deserve it as much as anyone I know." They were silent for a moment.

"Is she moving back to Eden Springs?" Colleen asked finally.

Wesley sighed. "She's considering it, yes. She may keep her place in Charleston. But there's a lot to think about... for both of us," he admitted. "But we can talk about that later," he said, patting her hand. "Right now, I want you to tell me about whatever is bothering you. What's wrong?"

"I don't know where to begin," she murmured. Then she sat up straight and resolute. "First of all, while we are being honest, there is something you need to know." She withdrew her hand from his and stood to face him, the distance making it easier to say what she had to say. "I had a very brief affair with Max Evans, a while ago."

Wesley's shoulders slumped. "What?"

"It's over now," she assured him. "It was never meant to get serious. And I am not saying this to hurt you, or Elizabeth, but if anything comes out about it, then at least you've heard it from me. It was a really stupid thing to do, it was only one time, and I really regret that it ever happened. I should have known better. I am very sorry. But I am tired of all the secrets—especially the ones I have kept from you."

He nodded. "OK. But now you will tell me the real reason you are here."

"I need your services—as an attorney."

Wesley sat back in his chair. "This sounds serious then. Tell me what's going on."

"I'm not in trouble," she quickly assured him. "Really. It's not that." She could see the relief in her father's face. "I have information about a crime. And I want you to go with me to the police." Colleen felt the burden lift from her as she related the story of Max's ruthless moves to get Howard's Walk away from Kate by using whatever means necessary, the reasons he wanted the property, and, finally, the possibility of Max's and Simon's role in the fire at Martini's Marvels.

Wesley listened intently and when she assured him that she had told him everything she knew, he went to his desk and picked up the phone. He punched one number on speed dial.

After a few moments, he said, "Sheriff Bailey, this is Wesley. Are you available for me to stop by? Yes, it's very important. Thank you. I'll be right over."

Colleen stood as he spoke on the phone. The wheels were now in motion and she knew nothing would ever be the same again. She silently prayed that it would all be for the better.

Wesley looked at his daughter. "We'll take care of this, Colleen. Don't worry." He held her tightly. "You did the right thing. I am very proud of you."

Her tears dampened his suit jacket. "You don't know how much that means to me, Daddy."

30

COLLEEN TOLD HER STORY TO THE SHERIFF. She handed over the note that she had found in her car and it was taken into evidence. The sheriff immediately called the DA and arranged for Colleen to be interviewed. As soon as Colleen's interview with the DA had ended, Wesley took her to her apartment where she quickly packed a carry-on bag.

"You'll have to come back for the trial, but I will feel better if you go away until then," he said as they drove to the airport in Winston-Salem. He handed her a phone and an envelope. "Take this; he won't be able to trace the calls. Don't use your phone or your credit cards. I'll set up an account for you."

Colleen put her hand on his arm. "Daddy, I know you'll take care of everything. Please don't worry about me."

He glanced over at her. "I will always worry about you. And I will not let Max Evans get away with this—he's deserved this for a long time. But I am not taking any chances with you or Elizabeth. Once Max is arrested, the judge will set bail and Max will be released, I'm sure of that. Simon will be arrested, too. But I am not sure his family will be eager to post bail."

"I know." They sat in silence for a while. "I can't believe that Billy was threatened, too. Now I know I did the right thing."

"They'll all be protected," he reassured her. "But Kate and Ben didn't feel that leaving Howard's Walk right now was an option, not with Billy being away from his mother like he is. The sheriff has assured us they will keep an eye on them. And he is a man of his word."

They arrived at the airport, parked, and walked to the ticket counter. Wesley paid for a one-way ticket to New York City where she had friends she could stay with and then walked with her to the security area. Colleen choked back her tears. "Thank you for everything." she whispered as she hugged her father goodbye. "Take care of yourself—and Elizabeth." She pulled away and looked him in the eye. "You both deserve some happiness."

Wesley replied in a voice full of emotion, "So do you, honey. So do you."

Colleen grasped the handle of her carry-on bag. "I'll see you soon," she said, then turned and walked into the security line.

Simon was arrested at his apartment. After only a few minutes of interrogation he confessed to everything and blamed it all on Max. "He's the one that hired me. He threatened me, too, if I said anything. Told me he could get me in a lot of trouble. He said nobody would believe that he had anything to do with it. I was scared so I did what he told me to do! Listen, we can make a deal here. What if I told you some other stuff about Evans? How would that go for me?" In the end, Simon told everything he knew about Max's scheme to get his hands on Howard's Walk, how he had even hired someone to scare Billy in the woods; the same man helped Simon in the arson job and had bragged about it that day.

The sheriff's next stop was the Woodlands to serve a warrant for Max's arrest. Max met him and two deputies at the door. "Hello, Sheriff," he said calmly. "What can I do for you? Don't tell me it's time for my yearly donation?"

Sheriff Bailey was undeterred. "Max Evans, you are under arrest for criminal solicitation to commit arson and criminal conspiracy."

"What?" he spat out as the deputy grabbed his wrists, clicked the handcuffs closed, and read out his rights. "This is outrageous! Angus, call my attorney at once," he called over his shoulder to his butler. Angus quickly went to the library while Max was shoved out the door to the waiting car.

"You will regret this, Bailey," he hissed. "I will have your badge. You have no business coming to my house..."

"Shut up, Evans," the sheriff interrupted, pushing Max into the back seat of the car. "I have every right to come to your house and the judge will be happy to explain why. It's time for you to be on the receiving end of some justice."

Twenty-four hours later, Max Evans was in front of the judge. His attorney noted Max Evans's strong ties to the community as well as his reputation as a philanthropist to the good people of Eden Springs, and insisted he was not a flight risk. But the judge regarded him levelly. "Mr. Evans, these are serious charges. But the law says I must grant bail in cases such as this. Bail is granted at $600,000." He turned his attention to the attorney. "He is to surrender his passport; he is not to leave the state, and my recommendation is that he does not leave town." He banged his gavel. "Trial is set for July 21st, 9 AM."

Max's limousine was waiting for him outside of the courthouse. He slid into the back seat and barked at the driver. "Take me home, Horace."

Kate, Ben, and Billy had not let themselves be separated since Max's arrest and release. But the stress was taking its toll, especially as they tried to keep everything as normal as possible for Billy's sake. After a heated discussion at the garden center later that evening, Ben agreed to let Kate head back to Howard's Walk ahead of him and Billy. "I think you should wait; we'll only be a minute," he argued. "It's not safe."

"I'll be fine," Kate assured him. "I just need to get these groceries back home and start dinner. It's getting late. You and Billy just come as soon as you can."

"I'm calling Sheriff Bailey to send a car by the house, then," he called out to her as she got into her car. She gave him a backhanded wave and drove off. Ben sighed and let her go. The last couple of days had been a blur. Simon and Max had been arrested. Max was out on bail, but Simon had not been so lucky. Colleen had left town for parts unknown and his mother was safely ensconced at Wesley's house—he knew no harm would come to her there. Wesley and his mother. Why hadn't he seen it, he asked himself over and over. He had met with them both on the day of the arrests and could tell that she was happy and that together she and Wesley would face whatever was ahead of them. But he still worried—until the trial was over, and that was a month away, he would not rest easy. No one had heard from Max since he was released on bail. *Good,* he thought. *Let him rot in that house.*

Ben watched as Billy helped unload bags of soil from the truck. He had seen a change in him since he had spent more time with him and Kate. He knew that Mimi loved him more than anything but now that he had been away from her, Ben was seeing a confidence and independence that hadn't been there before. He knew Billy was going to be part of their lives for a long time. And that was just fine with him. The future was full of promise for all of them.

Kate took note of the sun setting across the fields on Chilton-Franklin Road. The dark was settling in quickly, and she turned on her headlights. The truck that had been following her did the same and she glanced back at it. It sped up, starting to match her speed. Suddenly, it pulled up beside her. Kate swerved, almost losing control, when she realized it was Max. He sped up again and veered to the right in front of her, cutting her off.

Kate slammed on her brakes and slid off the road into the grass. Everything on the seat next to her flew to the floor of the car and she fumbled to reach her cell phone. Max screeched to a stop and jumped out of the truck. He strode up to Kate's car and yanked the door open.

"Get away from me!" Kate screamed. The cell phone fell out of her hand and as she reached for it again, Max grabbed her by the arm and dragged her out of the car. He pushed her up against the fender. She could smell liquor on his breath. She struggled against his strong grip.

"You are going to pay for what you did to me, you and your family," he slurred, grabbing her chin and twisting it toward him. "Did you have me arrested? Was it you? 'Cause no one comes after me and gets away with it!" Kate kept struggling, trying to get him off balance. He fought to keep his grip on her. "I'll see that house destroyed before your very eyes. You and that no-good son of mine…"

Max tightened his hold on her, and Kate kneed him hard. He fell back and Kate shoved him with her foot, pushing him to the ground. She jumped back into the car, jerked it into gear and sped off.

She grabbed her cell phone off the floor and punched in Ben's number. "Please pick up, please pick… Ben, he's after me! It's Max—he's… Oh, my God, Ben, he's following me again! Please hurry! I'm almost home. Please hurry!!" she cried.

"Kate, we're right behind you," he said, his voice urgent. "I've already called the sheriff—just get to the house and lock the doors!"

31

KATE TORE UP THE LAST MILE TO THE HOUSE knowing that even there, she would not be safe from Max. But she knew she had no choice. This place that she never wanted, this place that was supposed to be Becky's, not hers, this place that had brought her only hurt and pain from Becky's death... this was also the place that cradled her during her darkest hours and where she found her family and a love that she could never have imagined. But she was not looking to the house as a refuge now, as she did in the past. Now it was her life, her future—hers and Billy's and Ben's—and she flew towards it.

Headlights flashed behind her, growing larger as she slowed on the curves. She jammed her foot down on the gas and shot forward to the house. The car slid sideways as she swerved around the circular drive and hit the brakes. She got out of the car, sprinted onto the porch, and jammed every key at the lock until the right one fit. She ran inside. Light from Max's headlights and the sound of screeching tires filled the space behind her. Kate slammed the door closed and yanked at the deadbolt until it clunked into place.

It was silent then except for the sound of an engine, idling, then revving slightly, then idling again. A few moments passed. She stood paralyzed, waiting for the sounds of Max's footsteps.

Then, a screech of tires again. Headlights lit up the windows and Kate screamed as Max's truck exploded through the front door. Shards of glass and shattered wood showered over her. She screamed again, turned, and ran into the kitchen.

Suddenly, Max was there beside her, clamping onto her arm and swinging her away from the counter. He threw her to the floor, face down, knocking the air out of her and bore down on her with all his weight. Kate gasped for breath, clawing at the floor, reaching for anything she could get to protect herself. She felt Max's hot breath on her face, his wet lips on her ear. "I will destroy you, and I will destroy this house," he hissed.

His menacing threats were like a trigger going off in Kate's head. Another place, another time—so many times when fear and panic had come to take her captive, stealing the very breath from her and pinning her to the floor. It was inhuman then and it was inhuman now, even as Max's flesh and bone covered her.

But she would not give in to the fear this time, she would not beg for her life again. This time she would fight. The terror had been destroyed before and she would find a way to destroy it again. Max suddenly shifted his weight and Kate grabbed the leg of a chair, heaving it backwards with all her strength. But it was stopped in mid-air and before she could release it, Max twisted her arm towards him. Kate screamed as bones snapped. The chair slammed into her body. Everything went black.

Kate could only whimper "no, no," as she was lifted like a rag doll. Her breath came in ragged gasps, taking in the acrid taste and smell of smoke. She tried to scream but no sound came. She struggled to move but her arms and legs would not obey. She could not see where she was being taken. But the arms that lifted her now were strong and secure. They were carrying her away from the smoke, carrying her to safety and gently laying her down on the cool, damp grass.

She heard other voices then. Sirens wailed in the distance.

"Kate, Kate—can you hear me?" Ben gently pushed the tangled mass of curls from Kate's face. The sound of his voice and his hands on her face were a miracle to her. A sip of water came to her lips and she drank it in and then coughed it out again.

"That's enough," Ben said. "The ambulance is on its way."

"Miss Kate—I carried you. Is that OK, Miss Kate? You couldn't walk so I carried you." Kate finally opened her eyes and saw Billy leaning over her, his hands on his thighs. But he wasn't smiling. His face was solemn and worried.

"Billy, are you OK?" Kate finally got the words out before breaking into another spasm of coughs.

"I'm OK, Miss Kate. Are you OK, too? Will she be OK, Ben?"

"She'll be fine, Billy, thanks to you."

"Max—it was Max, Ben—he came after me and—what has he done?" Kate cried. She sobbed as she remembered it all—Max, chasing her as she sped towards Howard's Walk, plowing his truck through the front door of the house, attacking her in the kitchen.

"I smell smoke! What happened? What did he do? Did he...?"

Ben calmed her. "He tried, Kate, but I put it out. And I called 911. Everything is OK now. Don't worry about it. As long as you are OK."

"He can't get away with this Ben—he just can't! All our work—Becky's house—our house!" Kate sobbed in his arms.

Ben held her close and rocked her. "I know, Kate. But he can't hurt you anymore. We'll find him and he'll pay for this, I promise you."

The sound of the EMS and fire trucks signaled their arrival. Billy ran to meet them and directed them to the back of the house. "Hurry, hurry!" he shouted to the first responders. "Follow me!" Billy and Ben stood anxiously nearby as Kate was checked out and put onto a stretcher. Her right arm was secured, and an oxygen mask placed over her face.

"We need to get her to the hospital," the EMS technician said to Ben. "We'll take her to County General; you can follow us."

Kate reached out for Billy. She pulled off the oxygen mask. "You saved my life, Billy. And I promise you I will never forget that!" She turned to Ben. "Make sure he's OK. Don't let anything..."

"I won't. We'll be right behind you. I've got this, Kate." The doors of the ambulance closed, and Ben and Billy headed for his truck just as Sheriff Bailey pulled into the driveway after allowing the ambulance to pull out onto the road. He motioned to Ben. "I got the call; I'll take you and Billy to the hospital, so you won't have any problems on the way. Let's go." Ben quickly agreed. Billy got in the back seat and Ben joined the Sheriff in the front.

"You want to fill me in on what happened?" the sheriff asked Ben as they sped off after the ambulance.

"Can't right now, sheriff. It will have to wait," as he motioned towards Billy in the back seat.

Sheriff Bailey nodded. "No problem. We'll have time later. But just so you know, a certain individual has been found and taken into custody. Quite a struggle as I understand it. He'll be taken to another hospital for treatment."

"Thanks for letting me know," Ben said quietly.

"I'm sorry about how this turned out, Ben. Wish it could have been different. Being family and all, I mean."

Ben stared out into the night. "Family's a funny thing, Sheriff. I'm just glad I get to choose mine now."

EPILOGUE

KATE LOOKED OUT OVER THE CROWD gathering on the sloped lawn behind Howard's Walk. An expansive white tent adorned with tiny white lights lent a festive air to the long-awaited grand opening of the gardens. Rosie and the ladies of the First Baptist Church loaded the tables under the tent with salads of every sort, trays of fried chicken and pulled pork barbecue, weighty casseroles, and four kinds of banana pudding, each one touted to be the best of their mama's recipes. They were feeding an army of guests that day and had to impress.

John Hubert, who was running for re-election as mayor of Eden Springs, shook hands with each and every guest entering the tent. Stella and her committee were taking visitors through the newly renovated greenhouse. Kate waved as she saw Mr. Tower and Mrs. Mims in the group. She would be thanking them shortly for their generous donation to completely refurbish the greenhouse, in memory of Becky.

Wesley and Elizabeth had arrived early to help put the finishing touches on the historical displays inside the house. They had worked to put together a fascinating tour of the history of Howard's Walk and Eden Springs which was drawing the attention of history buffs locally and across the state as well. Colleen had sent her regrets about not being at the celebration, but she was on her dream vacation to Paris and wished Kate and Ben all the best.

Sam and Martin were happily sharing their knowledge of every plant, shrub, and flower on the property. They would soon be moving into the house on the property of Eden Springs Garden center to help Ben expand the business as new partners and add their own unique talents in gardens and ornamental sculptures.

Her gaze then fell on Billy, carefully maneuvering Mimi in her wheelchair across the lawn to the shade of the tent. He had changed, she thought, over these last few weeks. Working with Ben at the garden center and caring for Mimi, he had grown more self-reliant under their watchful eyes. She knew that Billy would always need her to look out for him. But she was confident that their life with Billy would be a good one.

Billy and Mimi joined two couples seated at a special table under the tent that had been laid out with the heirloom that had started it all, with its crimson poppies, emerald green leaves and vines and embroidered flowers scattered across the center. The tablecloth had found its rightful place again at the heart of a Howard family celebration.

At Wesley's urging, Kate had reached out to Bessie's family in England and their presence with them today was a dream come true. Quinn Corbyn and his wife Edwina fussed over Billy, and Orson and Flora Corbyn engaged Mimi in conversation, catching up on all they had missed over the years and sharing stories about their beloved Aunt Bessie. Kate and Billy now had aunts and uncles and cousins, all eager to visit and get to know their new family in America. They had very little knowledge to share about Jenny Howard and her whereabouts, but Kate was content knowing that when the time was right, she would begin the search for their biological mother.

And Ben. Her heart still stopped when she looked at him. Strong, tender, loving Ben, who knew loss and heartache like Kate did, but only gave love, who embraced family as the source of happiness, even when his own father had betrayed him. Ben proved every day—both in words and actions—his total devotion to Kate and to their future together, and she would love him forever.

Kate smiled as she thought back to Sam's vision of a garden that he shared so many weeks ago. A gate had been placed, as he had described, not to keep people out, but to invite them in. Rebecca's Rose Garden was an intimate place, filling the air with the perfume of roses. A lily pond with goldfish edged the garden, surrounded with flagstones carefully set out by Billy. She closed her eyes and breathed in the scent of newly turned earth and envisioned the extravagant colors of the spring flowers that would be greeting her in the months ahead.

The Gardens at Howard's Walk had become like that old friend whom you haven't seen in a while, who may seem different, but deep down is the same friend you knew so long ago. This was her heirloom, that treasured gift handed down from one generation to the next; the heirloom that Becky had so lovingly left in her care.

And Kate had never felt so alive. Not ever.

THE END

ACKNOWLEDGMENTS

I COULDN'T HAVE FINISHED THIS BOOK without the support of my family and friends who believed in my ability to complete a labor of love that started a long time ago! I appreciate you all more than you know. Thank you.

To my husband Dan, whose patient advice on all things horticultural was invaluable to the story. Your loving support over the years gave me the belief that I could write this book.

To my daughter Michelle, your advice and enthusiasm constantly encourages and inspires me.

To my editor, Anna Benn, your insight and patient reviews helped me fly when I was stuck on the ground.

To the team at Light Messages Torchflame Books, my heartfelt thanks for your guidance and professionalism at every step to make this book a reality!

ABOUT THE AUTHOR

AWARD-WINNING AUTHOR NANCY WAKELEY grew up in the New York State Finger Lakes region and now resides in Apex, North Carolina, with her husband. She completed her degree in health information management from Stephens College, Columbia, Missouri, and spent her career in the health information management and clinical research fields until the writing muse lured her into retirement.

Nancy belongs to the North Carolina Writer's Network, NC Scribes Writers Circle and the Military Writers Society of America and gives back to her community through volunteerism. She embraces all things fashioned out of musical notes and words as the ultimate reflection of life's exquisite journey.

Heirloom is Nancy Wakeley's award-winning debut novel in the *Kate Tyler Mysteries*.

Connect with Nancy:

Facebook @authornancywakeley
Twitter @nancywakeley
Instagram @nancywakeley2
www.nancywakeley.com

The Legend

BY NANCY WAKELEY

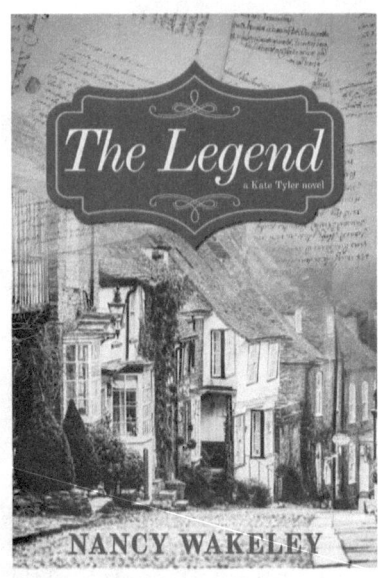

LEGENDS CLASH WITH REALITY at the Calloway House

Kate Tyler isn't sure she's living the life she was meant to live. Eden Springs has been wonderful, but she can't deny the wanderlust tugging at her heart. Desperate for a change of pace, she packs her bags and heads to the ancient town of Rye, England where she hopes she'll find inspiration for her new travel blog.

But when she arrives, mysteries follow her everywhere she goes. Strangers seem to know her, a book of ancient legends contains her mirror image, and Virginia Calloway is insistent that Kate come over to discuss the Legend of Arabella Courbain. Hoping to solve one of the many mysteries of this spontaneous trip, Kate agrees.

But the deeper Kate digs into the truth of what happened to Arabella back in 1766, the more she learns that the present may not hold the answers she needs. When legends cross with reality, Kate must find the truth before history repeats itself.